D0973189

FALL OF ANGELS

BY

KEARY TAYLOR

Third Paperback Edition: July 2011

The characters and events portrayed in this book are fictitious. Any similarity to real persons, living or dead, is coincidental and not intended by the author.

Taylor, Keary, 1987-
Branded (Fall of Angels) : a novel / by Keary Taylor. – 3rd ed.

Summary: Jessica, haunted by nightmares of angels, lives a life of seclusion until Alex suddenly takes over the house she lives in. When she starts to develop feelings for him, the mysterious Cole moves in next door, wanting nothing but Jessica.

ISBN 978-1450572378

For all of those who told me to keep writing.

CHAPTER ONE

When you go 108 hours, four and a half days without sleep, your body starts to do strange things.

Mine was panicking and shutting down at the same time.

My heart pounded despite the fatigue that consumed me. The ringing in my ears was so loud I couldn't even hear the breeze as it blew through the towering trees that surrounded me. My eyes ached so horribly I wanted to throw up. If I looked in a mirror I knew they would be bloodshot and swollen. I felt delusional and jumped at every shadow that danced on the black lake's surface, sure it was a demon come to carry me away.

I was so tired.

Don't fall asleep.

I paced on the dock, the moon shining brightly above me. I couldn't fall asleep; I wouldn't let myself fall asleep. To sleep brought terror no one could understand.

I counted my steps as I paced. Fourteen ... fifteen ... sixteen ... I never lost count despite the fact that I didn't consciously do it. I couldn't help it, the numbers just came.

Just a few more hours. That was all I needed. In a few more hours I would be ready to face the terror that came with sleep. I could face the judgments of the angels and those that had no right to be called such. I had made it 108 hours already; I could make it just two or three more.

I couldn't fight this any longer though. I was going to have to sleep and it was going to have to be now. I had learned better than to fight it this long.

My breathing increased rapidly as I forced myself to walk back toward the deserted house that looked toward the east side of the lake. My head spun and I feared I might pass out right then and there on the cold wooden planks.

Silent walls greeted me as I entered the house. I had been the caretaker for just over a year and a half and not once had the elderly owners come to stay. That was for the best. They would know I was crazy after only a few days.

Panic saturated my system as I stumbled through the door that led to my basement apartment. My eyelids were losing though. My legs protested in fatigue as I staggered into my bedroom. I barely made it to my bed before collapsing.

I've always counted. In a strange way it felt like the numbers kept me safe. I could block out the hell that surrounded me, that was my *life*, by concentrating only on counting. Numbers made sense. They fell into their right order and no matter how you rearranged them, you could still easily identify them as numbers.

I counted to 206 before he came to get me from the cell I was locked in. It was the same man each time. He was glorious and perfect, just like the rest of them. His chin was strong and square, his nose flawlessly straight. His lips were exactly the right fullness and housed straight, white teeth. His hair was a beautiful color of charcoal and the reflection of the flames danced across his intimidating muscular body in strange and beautiful ways. His wings, just like the rest of them, were graceful yet powerful. They always captivated me despite the chaos surrounding me. The feathers were beautiful, gently changing from the softest, purest white to shimmering, metallic silver.

His eyes were unique however, compared to the rest of them. Grey. An indication he was on neither side, neither the exalted nor the condemned. He was simply the one who transferred me from my cell to the judgment stand. He did not pass judgments and he had not been placed on either side.

I did not know his name or if he even had one, but I always thought of him as Adam. In the Bible, Adam was unique in that he was the first. I had never seen another angel with eyes like this Adam. He was the first and only as far as I knew.

Adam tied my hands in front of me with the same gold cord he always did. I shuffled behind him as we exited my cell. I was long past trying to fight him; I learned long ago that was useless.

He lead me down a long stone tunnel. Torches lined the walls, their flames dancing and licking out in mocking ways. They provided no warmth and no comfort. At the very end of the passageway was my cell that was nothing but a five by five foot area with steel bars and a locked gate. It ran on for sixty-two steps, nothing but an empty passageway. There was nothing visible at the other end of the tunnel, just an opening that appeared to lead into a lighter place than this.

Thirty...thirty-one...thirty-two... I counted and looked at my feet through the slits in the white hood that covered my head. The rest of me was sheathed in white as well, a simple shell that covered my body.

Adam said nothing as we walked, his gaze fixed on our destination. I always wished he would say something comforting. Anything to reassure me against what I knew was going to come. But he was always as silent as the stones that encased us.

Fifty-seven...fifty-eight...fifty-nine... Panic was rising rapidly in my blood like an acidic poison, eating away at my nerves. My breathing picked up, coming in sharp, painful spurts. I automatically slowed and Adam pulled on the remainder of the golden cord that hung between my two tightly fisted hands. I wanted to stop, to turn around and run back to my cell. Being locked in the cell for eternity was better than what I was about to face.

My count to sixty-two ran out and Adam pulled me from the safety of the tunnel. We entered into the middle of a tall cylinder. A narrow catwalk sprouted from the tunnel and extended to the other side of the cylinder, running into a solid wall. A slender staircase wound up and down its sides. Before me were ten magnificently carved stone seats, mounted directly onto the vertical wall. Adam walked me to the center of the catwalk then turned and walked back into the tunnel alone.

I tried not to look up as I stared intently at my bare feet. The sudden rustle of wings and the low murmur of

4

gloriously beautiful voices was enough to wash fear over me in a crushing wave. I knew exactly what my surroundings were. Above me was perfectly beautiful skies that were never ending beyond the rim of the cylinder. Below me, the cylinder plunged into never ending depths of fire and torture. Before me sat the council that would judge: five that were exalted, five that were condemned.

Each was breathtakingly beautiful, the men and women alike. Once they opened their mouths one could tell which side they were on though. The condemned said hateful things. If you looked close enough, one could see the physical difference as well. Those who were exalted had beautiful blue eyes, the condemned had eyes blacker than ink.

My hands twisted around one another in fearful anticipation. The gold cord that bound them was beautiful to the eyes but it was strong and would not give in the slightest. If I pulled against it too hard I knew it would cut into my skin till it drew blood.

"Jasper Wood," one of the council members started. It was a man I stood trial for tonight. *My name is not Jasper, my name is Jessica,* I chanted to myself internally. I often had to remind myself who I really was. It would be all too easy to lose my grasp on reality and fall to pieces.

The familiar sensation that I was about to pass out began and I wished more than anything in my life that I could.

"The deeds of your life have been accounted for and judgment will be passed. Your actions must be made known."

I fought back the urge to scream as I heard the rustle of wings again, heard the hysterical, deranged laughter come from below, and the whispers that sounded more like singing coming from above. I could feel hundreds of eyes settle on me as they took their places on the staircase that wound around me. My breathing was becoming so shallow and quick almost no oxygen was coming in or out.

"Jasper Wood, your deeds will now be revealed," the beautiful man before me continued. I finally looked up as two scrolls were produced. They were unraveled and terror sunk further into my heart. One was very long, the other all too short.

The items on the list were read aloud. One list recounted all the good deeds of Jasper Wood, the other all the bad. The latter was the longer list.

Next came the part that exemplified how unjust my presence there was. Sentencing. The council would cast their vote as to where I would be sent. Up meant exaltation and never ending bliss. Down meant a branding and never ending torment. Based upon acts I did not commit.

The five condemned council members squirmed excitedly in their seats. They knew what the outcome of this trial was going to be. Their eyes grew wide with anticipation and they leaned forward and waited anxiously for their turn to pass judgment.

"Down," the first of the exalted began.

"Down," the second sentenced.

"Down," the third.

As the judgments continued to be passed, I squeezed my eyes shut as tightly as I could and rattled the numbers off in my head. Twenty-one...twenty-two...twenty-three... I counted as fast as I could even though I knew it could not save me from what was to come.

"Down," said the tenth.

The scream finally erupted from my lips as the deranged laughter erupted from the walls, from the angels with the black eyes. They heckled and called Jaspers name, pointing and laughing at me, knowing I was about to join them in eternal damnation. I clasped my restrained hands to one ear, knowing it would do no good and would only make them laugh all the more.

My eyes were drawn back to the council, to the one who led the condemned. A wicked grin spread on his beautiful face, his black eyes nearly unfocused with glee. His great wings coiled before bursting and propelling him towards me. Another scream ripped from my chest and I shrank to the catwalk as he landed beside me. Another of the angels from below joined us and handed the first a rod, glowing red on one end. My eyes took in every detail of the beautiful and terrifying mark it held.

I wanted to run back into the safety of the tunnel, to find Adam and beg him to save me. I wished I could leap into the depths of the cylinder, find the bottom, and hide in the darkness forever. But there was no use in fighting what I knew was coming.

My entire body trembling violently, I made it to my hands and knees. I dropped my head before the dark angel and with my cuffed hands, swept my hair from my neck.

It seemed it should not have been possible but the laughter picked up all the more from the branded ones I was about to join. I could sense the grin on the face of their leader as he took another step towards me.

I took one short, shallow breath and squeezed my eyes shut again. A flash of white hot pain shot through my body as the red end of the rod was pushed into the back of my neck. I could hear the skin shrivel and melt as it gave way to the pattern I knew all too well. After what seemed an eternity, the rod was removed, and barely coherent from the pain, I was pulled to my feet.

"Jasper Wood," the first of the angels spoke again, the leader of the blue-eyed council members. "Judgment has been placed."

At his words a new sensation began. The feeling that giant sized insects were crawling just under the skin in my back overwhelmed me. Just when I thought I could bear it no longer, I heard my flesh tear and my own set of beautiful wings burst forth. Even the damned were given wings and made beautiful.

With this, hell finally broke loose. Those with the black eyes leapt from their seats and flew straight towards me. Their cold hands clasped around my arms and legs, pushing and pulling from every direction. There were too many of us on the narrow strip we stood upon. We were going to fall. And the only way to fall was down into the fiery depths. As the chaos continued to envelop me, an earsplitting scream erupted once more from my lips. As we slowly tipped sideways, I slipped into darkness.

CHAPTER TWO

I woke the same way I always did. Screaming in terror. I was sitting straight up, clutching a hand to the back of my neck. The other arm was extended across my body, under my other arm, my fingers stretching toward my shoulder blade, searching for wings.

I looked at the clock and noted I had slept for two and a half hours. It had been a short trial. It was still only five in the morning.

Working hard to slow my breathing, I rolled out of the bed and staggered to the bathroom. I flipped on the switch and squinted through the blinding light. The bathroom was generic. White walls, white baseboards. A sink, toilet, and shower/tub.

I stripped down and turned the water in the shower on. Knowing what I was about to see, I stood before the mirror and turned my back to it, peaking over my shoulder back at my reflection.

My parents had always insisted that nightmares weren't real. They couldn't be real. The scars that covered my neck and back suggested otherwise. A beautiful and detailed X was branded into the back of my neck and an intricate, rather realistic pattern of wings spread itself from the lower portion of my back, up to the top of my shoulders. Both were a fresh, scarlet red. The color wouldn't last long. After a day or so both would fade to a flesh color, no longer swollen but just a raised scar. I compared the wings to the African tribes I had seen who would cut their flesh to make the beautiful patterns that covered their bodies. I believed it was called scarification. Mine looked just like this but in the right light you could see a strange metallic silver in the wings, just like the angels from my nightmares. The X was a beautiful and terrifying scar, as if a red hot iron had indeed been pressed into my neck.

I stepped into the shower and relished in the hot water. If only it could burn the marks from my skin. Some would say my scars were beautiful, but I hated them. They were sore reminders of just exactly how abnormal my life was. I could never have a normal existence because of all this. I was a freak.

Shivering, I dressed quickly, pulling on a thick knitted sweater, a pair of thermals and my most comfortable jeans. As the shaking stopped I returned to the bathroom. I stared at my reflection in the mirror. Growing up I had been told I was a beautiful child, but I didn't see it. I had always thought I was fairly plain looking, ordinary in every way. My eyes were slightly larger than they should have been, a dark hazel color. The dark bags under them never faded. I wished my nose were just a little narrower, it wasn't big, it just wasn't perfect in my eyes. My lips were absolutely average, not luscious, and not thin. I suppose I did have good skin though. I had been lucky, now twenty-years-old, acne had never seemed to catch up with me.

Grabbing a brush, I tried to drag it through my hair. It fell around my face in a thick mane of curls that refused to be completely tamed. They seemed to have a mind of their own most of the time. It was time to get my hair cut; it hung nearly to my waist now. After a few minutes I threw the brush back into its drawer in frustration. It was useless.

I went to the tiny kitchen that occupied one corner of my apartment and eyed a box of cereal warily. Further proof of how much of a freak I was. I didn't need to eat often and never felt the need to do so. I never really got hungry and only ate maybe once a day, if that. The same went for sleep. I knew it was impossible for normal people to survive on as little sleep as I did. There was something wrong with me that made it so I required less sleep than the average person. For that I supposed I should have been grateful.

Reluctantly, I poured a bowl of cereal, drowning it with milk that would expire the next day. I sat at the card table I used for a kitchen table and flipped my laptop open. It took only a second for the screen to start to glow. I pulled up the internet browser.

"Jasper Wood." I typed the words into the search engine deliberately. It was likely too soon for anything to show up.

I hit search and quickly scanned through the hits. There was a musician by this name but nothing that looked promising. The obituary probably wouldn't be out for a few days. That was the way it usually worked anyway.

I was thirteen when I first realized the names I stood trial for weren't just random names my subconscious was making up. I stood trial for an Eliza Booth one night. She was a good woman; she had not been branded and was granted blue irises. A few days later I had glanced at my father's newspaper and saw Eliza Booth's obituary. She was eighty-five and had died in her sleep. I checked every name after that.

The most horrible experience had been when I stood trial for a boy at my high school. I had never liked the kid. He wasn't the kind of person your parents would want you hanging around with. He had committed suicide when he got into some drug problems. He been branded. Luckily, that was a singular incidence; standing trial for someone I had actually known. I didn't want to relive that again.

Nearly every name I stood trial for popped up in an obituary somewhere. Those I couldn't find I just figured never had one published in the papers.

I finished eating quickly. After I had brushed my teeth, I pulled my shoes on, grabbed my purse and keys and opened the door that led to the rest of the house. The remainder of the basement contained a large family room, each of the corners and closets containing a wide variety of toys and games, the room dominated by a pool table, a slightly outdated big screen TV, and every other form of entertainment one could think of. There was also another bedroom and from its contents I guessed it must have belonged to a teenage boy who was long gone. There was also a bathroom, similar to my own, completely generic. I made my rounds, checking that everything was in its order and headed upstairs.

The top floor consisted of a large open area, containing the kitchen, dining area, and a living area. The only slight separation in the room was the stone fireplace that stretched from the floor into the vaulted ceiling. Huge beam rafters spider-webbed across the ceiling, giving it the slight feel of a lodge. On the south side was a very large master bedroom and attached to it was a bathroom that was bigger than the bedroom. Once I was sure that everything was as it should be I walked out the door that led to the road.

It only took me a minute to walk to the next door neighbor's home, just ninety-one steps. I didn't knock, she would still be asleep. I simply removed the list that had been taped to the door. There was not a whole lot listed there, just things for Sal's basic needs.

I quickly returned home and looked at my watch as I slid into my car. Seven a.m. The stores should be opening soon.

I put the key in the ignition and smiled as the engine roared to life. Last year I had crumpled my Toyota like a soda can when I crashed it into a ravine, trying stupidly to stretch myself to the 120 hour mark. Of course I had fallen asleep. Considering I did not make much money housekeeping, my budget for a new car was limited. Ironically enough, I found one of the neighbors had died and his wife, not knowing or caring how much it was worth, sold me my 1967 Pontiac GTO for what I had on me. The outside was nothing pretty to look at but it had been rebuilt to mechanical perfection and the interior looked flawless. I wasn't sure how I felt about driving a dead man's car, no matter how much I loved it.

I threw it into reverse and carefully backed out of the garage. The road curved around the houses built along the water's edge. Once free of the homes, the evergreens towered along the side of the narrow road that led to the freeway, giving the effect of driving through a tunnel of evergreens.

It always seemed like it took longer than it should to reach the heart of Bellingham, considering I technically lived in Bellingham. Lake Samish was about as far south as you could go and still be within the city boundaries. Between the well-populated lake and the heart of town there was not much but towering trees and low mountains.

As I pulled into the parking lot of the grocery store, I closed my eyes and counted backward from ten. I could do this. In four days it would all be over and I could go out without being tormented. Until December anyway.

I had tried to avoid having to venture into town at all costs but my food supply was getting dangerously low and I knew Sal was going to be needing things as well. If I didn't take care of her who was going to?

As soon as I walked through the door I was confronted with what I had been trying so hard to avoid. All the Valentines' candy and gifts were set up right at the entrances, red and pink streaked throughout the building. I had nothing against Valentine's Day itself. It was the chubby-cheeked, pink little cherubs that smiled up at me from the heart shaped cardboard boxes of chocolates I hated. Each of them stared up at me like some cruel joke and I certainly did not think it was funny. I heard the sounds of mocking and demented laughter building up from inside of me, a reminder that I could never escape the angels of judgment.

"Please mom, can we just go home?" I begged. My nine-year-old hands trembled.

"We just got here," she said as she grabbed a shopping cart. It was frigid in the February Idaho air. "What's the matter?" she asked, turning her irritated eyes on me.

I shrunk under her gaze as we stood on the frozen concrete before the store. I looked at the entrance of the grocery store and saw the pink and red hearts with arrows through them on the windows. "Please, can we go home?"

My mom just shook her head and walked into the store. I had no choice to follow her.

I started hyperventilating as the doors opened automatically, a blast of warm air hitting my face. My mother veered to the right, heading toward the produce. I stepped forward to follow her. I only got half way there when I saw it, choking with fear.

A life-sized cardboard cutout of a cupid with a bow and arrow was propped up next to a display. Its cartoonish wings sprouted out of its back, making the angel looked suspended in the air.

As my eyes grew wide, taking its ludicrousness in, the mark on the back of my neck blazed. A choked gasp rose in my throat. I stopped breathing, unable to take my eyes from it.

A harsh hand on my arm brought me out of my state of frozen fear.

"What are you doing?" my mother demanded. "Come on!"

"Please," I begged again. As I looked around, I saw that dozens of smaller versions of the same cupid had been suspended from the ceiling. They all seemed to be watching *me, laughing at my fear. I could never escape them. "Mom, please! I can't be in here!"*

I broke away from her grasp, sprinting for the door.

Without even making sure no one was looking, I grabbed all the boxes that were placed standing up and stacked them one on top of another, face down.

Christmas was worse. Angels were everywhere in December, on top of trees, on ornaments, costumes in nativity skits, even in songs. If only people knew what angels were really like. They wouldn't be so quick to place them everywhere in their homes.

I quickly purchased everything I needed and made extra sure I had everything on Sal's list. There were always a few items on her lists I wanted to question her about but with Sal it usually seemed better not to ask too much.

The next stop was the independent bookstore down the street. Without a doubt it was my favorite store. It felt like a safe place where everything should be able to be rationally explained. There was so much wisdom and knowledge in one place, thousands of volumes of thousands of people's life's work. I often daydreamed that one day I would stumble across the answer for forever curing my nightmares in these walls. Surely the answer had to be out there somewhere.

I immediately went to the table containing the bestseller books and picked out three new ones for Sal. The woman read more than anyone I knew. I sometimes doubted how much she actually got out of the books but I was glad she had a passion in her disturbed life.

Next, I automatically headed toward the science section of the store. If I was going to find an answer here among so much wisdom, surely it would be there. The last few months I had been going through the psychology shelves, skimming for anything to do with dreams or even hallucinations.

I picked up book after book, skimming through their pages to see if there might be anything helpful. Each one frustratingly yielded nothing. I didn't know what I expected though. Why would anyone know anything about the anomaly that was my life? What I experienced should be impossible.

The sound of spiteful chuckling pricked at the back of my mind. If angels were supposed to be such wonderful and perfect beings, why were they tormenting me so?

Trying to ignore the sounds in my head, I put the book in my hand back on the crowded shelf and moved to the fiction section. I picked up the bestseller of the week, scanning over the synopsis on the back. It promised suspense and romance and I couldn't help but want to jump on the bandwagon and read it. After a moment of consideration however, I placed it back on the shelf. Reading about someone else's happy ending would only leave me feeling depressed and sorry for myself. Being just days away from the official lover's day of the year wasn't going to help either.

Before I could work up too much emotion over the fact that I was doomed to be alone, I purchased Sal's books and headed back out to my car.

The clouds sat low as I made the quiet drive home, resting near the top of the towering evergreens that lined the road leading into the lake. True to the nature of living in the

Pacific Northwest, it was sprinkling. This was the part I despised about winter in Washington, the almost total absence of the sun. I didn't mind the rain but I tended to get a bit depressed when I didn't get to see the sun for more than a week.

The ever silent walls greeted me as I arrived home and I quickly put my things away. It felt good being stocked up and knowing I wouldn't have to venture out for at least a week. By then all remnants of this misrepresented holiday would be cleared.

I grabbed the two brown paper bags and the books and walked the distance to Sal's house. It was still sprinkling slightly but by this point it was no more than a mist. I didn't mind going out in the wet, it wasn't like it could damage my hair. It was bad enough all on its own.

I gave two hard knocks on the door before I let myself in. Sal never answered but she was always home. And she never kept her door locked despite what I advised her time and time again.

Sal's home was beautiful inside. It was newer than the house I lived in, only seven or so years old. It had at one time been decorated lavishly. The walls were painted a nearly blinding white and windows were everywhere. Strong accent walls were spread throughout the house, red, purple, even black. But now its former glory was dampened, buried under the clutter that was everywhere. The house was kept immaculately clean but Sal never threw anything away. She always said she might need it later, no matter how insignificant or how much it looked like garbage to me. The walls would have been lined with garbage as well if not for the housekeeper that came every few days.

"Sal?" I called as I set the bags down on the black granite countertop. "Sal?" I called again as I finished loading things into the fridge.

I would have started to get worried but it was not uncommon for me to have to search for Sal. She often fell asleep in odd places, the strangest being in the rafters in the dining room once. How she got up there I never found out.

I peeled my jacket off and laid it on the back of a chair and set out on my search. The kitchen and main living room were connected, the view looking over the lake. Just off from the big room was the dining room.

Stairs descended from the living room into the basement level. On this floor there was only a large office and an even bigger master suite.

"Sal?" I called at the door as I knocked. After waiting a few seconds I let myself into her bedroom.

The furniture in Sal's room was elegant and grand, looking fit to be in a king's quarters. There were beautiful, elegant curtains that hung from the windows that looked over the lake. A large painting of Sal in her younger days hung above the bed. A sheet had been pinned over the picture though but I noticed it had been drawn back, as if she was trying to peek at it. But all this was marred by the things that littered the room. There were heaps of clothes, waiting for the housekeeper to come, most of them probably still clean. Piles of books, though neatly stacked, were everywhere.

"Sal?" I whispered as I listened for any signs of life. After a moment I heard what I was listening for and followed it to the grand master bathroom. The bathroom matched the rest of the house, elegant in every detail. And there she was, sleeping in the claw foot tub, a towel under her head for a pillow.

She looked so peaceful, her face so much more relaxed than it was when she was awake. Her hair was blonde and even though she was only thirty-five it was starting to grey slightly. Her skin at one time had been perfect and beautiful but now was in sad need of some TLC. Wrinkles were already spreading on her forehead, but this was more from the concerned look that crossed her face constantly than from age.

"Sal," I said softly as I put a hand on her shoulder. "Wake up, Sal."

She immediately opened her eyes and a confused expression crossed her face. She looked around her and the expression of confusion deepened at her surroundings. When her eyes landed back on my face she relaxed just a bit.

"Is it done?" she asked.

"Is what done?" I asked as I helped her out of the tub.

Without answering me, she walked back into the bedroom and I followed her up the stairs. She went directly to the oven and opened the door. As I followed her, I could hear her sniffing at something, her head halfway inside the oven.

"I don't understand," she said with a confused voice as she shut the door. "I put it in hours ago."

Without asking what in the world she was talking about, I opened the oven door and saw what was on the rack. There was a frozen lasagna sitting on the top rack but the oven was stone cold.

"Did you turn the oven on?" I asked her as I searched around for the box it came in.

"Oh," she said, dragging the word out. "I forgot about that part I guess."

I found the box in the cupboard that contained the dinnerware, shoved on the highest shelf. She was trying to hide it from the housekeeper so it wouldn't be thrown out. After reading the instructions, I pulled the lasagna out and set the oven to pre-heat, not even thinking twice about why Sal wanted to have lasagna at ten-thirty in the morning.

"I got you some new books today," I said as I picked them up off the counter and handed them to her.

Sal's eyes grew wide and excited as she grabbed them from my hands and walked to the couch in the living room. I followed her in and took my own seat.

Sally Thomas had once been a beautiful, perfectly normal woman. She married her husband when she was twenty-four and the marriage had been fairly happy for a few years. As her husband began making more and more money he became a very selfish and unkind person. He also took to drinking, a lot of drinking. And when he was drunk he became violent.

Sal happened to come home one day to find her husband in a drunken rage and she got in his way. He beat her silly. She should have left him then but like so many other women she was in denial that he truly had a problem each time he promised that it would never happen again. Some people shouldn't be allowed to make promises.

The beatings came several times a week for years.

About six years ago, a friend came over to check on Sal when she couldn't get a hold of her. She found Sal unconscious on the floor, in a pool of blood. She called an ambulance and Sal was lucky to have survived. The doctors said she was never going to fully recover and they thought there would probably be some brain damage.

Sal's husband had fled that night but guilt eventually caught up to him and he turned himself in two days later. He was arrested and sentenced to jail for a very long time. All his money and assets were turned over to Sal.

I couldn't understand how Sal had managed to take care of herself before I moved to Lake Samish. While she had her lucid times where she seemed absolutely normal, these occurrences were rare.

"Do you need anything, Sal?" I asked as I watched her flip through one of the books.

She shook her head furiously but after a second snapped her head up to look at me.

"Money," she said before she sprang to her feet.

"Oh," I said with a sigh. I knew what was coming. It was always the same.

Sal disappeared down the stairs and I heard her banging around loudly in the office below. After a few moments she reemerged with a broad grin on her face.

"Here you go," she said as she shoved a few bills into my hands. "Thank you, Jessica."

I looked at what she gave me and noted there was two-hundred dollars there. This was nearly twice what I had spent getting things for her. But I knew better than to refuse. I had done that twice and it had thrown her into a screaming fit. It had taken me hours to calm her down. I wouldn't make that mistake again.

"Alright," I said as I stood, tucking the bills into my back pocket. "I'm going to get going."

Sal didn't say anything back as she settled into the couch and flipped another book open, turning to a page three-quarters of the way into it.

"Call me if you need anything," I said as I opened the door. Still nothing. "See ya, Sal."

Getting no response, I closed the door behind me and started the walk back to my apartment.

I was ashamed to admit it, but being around Sal made me feel just slightly better about myself. I certainly felt terrible for what had happened to her. I had no doubts as to what would happen to her ex-husband come his judgment time. But I could usually hide my oddities. Occasionally numbers slipped between my lips but I knew I wasn't the only one who counted my steps; it was something plenty of people did. I felt pretty normal when I was around Sal. I was the sane, rational one.

Ninety-one steps later I was back in my apartment. It was simple but cozy. The living area, kitchen and non-existent dining area were all combined. The kitchen contained one row of upper and lower cabinets. The stove was one of those old units that were remarkably smaller and narrower than the modern appliances. There was a sink with a single basin. There was no dishwasher. The fridge sat at the end of the row and a microwave perched atop it. I didn't exactly like this arrangement, it made it difficult to use, but there was nowhere else to put it.

The card table I used for dining upon was against the wall, floating oddly between the carpet of the living area and the outdated tile of the kitchen. Again, there was not quite enough room. The living area was small but because I only had a small loveseat and a television that sat on top of a milk crate it didn't feel too cramped. My bedroom was set off from all this and oddly, it was as large as the other room, if not larger. There wasn't much int here either, just my full size bed, a dresser and my guitar, leaned in the corner. A walk-in closet led off the bedroom, as did the bathroom.

It wasn't much, but it was home, my own little haven where no one bothered me and no one could call me crazy.

The days passed slowly in the winter. There was nothing to distract me during the day as there was no yard work to be done and the garden had retired for the cold season. The rest of the house remained immaculately cleaned and would stay so considering I was the only one here. At least the days were slowly getting longer. One other major disadvantage Washington had is that in winter it starts to get dark at four-thirty. When one is trying to avoid sleep, darkness is the enemy.

CHAPTER THREE

I looked at the clock that hung above the kitchen sink as I wiped my hands dry on a towel. Two thirty-six. I felt pretty good despite the late, or rather early hour. The fact that *all* the dishes were now sparkling clean might have had something to do with that. I *hated* doing the dishes.

As usual, I had on every light I possibly could in the apartment. As I said, darkness is the enemy. The temperature was also turned down as low as I could stand it and still wear my usual tank top and cotton shorts. Wearing anything else this time of night was just too uncomfortable.

I grabbed a can of Dr. Pepper from the fridge. I hated to admit it but I was addicted to caffeine. In a way I had to be; how else was I supposed to go such long stretches without sleep? I may not have needed as much as everyone else but I didn't exactly have superpowers. I popped the top open and took a long draw. Bubbles swirled around my mouth for a short moment before they slid down my throat and fizzed in my stomach. I tried not to think about what all the carbonation might be doing to the lining of my stomach and my liver. It took me all of twenty seconds to down the can before I crumpled it and tossed it into the recycle bin under the sink.

I made my way to my bedroom, grabbed my guitar and flopped onto my bed, my back leaned against the wood headboard. I stared blankly at the light yellow wall ahead of me as my fingers wandered on their own over the strings.

An irritating prickling began on the back of my neck and I could somehow feel every detail of my scar. This happened almost every night. It was as if the demented angels were calling to me in my consciousness, whispering to me to come to them. They would not even leave me alone in my waking hours. It wasn't enough for them to torture me while I slept.

I stopped strumming when a small sound disturbed the otherwise silent house. The sound of a door creaking open. I knew beyond a doubt all the doors were securely closed and locked.

My heart started pounding as I realized what must be happening. Someone had broken in, picked the lock. My ears started ringing in a weird way as I dashed to the door that led into the rest of the house. I crept silently to the bucket in a corner that held a large stash of sporting gear and grabbed a metal baseball bat. Numbers were racing through my head almost faster than I could even subconsciously process them.

As I reached the bottom of the steps, I heard two or three heavy things drop to the ground. I inched my way up each stair, my back pressed to the wall as flat as I could make myself. The sound of keys jingling floated down to my ears and light found its way into the stairway as a switch was flipped on in the living room above. I thought I heard the sound of the fridge open and close. This made no sense. Why would the intruder be checking the empty fridge?

I heard steps cross the kitchen back toward the living room and approach my hiding place. My heart pounded so loudly, surely that was what brought the intruder to my hiding place. Another switch flipped on and the stairway was suddenly filled with blinding light.

"Stop right there!" I shouted as I held the baseball bat ready to swing away.

The intruder had just stepped onto the first stair when I shouted. He jumped violently, his foot slipping, and gave a yell. He held up his hands and I was glad to see they were empty.

"Who are you?" he demanded. "What are you doing here?"

"Me?!" I cried as I backed down another stair. "What are you doing here? There's no money here, I can tell you that so why don't you just leave and I won't call the cops."

"What are you talking about?" he said as he lowered his hands. "I didn't break in, although I'm starting to wonder if you did. What are you doing here?"

Nothing he was saying made any sense. "I work here! I'm the caretaker. Now please leave or I *will* call the cops!"

"Calm down," he said, a small smile almost spreading across his face. "I'm the Wright's grandson. Paul and Sue were my grandparents."

"Were?" I demanded, my brain not quite comprehending everything that was happening.

"Yeah," he said as he looked at the cream colored carpet at his feet. "They died a week ago in a car accident."

I didn't say anything for a few moments. Maybe he was lying. I hadn't heard anything about the owners of the house passing, but he did at least know their names. If he was breaking in he had either known them somehow or had done his homework.

"I promise I'm not lying," he said as he looked into my eyes. "I wouldn't make this up."

I actually looked at the man before me for the first time. He was tall, probably just over six feet. He was well muscled and certainly looked fit. His hair was a short, well-trimmed sandy blonde color, his features were strong and sharp. His eyes piercing blue. Had I not been so terrified I would have been tempted to stare open-mouthed.

"My name's Alex," he said and looked as if he were debating if it was safe to come closer or not.

Alex... the name rang a bell. I had seen the name somewhere in the extra room downstairs, engraved on a trophy or something. As I looked at his face a bit closer I vaguely recognized it. His picture hung in several places upstairs, mostly in the master bedroom. He was older now but he was definitely the same young man.

"You're telling the truth," I said plainly.

"Promise," he said, that same smile tugging on his lips again.

Realizing I was still holding the bat ready to swing, I lowered it to my side. I suddenly felt conscious of how I looked. I felt horribly exposed wearing a spaghetti strapped tank and knew my shorts were *quite* short. They were the same ones I had worn since I was thirteen and were covered in frogs.

He must have noticed me squirming and looked slightly away, that grin again begging to spread itself on his face. "Um," he said uncomfortably before looking back at me. "Do you happen to have anything to eat? I'm starving and the fridge up there is empty. Guess I should have expected that."

I was taken aback by his request. This seemed rather presumptuous, especially since I had just been ready to attack him with a bat.

"Uh," I stuttered as I tried to decide what my answer was going to be. "Yeah, I guess," I said, a disbelieving look crossing my face.

"Thanks!" he said as a dazzling smile finally spread across his face. It was if he had been stuffed full of sunshine and it was begging to burst out of him. It stunned me for a moment. A flock of butterflies swarmed in my stomach.

He followed me as I headed back toward the apartment. It kind of felt like I was dreaming, but my dreams weren't like this.

"Wow," he said as he looked around the dim family room. "Looks exactly the same as when I was here last."

I didn't say anything as I opened my door. I wasn't sure what to say.

"I decided to make the drive up here yesterday morning. Driving the entire west coast took a bit longer than I expected. I guess I should have grabbed something to eat on the way but I was ready to be done traveling."

Still slightly dazed by what was happening, I opened the fridge and examined its contents. After a second I shut it.

"I don't know what you'd like. Have whatever," I said as I walked past him toward my bedroom. I ducked inside for a moment and grabbed my pale pink bathrobe and wrapped it securely around myself.

"I really appreciate this," I heard him call, his head buried in the fridge. "I know this must be really weird for you."

I walked back into the living room and watched as he pulled the makings for a ham sandwich out and set it on the counter.

"I didn't realize you were here," he said as he unscrewed the lid to the mayo. "I should have guessed someone would be though when I read in the will about a big chunk of money being left to pay for the caretaker. I wasn't really thinking straight when I was reading it though. It was kind of a shock."

His sandwich made and the ingredients put away, he turned and sat at my shabby table. "You want one?" he said through a mouthful, his expression unsure, as if he realized he should have asked about sixty seconds ago.

I shook my head and didn't say anything. The last thing I expected to happen today was to have a man sitting at my table at three in the morning.

"What's your name?" he said as he swallowed.

"Jessica," I half whispered. "Jessica Bailey."

"Jessica," he said as if to test out how it felt on his lips. "I'm really sorry about this. If I would have known you were here, I would have waited until morning to come."

He scarfed the rest of the sandwich down in one bite. I waited for a few moments, still staring at him in disbelief. If there were any hints of tiredness in my system earlier they were gone now. It felt like my entire body was buzzing with awareness.

He swallowed his last bite and wiped his mouth on the back of his hand. "Won't you sit down?"

I moved stiffly to the other seat at the table. I could not even begin to search for words to say.

"Are you okay?" he asked as he looked at me. "You seem really shook up."

His words seemed to finally jar me from my stupor. *Way to make a good impression*, I thought to myself. He hadn't even seen the worst of anything yet and he already probably thought I was crazy. "Yeah," I finally managed to spit out. "You just... scared me. I didn't exactly expect to have a visitor in the middle of the night."

That smile tugged on his lips again. "I'm sure."

He seemed to be studying me for several long moments and I felt self-conscious again. I was sure my hair was a mess, its wild mane of curls everywhere. I wasn't wearing any makeup, though I hardly ever wore it. Even though I had gotten some sleep the night before I knew the bags under my eyes must still look frightening.

"I was in Africa when they called me." I almost jumped when he finally spoke. "I was doing volunteer work in Kenya. I got the call just a few hours after the crash and I had to fly back the next day to take care of the funeral arrangements. Wasn't exactly how I had planned for my week to go.

"They were buried in southern California and their lawyer told me that they had left everything to me. Including all their real estate investments."

"And that would include this house," I said quietly and wondered if he realized he was starting to ramble.

"I guess so," he said as he looked around. "This house was always my favorite. It's quiet here, peaceful."

I nodded my head without saying anything.

He said nothing else but stood and stretched. This was followed by a yawn. "Well I'm spent," he said as he headed toward the door. "Good-night, Jessica. Thank you for the sandwich."

He paused at the door for just a moment, leaving it half open. He looked into my eyes and it took me a moment to realize why fear and intrigue suddenly set into my heart. Those eyes, perfectly blue. Almost exactly like the exalted ones.

Just as he walked out and quietly closed the door, I managed to whisper, "Good-night, Alex."

I crawled onto the couch, wrapping my arms around my knees and listened to his movements. He walked up the stairs for a few moments before coming back down. I heard a door open and close and I had a sudden terrifying realization.

Alex was staying here: I had heard him bring in suitcases. He would be sleeping here at night. And in the room that shared a wall with my own.

I don't know why I had not realized this before. If I were to fall asleep I would seriously freak him out when I started screaming.

Of course as soon as I had this thought my eyelids became heavy. It sucks sometimes how the brain works, when you tell it not to do something, that is of course the first thing it wants to do. As if in response to this, my scar began to tingle again.

A door opened and another one closed. A few moments later I heard the shower in the other bathroom being turned on. After a minute or so I heard a faint humming, a song I did not recognize.

A thought occurred to me and I sprang from the couch and retrieved my laptop. As soon as it was up and running I opened up the Internet. I typed in the words and a fraction of a second later I was sorting through hits. The fifth one down gave me what I needed.

Alex had been telling the truth. Paul and Sue Wright had indeed died a week ago in a car accident. The article said Paul had likely fallen asleep at the wheel and drove into oncoming traffic, hitting a semi-truck. The truck driver had not been hurt but they had not stood a chance in their little compact car.

I heard the water shut off and I snapped the computer closed. I listened for his movements again and heard the bathroom door open and his bedroom door close. I counted to fifty and heard no more movement.

All my life I had been envious of everyone around me, just for the simple fact that they could sleep without fear, without having to face judgment for the dead. Absentmindedly I placed a hand on the back of my neck and ran my fingers over the scar.

After downing another Dr. Pepper, I sat back down on the couch and listened to the house breathe in the night. The wind picked up slightly, whispering to the house to let it in and warm itself. A light sprinkle began, giving the world a cleansing rinse from the day's grime. Finally the house sounded like it should this time of night. Silent.

CHAPTER FOUR

"Morning, Jessica."

I jumped violently when I heard his voice, slopping milk all down my front. I looked toward the door and stared obviously at the face there. Alex had showered again and gotten dressed. Perhaps I had not seen him clearly last night but the man before me was completely heart-stopping. I had been right the night before, he was well muscled but the shirt he wore that clung to his chest enhanced the effect blissfully. He was well tanned and I remembered he said he had been in Africa. His face nearly glowed with the effects of the sun and it complimented his facial features wonderfully. His jaw was square and strong, his nose was slightly broad, but it complimented his face perfectly. And again, those piercing blue eyes. A slight shiver worked its way up my spine.

I realized I was staring and embarrassed, looked down at my mess and was glad I had not gotten dressed yet for the day. At the same time I was beyond embarrassed to be seen in my pajamas again.

"Sorry," he said, trying to stifle a chuckle. "I didn't mean to scare you again. I guess I should have knocked."

"That might have helped," I said as I set the bowl down and grabbed a kitchen towel to dab at my soggy front.

"I'm going up to Bellingham to get some stuff," he said and I silently wondered if he was really staring at me or if I was just sadly wishing he was doing so. "It would be kind of nice to have some food in that fridge. I was wondering if you wanted to come with me."

I paused for a minute but didn't look up. The answer "yes" almost slipped through my lips before I could stop it. I quickly bit my lower lip and set the towel back on the counter. "I actually just went up yesterday to get some things. Thanks though."

"Ok," he said with a slight smile. "If you're sure."

I nodded my head, again biting my lower lip. I held my breath and counted to five so I wouldn't blurt out that I'd changed my mind.

"I'll see you later then," he said, flashing a brilliant smile. My heart gave a strange little twist as I watched him hesitate in his place for a moment. I hoped the expression that crossed his face for the briefest moment was disappointment. A moment later he walked out the door.

I gave a soft groan and flopped onto the couch. This was bad. How could I possibly make it work with Alex here? Things were going to get too complicated for me. And this was his house now. It could get really awkward really fast.

Or it could be really nice...

Stop it, I scolded myself. I couldn't let those kinds of thoughts surface. I couldn't let myself develop feelings like that again. No matter how just being around him these two short times felt like rain falling on a long dried out desert. I couldn't allow feelings like this to continue any longer. Relationships for me were impossible. I had learned that the really hard way once before. And besides, why would Alex ever be interested in someone as crazy as me?

My locker vibrated as I finally managed to get it open. The thing had never opened easily since I had been assigned it last year. I dug into my backpack, pulling out a book from my last period.

I heard the snickering across the hall, despite the steady flow of students that trudged through the halls of Bonneville High School. Two girls stood together, the queen bees of the popular crowd, whispering to Steve Fenn. My chest filled with flutters as his eyes met mine momentarily.

"She's so weird," he chuckled as his eyes darted away from mine, back to the Barbie's at his side.

"Doesn't she ever sleep?" one of the girls sneered. "Talk about bags."

I buried my head in my locker, pretending to be looking for something. Pretending like I hadn't heard their cruel words.

The wings on my back suddenly felt like a beacon. I felt sure that everyone in the hall could see them through my shirt. They might as well have been a billboard attached to my forehead stating FREAK.

I shook the memories off. This wasn't high school. The past was the reason why I had chosen my solitude. I could scream in peace here.

As I lay there patronizing myself, I had an important realization. I had the feeling Alex wasn't going anywhere any time soon. I was going to have to sleep sometime. The perfect time to do it was going to be while he was out.

I knew there wasn't going to be much time as I ran into my room and closed the door. I pulled the thick drapes over the window and crawled anxiously under the covers. For most, sleeping under pressure would be impossible, but when you slept as little as I did, it wasn't difficult. My body may not need as much as everyone else, but it still needed some.

I had never so willingly fallen asleep. The comfort that I might be able to hide the truth of what I experienced eased me into the darkness in just a few short moments.

My heart was beating painfully fast as I sat on the floor of my cell, my hands holding onto the cold, steel bars with every ounce of strength I had. After only a moment, I heard footsteps and saw Adam come into view. His face was expressionless as always and he walked at a slow, steady pace toward me, the gold chain hanging limply in his left hand. His wings nearly dragged on the floor. They were beautiful and menacing all at the same time as the light danced off them.

He reached the end of the tunnel, drew a silver key and unlocked my prison. My heart hammered and I was certain he could hear it. I drew in short, labored breaths as he bound my hands. Fourteen... fifteen...sixteen...

He tugged me down the tunnel and I restarted my count. Soft whimpers escaped my throat and I felt a tear roll down my cheek, but Adam did not turn and offer comfort. He stared forward, his expression solid as stone.

The count to sixty-two ended all too soon and I was brought to my place in the center of the stone catwalk. I closed my eyes tightly under my white covering and tried to block out the sound of rustling wings.

"Crystal Daniels," the leader of the council began. It was a female today. *My name is Jessica, my name is Jessica,* I chanted in my head. My ears started ringing.

"The deeds of your life have been accounted for and judgment will be passed. Your actions must be made known."

A soft whimper slipped from my lips and tears started rolling freely down my face as the sound of wings filled the air and the demented laughter began. I was ever grateful for the sack that covered my face. It would only make them laugh all the more to see my tears. It was almost impossible to hear the beautiful voices that descended from above. It seemed there were far more that came from below.

"Crystal Daniels, your deeds will now be revealed," the beautiful man before me said. I could not help but lift my head as the scrolls were produced and unraveled. To my slight relief they seemed almost equal in length.

By this point I should have known better than to hope. Crystal had obviously been some kind of prostitute and had done many unladylike things in her lifetime. I already sensed the few good things she had done in her life would not be enough to save her, or me.

When the end of the list was read, my breathing picked up to double. A strange wheezing came from my throat and my head spun. It was time.

The condemned council members were to cast their votes first.

"Down," the first said with a demented chuckle.

"Down," said the second.

"Down," the third and fourth sentenced.

There was a pause and I turned to the man who was the leader of the condemned. His hesitancy was surprising. Normally, the condemned voted for everyone, even the ones who didn't deserve it, to be cast down. The leader was the occasional exception.

He seemed to be studying me, debating what the fate of Crystal Daniels would be. There was something in his black eyes that made me shudder more than normal this time. I knew he could not see my face as it was covered but something made me feel exposed and vulnerable under his intense stare.

"Up," he finally said after what felt like an eternity.

My heart fluttered and I turned hopefully to the blue eyed angels.

The first shook her head, her mouth in a tight line. "Down.

"Down," the second.

There was a slight pause before the third said, "up."

There was an even longer pause and I could tell my face was soaked with tears. There had already been enough votes placed to grant me a branding.

"Down," the fourth finally said.

"Up," the fifth, and leader of the exalted said, the sadness in his voice evident.

I could not force a scream from my lips as the deranged laughter exploded from the walls. I heard Crystals name screamed until the name itself seemed a condemned word.

I looked up at the council and my eyes rested on the leader of the condemned. He stared at me with that strange expression on his face as if trying to understand something. He seemed to be searching for the answer to a question he had been asking for a long time. It only lasted a fleeting second though before the wicked grin spread on his face and his powerful wings projected him toward me.

I dropped to my hands and knees, both shaking so hard it was difficult to retain my position. I swept the hair from my neck.

The all too familiar searing white hot pain began on my neck and shot through my body. I could smell burned skin and hear it sizzle as the rod was pressed into my neck.

I was tugged to my feet and my eyes couldn't focus as I looked ahead to the council again.

"Crystal Daniels," the leader spoke again, his face still downfallen. "Judgment has been placed."

The terrifying sensation began crawling under my skin. It moved as if new bones were growing and rearranging under the surface. I heard my flesh tear and my own pair of wings burst forth.

The black eyed ones burst from their position on the wall and leapt at me. Hands covered every surface of my body and just before I thought I would pass out, the darkness came to meet me with mercy.

I was slightly disoriented when I woke, unsure of what time of day it was. I searched frantically for my clock on the nightstand. Ten forty-six. I'd been asleep for over three hours. This was longer than I had hoped for. I listened intently, searching for any indicators that Alex might have returned. When only silent walls answered, I lay back on the bed with a huff. If he had been home I had no doubt he would have heard me scream. I knew I had, I always did.

The trial came back to me and something disturbed me. I had stood hundreds of trials, but this one was different, just slightly. The leader of the condemned had acted strangely. Almost as if he wanted to see the face under the sack. My face. I shuddered at this thought. The sack was my only defense or protection in the nightmares. I did not want to think about what might happen if they were to see the person on trial was not in fact the face behind the mask.

I shook my head, trying to clear these thoughts. I was overreacting. I was over thinking this. What did it matter? It was supposed to be just a dream.

If only it were just a dream.

I heard the door open upstairs and I sprang from the bed. I wouldn't let him find me supposedly back in my bed at almost eleven o'clock. I ran into the bathroom and started the shower. After closing the door I quickly undressed and after a brief glance in the mirror at my reddened scars, I stepped into the scorching water.

I tried to listen for sounds of activity above me but couldn't make anything out over the sound of the water running.

Washing so much hair took time and it was a menace sometimes. I really needed to get it cut. It always took almost five minutes just to wash and rinse it.

"Hey, Jessica?"

A scream escaped my throat as I jumped and frantically wiped shampoo from my eyes.

"Alex?!" I screeched. "What are you doing in here?"

"I needed to ask you something. It's not like I can see anything."

I would have thought he was trying to be like most perverted guys who would try and sneak a peek, but his voice sounded so innocent and almost hurt that I couldn't tell him to get out immediately like I initially wanted to.

"You could have knocked first," I said. I was immediately grateful the shower curtain was a solid white vinyl instead of the common clear.

"I did but you must not have heard me," he said and I heard him take a seat on the toilet. "Sorry for scaring you. I seem to be doing a lot of that."

I found myself half smiling. He was right. Every time we had talked thus far he had scared me half to death first.

"I was wondering if you'd like to come up and have dinner with me tonight?" he asked. "I like to cook but it's not a whole lot of fun to cook just for myself."

A small laugh almost escaped my lips but I managed to hold it back. From first look at Alex I would have never thought he was the chef type. Or that this question was important enough to him that he felt the need to barge in here while I was in the shower.

"Yeah," I said. "I guess that would be okay."

"Great," he said as I heard him stand and could almost feel the grin the beamed from his face through the shower curtain. Somehow I was sure it was there. "I hope you like Thai food. It's my specialty."

"Sounds great," I chuckled. *Thai?* Even more not what I would have expected.

I heard the door click shut and then faintly heard my bedroom door close.

I shook my head in slight disbelief as I finished rinsing and turned the water off. The man knew no boundaries. He was incredibly presumptuous but seemed to be completely oblivious to this fact.

I wasn't going to admit to myself the extra amount of care I took in getting ready for the day. I did not even realize I was putting a little bit of make up on until it was already done. I had even chosen my favorite pink sweater to wear.

I shook my head at myself as I walked out the door. I was pathetic.

Part of my everyday routine was to check on Sal. She was reading one of the books I had bought her and she seemed to be near the end of it. She wouldn't say much, just a few mumbles and nods when I asked her questions. She was rather unsociable the last few days. But that was normal for Sal. She seemed to have cycles of either being a nonstop chatter box or almost completely mute. I wasn't going to pressure her. She'd already been through enough in her life; I wasn't going to add any stress.

I returned to my apartment and sat back at the table. Knowing I was only trying to pass the time until dinner, I pulled my laptop out and pulled my email up. There wasn't much in there as I didn't keep in touch with the very few friends I had in high school. I didn't belong to any social networking sites for the same reason. Most of the messages in my inbox were junk, but one caught my attention. It was the monthly newsletter from Stanford that I still continued to get, despite the fact that I had never actually made it to the university.

Having nothing else to do, I clicked on the message. I skimmed it quickly, my eyes freezing on a short announcement half way through it. The notice stated that one Jason Walker would begin teaching psychology in the summer. I knew that name all too well.

I had run away from home when I was sixteen and found myself in central California. I lied about my age to get an apartment, found a job, and learned to grow up very fast. Somehow I managed to stay in school too. Soon after I turned eighteen, in my senior year of high school, I met Jason. He was handsome and charming. He was older than I was, 24 and already almost finished with his masters. But neither of us seemed to care about the age difference. He looked younger than he really was; I looked slightly older, so people never really asked questions.

Jason was attentive and did not seem to mind my strange idioms. He was a great listener and I told him *everything* about myself. He told me he loved me often, and I did the same. I had even allowed myself to think of the possibility that we might end up married at the end of the year.

After six months of the happiest days of my life, the world exploded.

"Hey," I said with a smile as I placed a quick kiss on Jason's cheek. He only gave me a stiff smile and set his backpack on the grass. I tried not to worry about the crease in his forehead that only made an appearance when he was worked up, or the way he kept his distance from me.

The California air was warm, perfect for this time of year. I had survived graduation three weeks earlier. I was proud of myself for making it through all four years. Working a full time job to support myself wasn't easy, and when you add to that the pressure of finals and keeping up a solid 3.8 GPA, well, it had been hard. But I had done it. Jason had been in the stands cheering me on as I received my diploma.

"Do you want to go to the club tonight?" I asked, trying to lighten the mood that was already darkening, despite the fact that he hadn't said anything yet.

Jason looked at the ground, his lips pursed together in a tight line. His jaw was set hard and he seemed to be considering his words.

"I can't do this anymore Jessica," he finally said. He couldn't even meet my eyes. "I can't handle it anymore. It's just not normal. They aren't real."

"Jason," I whispered, my brow furrowing with the hurt that was only going to get ten times worse over the next few minutes.

"This is what I'm going to be doing, Jess," he said as he finally turned hard eyes on me. "I'm a psychology major for crying out loud! I should be able to spot when someone can't handle reality when I see it. I can't do this anymore. Good-bye, Jessica."

And with that he picked up his backpack and walked out of my life forever.

It was as harsh and dry as that.

I would never attend Stanford despite my acceptance.

Without even really realizing what I was doing, I had packed my few things and driven aimlessly north and ended up in Washington, almost to Canada. I spotted the lake to the west of the freeway and thought it was one of the most beautiful places I had ever seen. It looked so peaceful, a feeling I was desperate for. After driving to the west side of it I saw the sign in front of the house advertising the need for a house sitter. I secured the job the next day and had been there ever since.

With a deep sigh I deleted the message. I had gotten over Jason long ago. It had been difficult but I realized that someone who was going to throw me away like that wasn't worth pining away after.

I pulled open the search engine and typed in Jasper Wood's name again. The obituary popped up in less than a second. There wasn't much there. He was forty-eight, had worked at a mill for years and did not seem to be leaving any family behind. I retrieved my leather bound notebook and transcribed his name as well as Crystal Daniel's onto the page. I did not have a reason for doing this, but I had done it since I realized the names I stood trial for were real people. I suppose it seemed barbaric to simply forget them, no matter how the deeds of their lives haunted me.

CHAPTER FIVE

The rest of the day passed by in one slow swirl of anticipation and nerves. There wasn't much to do around the house so there was little to fill the time with until I went upstairs to see if there was anything I could do to assist Alex.

I stopped in my tracks for just a moment when I saw him in the kitchen. He was barefoot, wearing jeans and a red polo shirt. His entire front was covered with a faded white and pink checkered apron. Despite the ridiculous covering, he looked absolutely stunning. I often heard women talk about the attractiveness of a man who cooks but I had never been witness to that until just then.

"Oh, hey!" he said cheerily as he looked up from his work.

"Uh, hi," I said stupidly as I just stood at the top of the stairs.

"Everything is almost done," he said as he turned back to the steaming pots. "Just give me a few minutes."

"Could you use any help?" I asked as my senses started to come back to me.

"You could set the table if you'd like," he said as he wiped his hands on the feminine apron.

I just nodded my head before walking to the cabinet where I knew the dinnerware was and grabbed two plates and two bowls. I grabbed silverware and glasses as well and got the large oak dining table ready.

"That smells *really* good," I said as I laid napkins down.

"I hope you'll like it," he said with a grin as he poured something into a serving dish.

I stood to the side of the table and twisted my hands. After my year and a half of almost complete solitude, I could tell I had lost a lot of social skills. I wasn't sure what to say or how to act. Being around Sal was one thing, but being around Alex was completely another.

"You want to grab this?" he said as he took the apron off and held out a large silver bowl. I lurched forward just a little too quick to take it from his grasp and that little smile tugged at the corner of his mouth again. As I set the bowl of rice on the table I hoped I wasn't blushing horribly, but I had the sinking feeling that I was.

Alex followed me and set two dishes down. One contained strange, triangle shaped noodles and the other a steaming, spicy-smelling bowl of vegetables and beef.

"It's not got a lot to it but trust me, it's going to taste great," Alex said as he pulled out a chair. It took me a second to realize he was holding it out for me.

"Thanks," I said as I tucked a lock of hair behind my ear and sat down.

Alex took his seat and reached for my plate. "Do you care?"

"No, go ahead," I said shaking my head, feeling silly that he was dishing up my food.

He scooped a large pile of the noodles and rice onto the plate and topped the noodles with the vegetable and beef mixture.

"Oh, hang on," he said as he set the plate in front of me and stood up. "Forgot something."

He went to the fridge and came back a moment later carrying a bottle of soy sauce.

"Oh, thanks," I said stupidly, nearly dying from how awkward I felt. I hadn't had dinner with a man in a *very* long time, much less a man who looked like Alex. That was never.

"I'm glad you agreed to eat with me," he said as he piled food onto his own plate. "I hate eating by myself. I find it depressing."

I silently agreed with him despite the fact that I did it every day. I hesitantly scooped some of the food onto my fork and shoved it into my mouth.

"Wow!" I said as I chewed. "This is amazing!"

He chuckled as he took his own bite. "Glad you like it."

"Where did you learn to cook like this?"

He finished swallowing. "I studied in England for a few years and one of my roommates was from Thailand. His mother owned a restaurant and he had worked in it pretty much all his life. So, he taught me."

"England?" I questioned after swallowing another amazing bite. "You've done a lot of traveling it sounds like."

He wiped the corner of his mouth with his napkin. "I haven't been back in the states for more than a month since I was eighteen. I'm twenty-three now."

"Where were you studying in England?" I asked, realizing there was a lot more to this man than I had first realized.

"Oxford," he said softly before taking a long drink of water.

"Oxford?" I repeated and couldn't help but feel totally insignificant. I still had yet to attend *any* form of college.

"Yeah," he said, looking slightly embarrassed. "I somehow managed to get an international business degree. Pretty boring sounding, right?" he said with a chuckle. "It's kind of a miracle that I actually did get the degree. I kind of like to wander."

"Sounds like it," I said.

There was a moment of silence as we both ate but it was comfortable and easy. That was a quality I liked in people. There didn't need to be constant chatter and mindless talk. Sometimes it was nice to just sit in silence.

We each finished our food and sat back in our chairs, feeling stuffed to the limit.

"So what about you?" he asked. "Are you from Bellingham or something?"

"No," I said feeling instantly uncomfortable. Talking about my past wasn't exactly easy for me. "I grew up in this really small town called Ucon, in Idaho."

"Wow, not what I would have guessed. So what happened?"

I was taken aback by how quickly he seemed to have guessed there *was* something that had in fact happened. "Let's just say it was time to leave home or both me and my parents were going to regret things that were about to happen."

I hadn't meant for the words to come out that way and suddenly wished I had given a more tactful explanation.

"You don't have to tell me anything you don't want to," he said quietly.

"Thanks," I whispered as I looked at my hands in my lap. There was a moment of silence again but this time it wasn't quite so comfortable.

A thought occurred to me and I looked up to his face. "So now that you're here and have this house left to you, are you planning to stay or go back to Africa?"

"I think I'm going to stay around here for a while. We were about done in Kenya anyway and by the time I got back it'd be over. I had been trying to decide what to do when it was over. So, yeah, I think I'll stay around for a while. I like Washington."

I felt weird asking the next question but it was important. "I can find somewhere else to live now if you'd like. This is probably weird for you, moving back and finding someone living in your house."

"No!" he sounded almost alarmed. "Not at all. Please, stay as long as you want. Like I said, there was a pretty good chunk of money left in a fund to continue paying your wages for however long you want to stay. And honestly, I'm glad you're here. I don't do well being all by myself. I like people." That small grin was begging to break free again.

"If you're sure," I said cautiously.

"Yes," he said almost too quickly and this time the grin was trying to spread on my face.

As if to save us from any further awkwardness, the phone rang. I almost sighed in relief. Even though I was enjoying Alex's company and attention I still wasn't sure how to handle it. Alex rose to his feet just before I could and answered it.

"It's for you," he said as he extended the cordless phone.

I grabbed it from him and held it to my ear. "Hello?"

"Jessica! Where are you? I've been waiting for forever!"

Guilt instantly washed over me as I heard Sal's frantic tone.

"I'm so sorry Sal. I got distracted. I'll be right over."

Sal said a clipped "bye" before she hung up.

"I have to go," I said as I turned to Alex and hung up the phone. "I can't believe I forgot it's Wednesday. I go over to the neighbors every week and watch her show with her."

"Who?" he asked as he leaned against the counter.

"Sally Thomas," I said as I started for the stairs to get my things. "Do you know her?"

"Only a little," he said. "She moved into the house a little while before I graduated but we weren't always here. I know my grandma was friends with her."

I hurried down the stairs, trying hard to keep the numbers that flowed through my mind from slipping over my lips. Ten…eleven…twelve… Alex followed me.

"I feel horrible I forgot about this. We do it every week. How could I forget?" I said as I opened the door to my apartment and looked around for my jacket.

"Do you mind if I come with you?" he asked as he leaned against the doorframe.

I froze in my tracks, half bent, looking through a few things on the floor. Sal might not notice my strange behavior toward her show, but Alex just might. And I wasn't exactly sure how Sal would react to him.

"Um..." I debated internally. I found my jacket and straightened as I pulled it on. "I'm not sure how Sal will handle it if you come. Did you know her much at all?"

"I know she's different," Alex said nonchalantly. "She always seemed to like me whenever I talked to her before though."

I nodded my head. "I guess it might be ok. She's been really quiet lately and kind of out of it so she might not really even realize you're there."

"That's alright with me," he said as he ducked out and I heard him rummage around in his room for a second before he appeared back in the doorframe with a hooded jacket on. "If you don't mind me tagging along."

"That's fine with me," I said, trying not to smile. "Let's go."

We walked out the door and made our way to Sal's in silence. I gave a soft knock on the door twice before letting myself in.

Sal was already cuddled up on one of the couches, a blanket wrapped around her shoulders, remote in hand.

"Sorry, Sal," I said as I took a quick look around to make sure everything looked in order. Everything seemed to be in its proper placement of chaos. "I had a friend show up and got a bit distracted."

At this Sal's head popped up from staring at the blank TV screen. Her gaze went immediately to Alex and to my great surprise, a smile spread on her face. "Hello Alex."

Alex didn't hide his astonishment that not only did she recognize him, but she also remembered his name. "Hi Sal," he replied with a broad smile, making a quick recovery.

She didn't say anything more as she turned her attention back to the TV and pulled up her TIVO menu. I gave Alex a sideways glance before we walked into the living room and sat on the empty couch. After just a second the show started.

Sal did not really watch any television, but she had an unfortunate obsession with *Touched by an Angel*, and I *had* to watch it with her. Of all the shows she could choose to be obsessed with it had to be *that* show.

As the episode started, I realized it was one that we'd already seen from an early season. I guessed by now we had probably watched all the seasons and every episode to ever air. I tried very hard to focus my attention on the show. Normally I was able to ignore the show completely, but with Alex there to observe, I thought it best to show some interest. It was not that I did not like the show. I thought the messages in it were good and had worthy origins, but why did they have to call them angels? If they were called anything else I probably would have actually enjoyed watching the show. Obviously the creators knew nothing of the true nature of the beings they were trying to portray.

I couldn't help it as I diverted my attention to anything other than the television screen without taking my eyes from it. I noticed that somehow Alex's arm had ended up draped across the back of the couch. Trying to be discrete, I glanced at his face, searching for any signs of a sly grin but found his face oddly attentive of the show before him. He wasn't trying to be sneaky or make a move. I somehow doubted he even realized his arm was there, resting just an inch or so above my shoulders.

I tried to turn my attention back to the television but caught a glimpse of Sal out of the corner of my eye. To my great shock and embarrassment she was staring intently in my direction, a slight smile spread across her face. It almost startled me at first, Sal almost never smiled. And she never lost attention in her show.

A confused expression spread on my face as I shrugged my shoulders just slightly as if to ask her, "What?" Her grin only got a little bigger before she turned her attention back to the television.

I didn't see it; if it was at all possible I just felt it, the small smile that crept onto Alex's lips.

The rest of the show passed by unbearably slow and I nearly sighed in relief when the credits started rolling. Feeling ready to snap at any moment from the tension I felt inside, I sprang to my feet and grabbed my jacket. Sal turned the television off and stood to face us, that strange grin still spread on her face.

I tried to ignore it, however impossible it was to do so. "Do you need anything Sal?" I asked, as I always did before I left her house.

"I'm okay," she said, her grin still plastered on her face. "Good-night Jessica. Good-night Alex." Without another word she walked to the stairs and headed down to her bedroom.

This time I did sigh in relief as we turned for the door and walked out.

"What a nice evening," Alex said as we walked up the stairs that ascended the sloped lawn to the road.

It was freezing. Small puffs of air curled out from our lips and noses and rose into the air in delicate patterns.

"Sal seems like a really wonderful person," he continued as we took our first steps down the road.

"She is," I said as I wrapped my arms around my torso. "She's different but I suppose that's part of why I care about her so much. She's so innocent."

Alex nodded his head. "It's really good of you to take care of her like that. My grandma tried to help her out, but we were gone so much it made it difficult."

By this time we reached the stairs that led down to the house and I kept my silent count to ninety-one to myself. As we walked back into the house the smell of our recent meal filled my nose.

"Oh shoot," I said as I closed the door behind us. "I forgot about all this. I'll help you clean it up."

He didn't argue with me and we quickly cleared the table and started to load the dishwasher.

"I really enjoyed tonight," I said as I put the plates onto the rack, speaking before I thought about what I was going to say. I immediately felt blood rush into my face.

"I did too," Alex said. As he rinsed a pot and handed it to me, his eyes met my own and I felt a small quiver run down my spine as that smile spread on his lips. He turned his attention back to another pot. "Thanks for letting me come with you to Sal's. It was nice."

I had to hold back a little chuckle as I put the pot into the dishwasher. *Awkward maybe*, I thought to myself. "I was surprised she remembered your name. She barley remembers her own most days it seems. You must have left a good impression on her before."

"I guess," he said simply as he handed me the last of the silverware. I loaded it into the rack and closed the door.

"Thanks for the help," Alex said as he leaned against the counter, his arms folded across his chest.

"You're welcome."

Alex glanced back at the clock that hung above the sink. It now read eleven o'clock exactly. "Well, I think I'm going to hit the sack. I've got to meet with an attorney in the morning. Something to do with my grandparents will and having the assets transferred to my name."

"Sounds fun," I said sarcastically.

"You'd better believe it," he said as he rolled his eyes and started for the stairs. We walked down in silence and said a brief goodnight before we went our separate ways.

When all was quiet, I pulled my laptop out again and pulled up the internet. After only a few moments I found the gruesome answers I was looking for.

I was right when I assumed Crystal Daniels was a prostitute. She had also been murdered last night in an alleyway. Stabbed four times in the chest. The murderer was still at large and they currently had no leads.

Could one really call that getting what another deserved? I didn't know if anyone deserved to die like that.

The next morning the house felt oddly silent. It was strange how I had grown so accustomed to having another person around after just one day. I thought I was happy being on my own. I had become independent and I needed no one. Apparently I was wrong. Humans are social creatures by nature and while I may have been a freak, I was still human. At least I hoped so.

I was restless and anxious with how empty the house felt so I headed to Sal's early. She may not have been the company I was craving, but anything was better than sitting at home alone at this point.

"Sal?" I called as I opened the door and peaked in.

"Come in," I heard her call faintly from inside.

As usual, I quickly glanced around and noted that everything looked in order.

"Sal?" I called again when I saw no signs of her.

"Down here," I heard her voice float up the stairs.

I found her in the office, sitting at the great oak desk, a shoebox open in front of her.

"What are you doing?" I asked as I sat in the chair in front of the desk.

She didn't say anything but pushed a photo across the desk towards me. I picked it up and examined it.

There were two people in it. The first was Sal. She appeared to be several years younger, her skin more youthful and her hair a bit more lively. Yet there was something all too familiar about her eyes, they looked haunted, hurt.

The second woman was slightly familiar and it took me a moment to recognize her. I had never actually met Sue Wright in person, only talked to her on the phone, but I had seen one or two pictures of her. She was a kind looking woman, pure white hair, wrinkles all around her eyes and sprouting from her sunny smile. Her face was tanned and warm looking.

Sue's arms were wrapped around Sal's waist, her head resting slightly on her shoulder. Sal looked hesitant but she was smiling as if in acceptance of the woman's affection.

"Alex said you were friends," I said quietly as I pushed the photo back towards her.

"I miss her," Sal said and I was surprised to hear the emotion in her voice. As I looked into her face I saw a single tear rolling down her cheek. I had never seen Sal cry. I also silently wondered how Sal had found out about Paul and Sue's death as neither Alex nor I had said anything at all about it.

Sal didn't look up again from the box as she pushed another photo towards me. This one held two men standing next to a barbeque, both wearing aprons. Paul and Alex. Paul was tall, just as tall as Alex. He was very fit for a man his age and his build was similar to Alex's. His hair was very dark, almost black, yet speckled with dignified silver. His face was tan as well, a leathered look as if he had spent too much of his life out in the sun.

"When were these pictures taken?" I asked as I noticed Alex looked much younger. He was exactly the type of guy that every girl in high school would have had a crush on. I certainly would have.

"That was Alex's eighteenth birthday," Sal said as she pushed another picture towards me. This one was of Alex blowing out candles on a birthday cake. "He graduated a month later. That was the last time I saw him."

It seemed strange to me that there didn't seem to be any friends around in any of the pictures. What eighteen-year-old guy was content to spend his birthday with just his grandparents and the odd neighbor? To me this spoke loads about his character.

"Alex is a nice boy," Sal said as she finally looked up at me, a serene smile on her face. "I'm glad he came back home."

The thought *I am too*, ran through my mind all too quickly. I tried not to think too much about how ridiculous I was being.

Sal continued to pass pictures to me. She starred in a few, but for the most part they were of Alex. There were several of him eating a hamburger, opening a few presents, and a few candid ones of him laughing with his grandfather. It took me a while before I thought to wonder where Alex's parents were. I had never heard him say anything about them yet.

After an hour or so I could tell Sal was getting restless and ready to be alone. I took this as my cue to head back home.

"Do you need anything, Sal?" I asked as I rose to leave.

She shook her head as normal and I bid her goodbye.

I didn't see Alex the rest of the day, much to my disappointment. The day passed painfully slow and when I finally heard the door open and close at eleven thirty, I knew it was too late in the night to rush out and see how he was. Not only was this desperate but I should probably be asleep.

X

The store was still fairly quiet, not a surprise considering we had gotten there just minutes after it opened its doors. Just after I had thrown a load of laundry into the washer Alex had come in and asked if I would mind doing some shopping with him. At first I had been hesitant, with it being the day before Valentines but when he told me he would be shopping for new appliances, it seemed less threatening.

"This would be *so* nice," Alex mused as he ran a hand over the glossy sterling silver range that was on display. "So much better than that old unit at home."

I couldn't help but chuckle. While I had to agree that the house could use some updating as it was twenty something years old now, it seemed humorous that a twenty-three-year-old guy would care.

"What do you think about this one?" he asked as he looked me in the face. His brow was furrowed but I could see the excitement in his eyes.

"Um…" I stammered as I struggled to look away from his face. The unit certainly did look nice, it was shiny and pretty but it was just another range to me, the only difference being that it had six burners instead of the normal four. "Are you ever likely to be using that many burners at a time?" *Nice,* I scolded myself. *That sounded real smooth.* I was such a dork.

A smile cracked on one side of his lips. "This is the one I'm going to get then," he said gleefully.

I only chuckled and shook my head as we walked over to the refrigeration units. Alex quickly got down to business, opening and closing the doors of almost every unit. At one particularly fancy one that contained some kind of touch screen in it, Alex started chuckling and shook his head.

"What's so funny?" I asked shyly, yet curious as to what the answer would be.

Alex chuckled again before he gave a little sigh and closed the door. "Just an old memory," he said as he moved onto the next unit. "I remember when I was about six, my grandparents got a new fridge that had the ice and water in the door and my dad was absolutely fascinated by it. He thought that was the coolest thing ever invented. I wonder what he might have thought if he were to see this."

This was the first time I had ever heard Alex mention either of his parents. "Where do your parents live now?" I couldn't help asking.

As Alex looked at me I saw a certain sadness spread in his eyes. It made me sad too, those startlingly blue eyes should never look sad.

"I have never actually met my mom," he said as he continued walking slowly through the isle. "She took off when I was only a few weeks old. My grandparents never had anything good to say about her and alluded to a drug problem she had struggled with for years. I guess I was lucky it didn't affect me at all when she was pregnant with me. I have no idea where she is or what last name she might be using to even try to track her down. I only know her first name is Caroline.

"When I was about three my dad was diagnosed with lung cancer. He smoked while he was in the army and it caught up to him, though he had quit long before I was born. His body wasn't handling it too well and we had to move in with my grandparents. It was a nasty battle with the cancer and of course they didn't have the treatments for it back then as they do now. He died a week before my seventh birthday."

He was quiet for a long moment after that and I could feel tears welling up in my eyes. "I'm so sorry, Alex. That's terrible."

His own sad eyes met mine. To my surprise, a smile spread on his face and to my relief it spread to his eyes. In a gesture that totally took me off guard, he draped an arm across my shoulders. "It's alright," he said casually. "My grandparents were amazing people and I was very happy growing up with them. I don't remember too much of my dad but what I do remember is nothing but good memories."

I tried to smile and gave a little sniffle. He looked back down at me and giving me a quick squeeze, turned to another fridge. "How about this one?" he said with a sarcastic smile. I couldn't help but laugh as I saw the one he indicated was maybe half the size of a normal fridge.

He didn't take too much longer to pick out the rest of his new appliances. My jaw nearly hit the floor when I saw the total price. I thought I saw Alex cringe slightly as well, but he simply pulled out a card. "Thanks Grandma and Grandpa," he said with a chuckle as he swiped it.

CHAPTER SIX

Morning dawned with an oddly bright hue. As I peered out my bedroom window, I was surprised to see several feet of fluffy-looking snow on the ground. One more thing about Washington in the winter; it can rain buckets and dump large amounts of precipitation in a short time, but if the temperature drops below freezing it makes for a lot of snow. Lake Samish was located in a bit of a pass and the roads were difficult to keep clear in snow storms. I knew what the conditions were going to be like. Smart people would be staying home today.

I had just poured a large amount of cereal into a bowl when I heard the door crack open.

"Jessica?" his voice was surprisingly quiet and hesitant. It seemed unnatural for him.

"Yes?" I said as I felt slightly frantic that I was getting caught yet again in my pajamas.

He rounded the corner and I was slightly surprised at his appearance when he came into view. He was wearing a threadbare white tee-shirt that seemed several sizes too small, with the mascot from some high school in southern

California. His bottom half was covered in red and black checkered pajama pants.

"Would you care to join me for breakfast?" he said, that smile playing on his lips again. "You know I had to try out the new goods."

I glanced at my bowl of still dry cereal and nodded my head.

"Great," he said, a dazzling smile breaking on his face. "It's all ready."

I considered putting something more covering on but after a moment decided there really wasn't much point. He'd already seen me as I was, several times.

I followed him up the stairs and my mouth started to water as the scent of bacon filled my nose. My stomach instantly growled, in an embarrassingly loud manner. Surprising, considering how infrequently I did eat; I didn't think I was actually hungry.

Alex chuckled as we came to the main floor. "Just in time it sounds like."

Shock spread on my face as I took a look at the table. He must have been up for much longer than I had realized. The table was filled with piles of bacon, sausage, eggs, and pancakes. The new look of the kitchen was surprising. Everything had a new bright gleam as the light danced across all the sterling silver surfaces.

"Hope you're hungry," he said as he walked to the table and pulled a chair out for me. "I got a little carried away this morning."

I took the seat he offered and noticed as my cheeks flushed red that the pancakes were pink and shaped into hearts.

Alex took the seat next to me and started dishing food onto his plate. "Happy Valentine's Day," he said as he glanced up at me for a moment.

I stiffened for a moment. The pancakes and the big breakfast instantly made sense. I had almost forgotten that this day was upon us. It took me only a moment to calm down by reminding myself that I didn't have to face the hypocritical novelties of the holiday as long as I didn't go out. The white fluffy stuff on the ground was certainly going to prevent that.

"And to you as well," I finally managed to squeak out.

"How'd you sleep last night?" he asked after swallowing a huge bite of eggs.

I nearly choked on my orange juice as it went down. I coughed violently for a second before I could speak. "Fine," I lied as I put the glass back down, before I could accidently spill it.

"You okay?" he asked. I couldn't tell if his tone was sincere or slightly amused.

"Yeah," I said as I dabbed a napkin at my mouth to make sure there was nothing embarrassing there. "How do you like your new fancy stove?" I asked, trying to very quickly change the subject before I had to lie any more.

This instantly brought a smile to his face. "It's awesome," he said with that huge grin on his face. "And I even had all six burners on this morning. Though I may not have actually been using them all," he added a little more quietly.

Food threatened to spray across the table as a laugh burst from my lips. Embarrassment washed over me immediately and I tried to cover it by shoveling another forkful into my mouth. I savored every bite as it went down. I couldn't remember the last time I'd had a hot breakfast, much less one that was this good.

"So what are your plans for the day?" he asked.

I swallowed a large bite of bacon before I spoke. "Don't really have any. I certainly won't be going anywhere," I said as I looked out the window.

"There's no lucky man on his way to take you out for a romantic Valentines?" he said with a wry smile.

I felt myself blush again under his gaze. "Nope, can't say there is," I said. "What about you? Is there some woman you're going to rush off to later to pick up?"

He gave a slight laugh. "Relationships have been pretty hard to maintain for me. It's a little difficult to have them when you're running all over the world. And I learned very quickly that long distance relationships just don't work out."

What he said made sense, but part of me was shocked that this gorgeous specimen before me could possibly be single.

"At least we've got each other today," he said as he looked back into his plate. I wasn't sure how he had meant for me to interpret this. His tone was innocent and did not imply anything. I tried to ignore how my heart gave a faint flutter before bursting into a throbbing race.

"It's been a long time since I've seen snow," he continued casually. "I was thinking it might be fun to venture out into it for a while today. You want to come?"

I looked out the window again. The snow would easily come above my knees. "I guess," I said with a hesitant grin as I continued to look out the window, trying not to think about how cold it had to be outside.

A boyish grin spread on his face as he turned his full attention back to his plate. He began shoveling his food down at an impressive speed.

"Whoa!" I laughed as I watched him. "Slow down, you're going to choke! A little excited, are we?"

"Not going to waste any time," he said through a mouthful of food.

His enthusiasm was contagious and I couldn't help but be swept up in it as I too scarfed down the rest of the food on my plate. It was too bad; I would have liked to have taken my time to enjoy it. But more than my desire to savor every bite, I wanted to go and have some fun with this pretty amazing man next to me.

As soon as we were both finished, we sprang from our seats and raced down the stairs, neither of us bothering to even clear our dishes from the table or put any of the extra food away. As soon as I reached my door I froze.

"I don't have any snow stuff," I called to Alex who was already in his room. "What should I wear?"

"I don't either," he said with a laugh. "I'm just going to put on as many layers as I can."

I gave a shrug before going into my room and following his advice. A minute or so later Alex entered the apartment and I couldn't help but laugh at his appearance. His legs were bulging and looked oddly swollen due to the multiple layers of pants. I could tell he had on several sweaters under his rain coat and he had a scarf wrapped around his neck and covering half his face. All this was topped with an orange wool hunting hat.

"How do I look?" he said using a dramatic Spanish accent as he struck a manly pose.

"Amazing," I said with a stupid giggle, not being completely sarcastic. I suddenly felt like a fourteen-year-old girl.

"You don't look so bad yourself," he said with a wink as he looked at me.

I was dressed similarly, with so many layers of clothing it was difficult to move.

"Shall we?" he said as he indicated the door.

"Let's go."

As I expected, as soon as the door was opened, a large pile of snow dumped itself onto my floor. After a few moments we had both scooped it up and plowed our way through the wall.

I had never seen any place more beautiful in the winter than Washington. It did not snow more than a dozen times in the winter but when it did, the effect was enchanting. The way the snow left a soft dusting on the towering evergreens never ceased to stop me in my tracks for a moment and take in its beauty. It was breathtaking.

The property the house was set on was a fairly steep hill, dropping quickly from the road above down to the lake, the house clinging to the sloping side. One wrong step and it wouldn't be too difficult to slide all the way from the top toward the frigid waters.

"This is why I love Washington," Alex said as he paused on the deck to overlook the view before us. "Southern California is nice in its own way but it doesn't have half the beauty this place does."

"I couldn't agree more," I said, watching the stream curl from my mouth, drift upward, then disappear.

Alex glanced over at me and that sly smile threatened to break through. Just as I caught the mischievous gleam in his eye, I knew it was already too late.

"Gotch' ya!" he bellowed just as he dumped a handful of snow on my head.

By the time I screamed and wiped the snow off he was already half way up the hill, running toward the road. I bent down and picked up a handful of the powder and formed it into a ball. My aim was surprisingly accurate considering the many cumbering layers I wore and the snowball landed square on the back of his head.

I couldn't remember the last time I had felt so lighthearted and care free as we chased each other around the yard, throwing snowballs as fast as we could. There weren't many times when I had allowed myself to be so relaxed around anyone, parents and friends included. It seemed so easy for Alex to bring out a side of me that I didn't think existed, a part of me that just wanted to be me and felt *free* to be just me.

"I don't think that's the best spot to lie down," I said with a chuckle as I watched Alex lay right in the middle of the road.

He sat back up and looked to his left then to his right before looking back up at me with a smirk. "I really don't think anyone's going to be driving on this road for quite a while."

I had to admit he was probably right. Even though it was nearly ten, there weren't any tire tracks on the road yet. We were pretty well snowed in.

With a blissful sounding sigh, he tilted his head back until he fell perfectly flat on the snowy road. I chuckled at him and shook my head. I looked across the road to the hill that rose up from it, wondering if we would be able to find a straight enough path to sled between the trees.

"Come make a snow angel with me, Jessica!" Alex said in innocent delight.

As I looked down, I was fairly sure my heart stopped beating for a moment. Flashbacks from my nightmares filled my head as I beheld the perfectly beautiful man with piercing blue eyes and brilliant wings newly formed at his side.

"I...I..." I stammered, frozen in terror. My hands started shaking and I felt slightly weak in the knees. My ears started ringing and I couldn't concentrate on any other sound. My breath came in sharp, painful bursts. The scar on the back of my neck prickled and started to burn.

"Jessica?" a voice called but it sounded muffled and very far away.

And then darkness swallowed me whole.

CHAPTER SEVEN

I always felt sure I knew terror as no other person did, but the terror I felt now could not even compare to what I had experienced before.

It was completely dark, wherever it was I might be. It hid things from my eyes and it seemed to be in alliance with the voices I heard. It unmercifully veiled them in its impenetrable folds.

The laughter was maddening as the voices heckled, rising in volume and dementia with each passing moment. Cold clammy hands reached out at me, tracing fingers along my cheek, down the back of my neck, across my thigh, grasping my ankles. The feeling of the condemned pressing closer in on me, nothing but hands touching, was beyond petrifying.

Through all these sensations a new one began. The feeling that a more solid and lucid being was standing directly before me, cloaked cruelly in the darkness. A new distinctive set of hands reached forth, just as frigid and clammy as the others but more deliberate, more powerful.

They placed themselves on either side of my face and I felt my insides chill as I had the feeling that eyes were boring into my own. Those hands slid slowly down to my shoulders, down my arms and I felt myself being pulled closer to the unseen being. The arms that started to wrap around me were just as cold as the hands attached to them.

I wanted to run, to disappear, to die, but could do nothing as those arms forced me into an arctic embrace.

I sensed rather than heard as the thing seemed to be inhaling my scent and felt as if death had finally found me when a pair of lips brushed my ear.

"You shall be mine," a voice clear and sharp as ice whispered.

As soon as the words were spoken I was released by the mass of cold hands and felt instead that my body was being shaken violently, the air around me warming quickly.

"You shall be mine," the voice again whispered into the darkness. It was followed by a chilling low chuckle.

"Jessica?" the voice was quiet but frantic.

I realized the shaking was coming from a pair of large hands on my shoulders. My heart was pounding and I felt like my body was trembling violently. I had to get my eyes open. I had to escape from the cold.

"Jessica?" the voice called again, this time a little louder.

The muscles in my eyelids finally started working again and I opened my eyes just slightly and gasped at a pair of blue eyes only inches away from my own.

"You're awake!" Alex cried as he gathered me up in his arms and crushed me to his chest.

"Can't breathe," I gasped as the air was forced out of my lungs.

"Sorry," he said as he immediately lay me back down. "Are you alright? Do you want me to take you to the hospital? I nearly called 911!"

As his questions registered I had to think if I *was* actually alright. My scar burned as if it had been freshly branded, but the rest of me felt only slightly shaky.

"No," I said after only a moment of hesitation. "I'm fine." Doctors were to be avoided at all costs. They would ask questions I had no logical answers to when they saw my bare back.

"Are you sure?" I could see the genuine concern in his eyes as he looked closely at my face. "I'm pretty sure my truck could make it through the snow if it had to."

"I'm fine, Alex," I said again as I struggled to sit up. A thick quilt fell off me and with a horrified gasp I realized I was wearing nothing but my underwear and bra.

"Alex!" I shrieked as I pulled the blanket back up to cover me. "Did you do this?"

"Yeah," he said, no embarrassment in his voice. "After you passed out you started shaking like crazy, your teeth were chattering even. Your clothes were pretty well soaked, so when I brought you inside I thought it best to get them off before you froze to death."

His explanation, however embarrassing it was, made sense. I registered that he himself was down to one pair of partially wet jeans and a tee-shirt.

"Oh, well, thanks, I guess," I said as I realized I was in the living room on the couch. I noticed it had been pushed in front of the fireplace and a fire was roaring in it. Even though I knew the temperature had to be at least ten degrees above the normal of the house, it felt wonderful on my skin and the shaking started to die down.

"What happened?" he asked as he took a seat on the couch down by my feet.

I hadn't thought up an explanation as to what had indeed occurred. I didn't even know. So I blurted out the first thing that came to mind. "I got a little light headed all the sudden. I'm not really sure."

He looked at me sternly for a long moment but seemed to accept my answer after a moment.

"How long was I out?" I couldn't even begin to guess, it could have been seconds or hours as far as I could tell.

"Only about five minutes or so," he answered as he stood. He walked to the kitchen and a moment later walked back with a tall glass of water and a pink, heart-shaped box.

"Drink this," he said as he handed me the glass and sat back down. "I was going to wait until later to give this to you. I didn't think it would actually be benefiting your health," he said with a chuckle and handed me the small box that I knew would contain chocolate. Mercifully it didn't have any chubby-cheeked cherubs on it.

"If your blood-sugar was low, this will help," he explained when I gave him a confused look. "Though that seems unlikely since we had just eaten. That could be the reason you passed out."

"Thanks," I said before I downed half the glass in one breath. I tried to ignore the intuitive way Alex was staring at me as I opened the box and popped a chocolate in my mouth. I extended the box toward him and, never breaking his stare, he took one.

"Alex," I sighed as I leaned back on the couch. "I'm fine, really. I'm not sure why I passed out all the sudden but I promise I'm ok."

"You gave me a scare there. We were just goofing off and then you looked at me and got this terrified expression on your face and collapsed, out cold."

Crap. I was hoping the terror I irrationally felt had not shown on my face. Apparently I wasn't so lucky.

"I think I'd feel better if you went and laid down for a while. You should get some rest."

My brand burned as I shook my head. "I'm fine. Really."

Alex shook his head and that mischievous grin spread on his face. Before I realized what was happening, he had scooped me into his arms, thankfully keeping me covered with the quilt, and slung me up onto his shoulder.

"Put me down!" I shrieked as he started his descent down the stairs. "Alex!"

"Don't argue with me, Jessica," he said and I could tell there was a smile on his lips. He was enjoying this. "You passed out for no good reason. You really need to take it easy for the rest of the day. Or at least a few hours."

Seeing that my pounding on his back wasn't getting me anywhere, I fell limp and let him carry me. He ducked as he walked through the door to my apartment and again into my bedroom. He set me down gently on my bed, pausing for just a slight moment to stare into my face again. This time however, it was not a stare of disbelief, searching for signs of my ill health. There was true concern there and I was surprised by the emotions that played across his face. First and foremost was the concern, but there was a hint of curiosity, and perhaps my mind was seeing things it wanted to, longing.

After a moment that seemed to stretch on for several mixed emotional minutes, I realized I had become partially uncovered and quickly rearranged the blankets to become appropriate. As I did so, a terrifying thought hit me like a semi-truck.

"How much did you see?" I asked with a shaking voice. "When you were taking my wet things off?"

If the answer to this question had not been so important I would have regretted asking it instantly by the hurt that spread on Alex's face.

"I generally like to think of myself as a gentleman, Jessica," he said as he straightened and stood, a stiffness filling him that didn't fit. "I didn't look any more than I had to."

"Alex, no, I didn't..." I trailed off realizing that I could not explain why I was suddenly so afraid he might have seen the brand or the impossible wings raised in my skin. "I didn't mean it that way."

He relaxed slightly, but the offended expression was still too present on his face. "Just a second," he said as he slipped out the door. I heard him rummaging through some things in the family room and he came back in after just a minute.

I was glad to see the hard expression was gone when he came back, replaced by that half smile that knew so well how to send my heart into a pathetic flutter.

"If you need anything," he said as he extended something to me. I rolled my eyes and laughed when I reached out and found it was a bell. "Just ring this and I'll come running."

I couldn't help but smile as I looked at it, shaking my head. "Thank you, Alex," I said as I looked back up at him, meeting his dazzling smile.

"You're welcome," he said and headed toward the window, pulling the drapes shut. He then walked to the door.

"Get some rest," he said as he looked back at me. "Please."

"I'll try," I said, truly wishing I could do as he asked.

He gave a weak smile and just before he closed the door a thought occurred to me.

"Alex?" Had I just imagined he snapped his head to look back at me just a little too fast? "Will you check on Sal for me? I just realized I haven't gone to see her today."

Alex nodded his head with a soft smile then left.

Now alone with my thoughts, I had to consider the terrifying thing that had just occurred. It would seem that I had passed out but instead of being thrown into a trial, something else had happened. I had no explanation for what occurred; I wasn't even sure what happened. But *that* had *never* happened before.

If there was any comfort in this terrifying curse I couldn't escape it was that it was always the same. The final verdict may vary but the trial itself was predictable in its events and order. The fact that there was a new factor in all of this was just as terrifying as the dream itself, or whatever that was.

After a few hours of mulling over what happened I had pretty well convinced myself not to think too much about it. It was just something my mind made up, a nightmare of my own making, a simple response to my fear of seeing Alex with wings a few moments before. And besides, no matter what it was, dreams weren't real.

If only I didn't know better.

The hours passed slowly. I knew I had to stay in my bed or risk having Alex carry me back down here. Twice he peeked his head through my door and I pretended to be asleep for his benefit. It was easier than arguing with him. In a way it was endearing. It was nice to have someone watching out for me for a change.

At four o'clock I decided I'd rested enough. I climbed in the shower and stood under the stream until the water ran cold. The contrast in heat felt refreshing but I pulled on my warmest sweater and put a pair of long johns on under my jeans.

When I found the basement empty I made my way upstairs, a delicious smell wafting through the house.

"Am I allowed to come out now?" I said, trying to keep my face serious as I stood at the top of the stairs.

Alex was in the kitchen again, that same silly pink and white checkered apron covering his front.

He looked up from whatever he was stirring in a giant pot and smiled. "Yeah, I guess."

He put a lid on the pot and wiped his hands on the apron before turning to something on a cutting board. "I hope you don't mind having dinner a little early tonight. I was getting a kind of bored I'm afraid. I don't much like being trapped in the house and it's been a little too quiet for me."

"It didn't have to be so quiet," I said as I took a seat at the table to watch him.

"Jessica," he growled. He turned his attention to something in the oven. "I hope you don't mind but I invited Sal to join us for dinner."

"And she accepted?" I took no cares to hide the shock in my voice. I had never known Sal to leave her house.

"Yep," he said, adding a few herbs to another pot.

"Wow," I muttered. "She must really like you."

"I was just nice to her. It took a little convincing but she didn't give me too much trouble. Speaking of which," he said as he glanced at the clock over the sink. "If you really are feeling better would you mind going over there and getting her? This will be done in just a minute."

"Sure," I said and jumped up to retrieve my boots and coat.

I couldn't help but smile as I walked out the front door and saw a path had been shoveled from our door straight to Sal's. He'd planned ahead.

I knocked and waited for a few seconds before letting myself into Sal's house.

"Oh boy," I breathed as I took the front room in.

I had seen it worse, but the place was a mess. It looked as if Sal had brought everything from all the cupboards and shelves and strewn it across the floor. Pots, pans, ancient looking phonebooks, CD cases, everything.

"Sal?" I called as I began the search for her.

"Ah ha!" I must have jumped two feet in the air when I heard her shout from the dining room. "Found you."

I rushed into the room just in time to see her tip over a vase and see two shiny things fall into her waiting hand. After setting the very expensive glass vase down, she slid the things into her ears and I realized they were earrings.

"I've been looking for these for the last hour," Sal said as she looked up at me.

I was shocked by Sal's appearance. Her hair was combed and even slightly curled. There were traces of makeup on her face and her clothes matched and looked like she had ironed them. I had never seen her look so put together.

"You look very nice, Sal," I said as I followed her out into the living room.

"Thank you, Jessica," she said as she began searching around in the mess. After a second she stooped and picked up a pair of shiny black dress shoes. "Is it time to go then?"

I still had not gotten over the shock of how normal Sal looked as I nodded that it was. Without hesitation she walked to and out the front door.

As I walked behind Sal my mind reeled, trying to recall even one occurrence when I had seen her leave the safety of her home. I was coming up blank. When I had first met her I had suggested she go shopping with me but she nearly broke down in tears and screamed at me to leave. I only made that mistake twice, the second time I had been hoping the first had just been a bad day.

Sal let herself into the house without hesitation, taking her shoes and coat off in the entryway. I had never felt underdressed around Sal until now.

"That smells really good," she said as she followed her nose to the kitchen.

I followed her, still not believing what I was seeing.

Alex had just finished setting all the dishes on the table when he looked up at us with that dazzling smile.

"I'm glad you came, Sal," he said as he extended an arm to her, draping it over her shoulders. I hoped he wasn't offended when she cringed slightly. She didn't like to be touched most of the time. Considering her past, I couldn't blame her one bit. "Happy Valentine's Day," he smiled.

"Well," he said as he clapped his hands together, his face practically beaming as he looked at each of us. "Dinner is served."

Being the perfect gentleman, he pulled each of our chairs out for us before sitting down himself. I couldn't help but gaze at the feast before us. Steaming plates of spaghetti and meatballs, breadsticks, a complicated and delicious looking green salad, and several bottles of sparkling cider.

The evening passed in a blissful state of ease I had not experienced in a very long time. Alex kept the conversation light and easy and I could tell he was always mindful of Sal's constantly changing state of mind. Sal was quiet but she looked happy. She never seemed completely relaxed but I had never seen her so, unless she was sleeping.

As I watched the evening unfold I realized something within me was changing. Ever since Jason had so cruelly broken up with me, I had locked my heart into an ice chamber and was determined to never let anyone near it again. Without my permission, something was happening. I knew I was developing feelings for Alex. I didn't see how I could help it though. Who wouldn't start to fall for this overwhelmingly attractive, single, considerate, fun guy?

Alex apologized for the simple dessert of brownies and ice cream, claiming he had run out of time to make anything fancier. It was slowly eaten as each of us had already consumed more than our limit.

It would have been nice to simply sit back and relax for a while after all the food before us was devoured, but I could sense Sal was getting uneasy and eager to get back home. I was already impressed with how long she had lasted.

"Come on, Sal," I said as I stood. "I'll walk you home."

Relief washed over her face as she walked hurriedly to the door and grabbed her coat and shoes.

"I'll come with you," Alex said as he stood.

I wouldn't admit it to myself but I smiled just slightly when he joined us at the door and we pulled our coats on.

It was still cold outside, but it did not feel any colder than it had during the day. Nonetheless, below freezing was still below freezing.

It did not take long to reach Sal's house as she nearly ran back to her front door.

"Good-night," we called as she practically shut the door in our faces.

I chuckled slightly as we turned back toward the house.

CHAPTER EIGHT

The night felt peacefully still as stars struggled to break through the clouds overhead. The soft blanket of snow that draped over everything gave it almost a warm feel. I could hear snow dropping off branches somewhere in the distance.

Neither of us said anything as we took the short walk back. I was learning to like that about Alex; he didn't feel the need to constantly fill the silence.

The way my body felt so constantly aware of his presence next to mine unsettled me. I had only known the man four days. I shouldn't be having the overpowering desire to reach out and take his hand in mine so soon, or ever really. We lived together. I had serious issues that were completely out of my control. There were way too many complications that could and would arise from letting something become of my feelings.

We were nearly to the door when the wind gusted in our faces, nearly knocking the breath from my lungs. Just as we opened the door the snow began to fall again.

As we shoved the door closed, we both broke out into laughter as I tried to tame my hair back into order. I closed my eyes as Alex pulled strands of hair from my face, enjoying his nearness far more than I should.

After a moment, I opened them again and was almost startled to find him still only inches away, his brilliant blue eyes staring intensely into my own.

My breath caught in my throat as I thought he leaned in just a fraction of an inch closer and I could see the struggle that was taking place in his eyes. My heart hammered and I silently prayed he couldn't hear it.

"I have something for you," he finally breathed after an intense moment, backing away slightly and removing his coat.

"Really?" I stammered. I took my coat and boots off, feeling suddenly embarrassed.

"Hang on," he said as he finished taking his outside things off, heading for the master bedroom.

I took a seat on one of the two couches before the grand fireplace and only had to wait a short moment before he came back into the room, a thin black case in his hands. As he sat next to me, my heart started to hammer again in anticipation.

"When my grandma died, she left quite the collection of sparkly things to me. Obviously I am never going to have any use for them so I'd like to give this to you."

He seemed slightly uncomfortable as he handed me the case. "I didn't get you anything," I said, dismay obvious in my voice, as I took the box.

"Seriously, don't worry about it," he said with a chuckle. "And like I said, it's not like I actually went out and bought something."

I opened the box and stared at the shiny object that lay within it. It was a bracelet, intricate and delicate. Tiny silver colored leaves wrapped up and down the entire thing, shiny jewels that looked dangerously like diamonds set between each one.

"Alex, it's beautiful," I whispered as I pulled it out.

"May I?" he asked as he reached for it. Despite the size of his hands, he had little trouble with the tiny clasp. "I thought it suited you. Kind of reminded me of you when I saw it."

Just before I snapped the box closed I noticed the name of the designer on the inside of the lid and a little gasp escaped my lips. I didn't know of any designers who made higher quality or more expensive jewelry than this. It had to be worth thousands of dollars.

"Alex, I..." the words came out stammered. "I can't."

"Jessica, please don't argue with me. I want you to have it. And really, what am I going to do with it? I hate to imagine what you might think of me if I started wearing it."

I couldn't help but laugh aloud as that half grin broke on his face.

"When you put it that way I guess it doesn't seem so bad," I said as the laughter died out.

He reached for my arm and held my hand lightly as he observed his gift there. My heart shuttered and my skin warmed under his touch, making it tingle.

"Perfect," he said with a smile.

We sat in silence for a moment, both just staring at the beautiful bracelet. It was getting harder to resist the temptation to lift my head and let my lips find his by the second. Actually it felt like pure torture.

Just as my will power was crumbling, the wind whistled against the windows, hissing at the house to let it in. In the same instant, my scar suddenly prickled and burned and without thinking, the hand Alex had been holding shot to cover it.

"I'm sorry..." Alex started as he looked up into my face, his expression slightly startled.

"No," I said, suddenly panicking, as I stood up. "The wind just startled me, I guess."

The confusion was obvious on his beautiful face, but at least he didn't seem hurt or offended.

"Um..." I said as I knew my face was flushing bright red. "I'll help you clean dinner up."

Alex only nodded and stood to follow me to the kitchen. Neither of us said much as we worked to clean and clear the dishes. I wasn't sure what to say or how to recover after my strange reaction. Talk about ruining the moment.

As we worked, my scar continued to prickle and I could feel my eyes growing heavier by the moment. I silently added up the hours in my head, realizing it had been more than eighty hours since I had slept. Strange, normally I could make it to almost one hundred before I felt the effects this strongly.

"I'm about ready to hit the sack," Alex said as he closed the dishwasher and started it up.

"Me too," I replied, wishing it wasn't so true.

Without saying anything else, he started down the stairs. I couldn't help the feeling of growing dread that spread through me as we descended in silence. Not so much over the fact that I was growing dangerously tired, but for the fact that

Alex was getting the first hints of how strange and messed up I truly was. I had hoped before that I might be able to hide everything and was now realizing it had been a stupid thought. The scars on my back controlled my life. It wouldn't be long before they would drive Alex away too, just like they did Jason.

Alex said a quick and quiet goodnight before we went our separate ways. I closed the door behind me with a small click, leaning against it and letting a frustrated breath out.

How could you be so stupid? I chided myself. I had been down this road before. I should know better. With the way my life was I couldn't let anyone in too close. And it would be wrong of me to expect anyone to accept the madness that followed me. It wouldn't be fair.

Trying to work some resolve into my thoughts, I went to the fridge and pulled out a Dr. Pepper, downing it in less than thirty seconds. I hated to admit it to myself but the effects of the caffeine didn't really work much anymore. I refused to upgrade to something that contained higher levels of it like coffee, the taste was terrible and I couldn't even stand the smell of it. And energy drinks always tasted like liquid Smarties to me.

My eyes were growing heavier and heavier by the moment though, and I paced the floor.

Seventeen...eighteen...nineteen...

Stop it, I scolded myself. But as soon as this thought processed another pushed it aside. It had been a few days since I had counted, aloud or internally. I couldn't remember a time when I had gone so long without counting. It was something I always did but now I couldn't recall the last time I had done it.

My panic was rising as I stretched my arms high above my head. I hated this time of the constant twenty-four hours that made up a day. I considered that maybe I should move to some place like Alaska. In the summer it was light almost all the time and in the winter I could find some secluded place where it didn't matter if I slept. No one would be around to hear my screams when I woke. But I hated the cold. I learned that from living in Idaho for sixteen years.

I knew I was coming down to my last ditch effort as I changed into my skimpy, worn out pajamas and walked out the back door to the deck.

The wind blasted into my face as soon as I stepped out, making my eyes water and sting. I could feel the goose bumps rise on my arms, felt the hair stand straight up. Everywhere but on the back of my neck, which burned and twinged uncomfortably.

The effect of waking my senses was instant but I knew it wasn't going to last long if I were to instantly walk back into the warm and comfortable house. Despite the cold and every cell in my body telling me to turn around, I walked down the deck and out onto the dock. It thrashed violently as the water churned around it and I had to place a hand on the beams that ran into the water to keep from being thrown into the blackness.

I sat at the edge of the dock, my legs dangling over the side. Small lumps of melting snow dotted the planks. The water jumped up at my bare toes and my teeth began to chatter as the icy water sucked all heat from them. There was no possible way I was going to fall asleep out here.

It wasn't fair for me to hope that someday Alex might be able to accept what was happening to me. People weren't made to handle this kind of thing. I knew that all too well.

I came in the back door in an effort to avoid the girls that had paused in front of my house, chattering away about the dance coming up, the one I didn't get asked to. The door closed noiselessly behind me as I stepped into the hall and headed toward my bedroom.

"I just don't know if her being at home is a good idea anymore." I heard my mother's quieted voice coming from her bedroom. "She just isn't moving on from this."

I swallowed hard as I crept silently to her door. Even though it was closed I didn't have a difficult time overhearing her.

"How many patients do you have there?" She was quiet for a moment as she listened to the person on the other line. "I just want to make sure there is adequate staff to handle such an extreme case."

She was quiet again for a while. My stomach knotted and my fists clenched. I heard the stiffed sound of my mother's sob.

"Thank you. We will bring her in on Monday."

As I heard the beep of the phone being hung up, I slipped into my room. Tears soaked my cheeks, my hands trembled with the anger I felt at my mother's betrayal.

So this is how the end happened. This is where all the fights, all the begging, and pleading finally led. I closed the door to my bedroom and pulled my suitcase out from under my bed.

I had never felt more alone than I did in this moment. There would be no good-bye. There was no one to say good-bye to.

I had no idea how long I sat on the dock, listening to the sound of the wind screaming through the trees in order to distract myself from my worst memory. Numbness was quickly spreading through my limbs. I knew the temperature had to still be hovering around freezing and when the ache and stiffness settled firmly into my joints I pulled myself painfully to my feet.

Feeling confident I could make it until morning now I made my way back to the house.

X

The deranged laughter erupted from all sides as the final judgment was passed. They stretched their hands toward me in greedy eagerness and their eyes grew wide in anticipation.

I could not bring myself to look up from my bare feet but I heard as his wings coiled then released and he landed softly beside me on the narrow bridge I stood upon. I dropped to my hands and knees without being forced, sweeping my hair away to expose the flesh there.

Despite how hard I tried to keep it contained, I could not fight the cry that leapt from my throat as the white-hot searing pain sizzled into my flesh. Unable to make my brain focus on anything but the pain, I was yanked to my feet. My head lolled from the right to the left, my neck unwilling to support its weight.

"Judgment has been placed," I heard the voice before me sing.

I could not hold it back even if I had the will to try as another blood curdling scream erupted from me and my own set of beautiful and powerful wings ripped from my skin. Even the damned were given wings.

Those with the black eyes sprang from their seats and flew at me. Cold, clammy hands were everywhere on me and I could not shake them off.

My breath suddenly cut off completely as I was unable to make my throat open back up. It took me a moment to realize why this new sense of terror disabled me so.

One of the cold, dead sets of hands had ripped the sack from my head, leaving my face in full view.

My eyes were suddenly in a dead lock with their leader who had branded me hundreds of times. The eyes, dead as night and enchanting as black pearls, stared straight into my own and I could not look away, nor could I find the will to. They were so beautiful, so captivating, so… imprisoning.

I almost struggled against them, those with the black eyes, tried desperately to learn to use my newly given wings as the pulsing, groping mass that surrounded me tipped sideways. Anything to stare back into those eyes, the eyes of their leader. There was something in them that made me want to stare back for as long as he would allow.

As we fell over the side, the man with such captivating eyes peered over the edge and watched me fall into blackness.

I batted wildly at the strong hands that grasped my shoulders, though my panic came from another source.

"He saw me!" I screamed as my eyes tried to adjust to the darkness. "He saw me!"

"Who?" a smooth but slightly frightened voice asked in the dark.

I immediately stopped hitting the hands away and tried to make sense of my surroundings. I was laying on something soft and realized it was my own bed. My eyes finally started adjusting, a soft glow coming from a candle set on my dresser.

As Alex's face came into view a new wave of panic settled into the pit of my stomach. I had fallen asleep and Alex had heard my screams.

"Are you okay, Jessica?" the worry in his voice heart-sinkingly evident.

I couldn't bring myself to answer his question, couldn't make my lips move.

"Oh, Jessica," he whispered and wiped his thumb across my cheek. I was horrified to realize it was wet with stray tears. "It was just a nightmare. It wasn't real, whatever it was."

His words should have been comforting, but it only brought on a fresh round of tears. I had heard those words from my parents far too many times. If only it *wasn't* real.

As Alex saw the tears that poured down my face he pulled me into his arms and I buried my face into the gap between his neck and shoulder. He ran a hand soothingly down my hair and I tried not to wince as it ran over the welted, burning, fresh scar on my neck.

"You want to talk about it?" he whispered in the darkness.

I shook my head but pulled him tighter to me with my arms.

My teeth started to chatter as the chill settled into my skin. "Why is it so cold in here?" I asked through my teeth.

"The power went out. I woke up a while ago and realized the wind must have made it go out. I was building a fire upstairs when I heard you scream."

I didn't say anything in response to this. There was no logical response I could give him. A twenty-year-old woman shouldn't wake up screaming from a nightmare.

"Come on upstairs," he said as he released me and sat back to look me in the face. Again he brought his thumbs to my face and wiped my cheeks dry. "It's much warmer up there."

I still didn't say anything but nodded my head. He took my hand and pulled me up from the bed, the other hand grasping my quilt. He nodded his head in the direction of the candle, and understanding, I grabbed it and we made our way up the stairs.

It was warm in the main living room and I felt myself relax as we stepped in. My head cleared slightly and I knew my tears were done falling. My nerves were settling with every passing second though a different tension was welling under my skin. I was going to have to come up with some kind of explanation for Alex. This wasn't going to be just a one-time occurrence.

Alex had already brought up a large pile of blankets and pillows, thrown on the floor in front of the couch like a half-asleep man would.

He dropped my quilt on one of the couches and proceeded to push both of them closer to the fire place. Feeling the need to help, I set about making up the beds.

"Here," Alex said as he handed me a glass of water.

I wanted to refuse the glass. Eating or drinking anything at that moment was about one of the last things I wanted to do but it seemed easier to accept it with thanks than refuse. "Thank you," I whispered as I accepted it, taking a few small sips. I watched as he settled himself into one of the couches, pulling the blanket up to his waist, his head resting on his arm, using it instead of a pillow.

Setting my glass on the floor, I too slipped under the covers and sighed at the warmth and comfort.

Through the comfortable, orange light that danced on the walls from the fire, I stared at the beautiful man's face that lay only feet away and he stared silently back.

I realized I had two options now. The first was to pack up and leave. I could tell Alex that I had just had a scary nightmare but this was going to happen a lot. I was always going to wake up screaming. I wasn't required to stay and I knew I was free to go at any time. This might be the smarter option; it would make my life less complicated. I could simply tell him that I had to go, walk downstairs, pack up my things, and get in my car and drive away. I didn't *have* to tell him anything.

The second was to take the risk and go after what I knew I wanted. I could tell Alex the truth and explain why I would wake up screaming every time I slept. There was a ninety-nine percent chance he would think I was insane and tell me to leave. But wouldn't that small one percent chance make it worth divulging the truth? The worst that could happen was ending up back at option one and having to leave.

"I have nightmares *every* time I sleep," I said deliberately, having made up my mind. "I try to sleep as little as possible so I don't have to have them. Every night when you go to sleep, I stay awake in this silent house so I won't do what I just did. I always scream when I wake up."

Alex was still silent when I paused but his face remained calm and I could not see any judgments being passed in his eyes.

"I dream about angels and stand trial for people who have died. They are either granted exaltation or are condemned for the acts they committed during their life.

"Angels are beautiful and have beautiful wings but they're not what people think. Most of them are wretched, wanting only for everyone to join in their misery. If people knew the truth..." I trailed off, a hand reaching toward the raised wings imprinted onto my back.

"I've had these dreams for as long as I can remember. My parents always thought I was making it up. They told me nightmares weren't and couldn't be real. When I discovered the names of those I stood trial for were real people who really died, I knew they were wrong. I also knew the dreams had to be real in some way from the condemned mark that was branded into the back of my neck

97

every time I woke up." I paused here for a moment, taking a deep breath and trying to find the courage to continue.

"I heard my parents arguing all the time. My father insisted it was just a phase I was going through, that I would grow out of it eventually. My mother thought I needed some professional help, possibly some kind of medication.

"When I was sixteen I overheard my mother on the phone. She was going to have me institutionalized. She couldn't take it anymore. She was tired of hearing me scream every night yet tired of always fighting me to get some sleep.

"I left home that night and I haven't been back since."

With this I could not find the will to continue, though there was little left to tell without going into impossible details. I closed my eyes and waited for his reaction, waited for him to ask me to leave.

I heard rustling and when I felt my quilt being lifted, I opened my eyes to see Alex crawling onto my couch. Without a word, he slid in behind me under the quilt. He wrapped one strong arm around my waist and pulled me in closer to him.

As we lay there in silence, I felt a sense of peace I had never felt before in my life. I suspected his silence was because he was not sure of what to say. What could he say after having information like that dumped on him? But he had not told me to get out and leave that instant. Instead he had expressed the kindest and most gentle display of comfort I could have asked for at that moment.

Lying in Alex's arms I found hope. Perhaps there was a way for me to have some semblance of a normal life. I felt it might be possible for me to achieve some higher level of happiness than what I had previously settled for.

But I understood that Alex's gesture was in no way a promise of anything to come. I still did not know exactly what he was thinking about the information I had given him. I had no idea what was going to come in the morning. But for that moment, lying there in his arms was enough.

CHAPTER NINE

That night passed blissfully for me. When your nights are never pleasant you learn to appreciate the ones that are so perfect you never want them to end. It did not take long for Alex to drift off into sleep, but he never let me go, never released that strong arm from around me. It was easy to imagine that the horrid truths I had just revealed to him did not exist and to pretend that this was the way my life was. It was easy to imagine that I loved and was loved. That life was normal.

I had never been so sad to see morning dawn in all my life but I rose as the sun started to appear over the tops of the mountains, taking care not to wake Alex.

Unsure of how the day was going to unfold or what it might bring, I tried to go about a normal routine. I took a quick shower, dressed warmly, and checked my empty email. Afterwards I sat on my tiny couch and looked out the window. The sun shown brilliantly, all the wind had ceased. I'd heard the power come back on sometime around five. It sounded almost as if there was a downpour outside as the snow melted and rolled off the roof in torrents. The snow never lasted long here, for which I was grateful. I hated the snow, except when it involved Alex.

I heard the phone ring but let Alex answer it. He had started to stir about a half hour ago but he remained painfully quiet and aloof. Even though it was unbearable to think what it might mean, I could not put any blame on him. He had a right to think about what I had told him and to make his own decisions as to what to do with that information.

Unable to take just sitting there and torturing myself with thoughts and possibilities any longer, I decided to go check on Sal. I walked out the lower door that led from my apartment, trying to be careful not to cross paths with Alex by accident. I didn't feel ready to face him yet.

When I let myself into Sal's house I was glad to find it was warm. In my panic last night I had not even considered Sal's need for heat. I was grateful her heater had kicked back on with no problems.

Everything was quiet in the house, though still in disorganized chaos as it had been the night before. After a quick search I found her sleeping soundly in her bed, still dressed in the clothes she had worn the night before.

Knowing full well I was simply avoiding going back, I set to cleaning up after the mess she had made. I had only gotten about halfway through when the house cleaner showed up and feeling stupid, knowing there was no need for me to be there, I left.

I came back in through my door, trying to close it very quietly behind me. I jumped violently when Alex suddenly strolled out of my bedroom.

"There you are," he said with that half grin. "I was looking for you."

I stood with my back pressed against the door, feeling a strange need to keep some distance between us. My heart pounded in my chest and I hoped and prayed he could not hear it.

"You want to come upstairs for a minute?" he asked, his voice cautious.

Here we go, I thought. *Get ready to pack.*

Despite the panic that was rising in my blood and the sharp ringing that sounded in my ears, I nodded my head and followed him silently up the stairs. I noted he had cleaned up the bedding from last night and had moved the couches back to their normal place. I took a hesitant and terrified seat on one of them.

Alex walked casually to the dining room table and started to shuffle through some papers.

"I got a call yesterday and then again this morning. I guess there are some discrepancies with my grandparents' will and I need to go meet with a few lawyers in California. My flight leaves tonight, the last one out. I'm not really sure how long I'll be gone but I would guess about a week or so."

It took me a moment before I could make my brain process what he had just said. He wasn't making me leave. *He* was leaving. I wanted to protest, to tell him he didn't need to make excuses. This was his home now; I would leave if he didn't want me around anymore. But I sat frozen and unable to say anything. I could feel that brick of ice forming around my heart again.

He shoved all the papers in his hand into a folder and then into a backpack. I then noticed the suitcase at his feet. A heavy stone settled itself into the pit of my stomach.

He was leaving.

Knowing I only had about a minute or so before a meltdown was going to consume me, I stood and was about to go.

"Wait, Jessica," he said and I was surprised at the strain and eagerness in his voice. I turned slowly back toward him, hoping my eyes hadn't turned red yet. "I want to leave my truck here for you, just in case the weather decides to go ballistic on us again. If you or Sal need to get out sometime I want to make sure you can. I was wondering if I could take your car down to the airport?"

It took me a moment before I fully understood his request. If he was leaving me his truck and taking my car then surely he wasn't leaving permanently.

"You'll bring it back in a week?" I asked stupidly, wanting him to give me some kind of reassurance.

"Of course I'll bring it back," he said with a little chuckle. "Your GTO may be a cool old muscle car but I've grown kind of attached to that truck since I got it. I'm going to want it back."

I couldn't help it as a slightly relieved chuckle escaped my lips. "Yeah, I guess that would be fine."

That dazzling smile spread across his face. "Okay, good. Come on."

Feeling a little dazed and a bit like my head was spinning, I followed him out to the garage. I realized then that I had never seen what kind of vehicle Alex drove. When we had gone shopping before we had taken my car. The shiny black truck before me was a little more than intimidating. I didn't know too much about cars but I could tell it had a lift on it and there were monstrous tires attached to it. And it looked brand new.

"You expect me to drive that?" the intimidation was obvious in my voice.

"It's not any harder to drive than your car is. And this is an automatic so it should be even easier," Alex said as he gestured for me to join him. Hesitantly, I did.

"Call it a little indulgence," he said with a grin as he opened the driver's door. "I've always wanted a truck like this but never had the money, so when a lot of it was suddenly dumped on me, I couldn't resist." The smile on his face looked like it was almost painful. "Hop in."

I hesitantly accepted the hand he held out to help me and mounted the enormous beast. The interior smelled strongly of new-car and leather.

"It's a diesel so should you have to put gas in it, please, *please* remember that," I could see the terror on his face at that possibility. "You shouldn't have to put anything in it though. It's full right now. Just push that if you need the four-wheel drive," he said, pointing to a button on the dash.

"Trust me," I said as I held my hands up. "If there is a need for four-wheel I will *not* be going out."

He just chuckled and nodded his head. "Really, it's not that hard to drive. You just have to remember you're a lot bigger than you would be in the GTO."

"Don't think I could forget that," I said as I slipped out and closed the door.

"Anything I should know about your car? Tricks or secrets?"

"It runs great. Don't try anything too wild in it. As long as you know how to drive a stick you should be ok."

Alex rolled his eyes. "I know how to drive a stick."

We both laughed for a moment as we headed back inside.

We passed the afternoon quietly but with much less tension than the morning had brought. I found myself back in the apartment when Alex popped his head in.

"Well, I'd better head down to the airport now," he said as he walked through the door.

I nodded my head, a bit unsure of what to say. He looked at me expectantly and after a moment I realized what he must have been waiting for. I grabbed my purse off the card table and dug my keys out. Slipping the one for my car off, I tossed it to him. He caught it easily with a grin. He tucked it in his pocket and when he pulled his hand back out, a piece of paper was clutched in it.

"This is my cell phone number," he said as he handed it to me, along with a set of keys. I hoped I wasn't imagining that his hand lingered on mine for just a moment longer than necessary. "Call me if you need anything."

"It would be hard for you to do anything for me when you're fourteen hundred miles away," I said with a chuckle.

That half grin spread on his face. "Yeah, I guess you're right. Still," he said as he took both my hands in his. My heart suddenly started hammering. "You can call me anytime."

How could those piercing blue eyes strike such terror and longing in my heart at the same time? It was a confusing and complex emotion.

His eyes never broke from mine as he slowly raised one of my hands in his and gently pressed his lips to my knuckles.

"Take care of yourself," he whispered as he lowered it and let go.

"I will," my voice was barely audible.

That half smile played in the corners of his lips before he tucked a stray lock of hair behind my ear. And a moment later he walked out the door.

CHAPTER TEN

I was bound and determined that I was not going to sit around and obsess over Alex or the fact that he was going to be gone for a week. I wasn't that pathetic, or at least I was going to pretend that I wasn't.

But a week had never looked so long.

I had a new issue to consider for distraction, thankfully, but very unthankfully. Something else had changed about my whole angel experience. This was the third thing that had differed from the normal experiences I had. I couldn't even begin to theorize about what this might mean. I shuddered when I considered the possibility that things might continue to change even more.

This last trial was a new kind of nightmare. The leader of the condemned had seen my face, looked straight into my eyes. If there had ever been some kind of comfort the nightmares provided it was that thin sack that protected my true identity. That had been ripped away. What would this change? I had no disillusioned thoughts that it might make the nightmares stop. I had already settled myself on the fact that it was something I was just going to have to deal with for the rest of my existence. But how would it effect the trials? At least one of the council knew the person beneath the bag did not belong to the name they were judging.

As terrifying as it had all been, I could not help but remember the strange emotions that spread through me as I stared into those black eyes. I had been so captivated by them. It had been as if I physically could not have looked away, had the mob not pulled me over the edge.

And for the first time, I could not remember the name I had stood trial for.

I reminded myself as I walked through the glass doors that I wasn't going to continue to be a hermit. If I wanted a shot at a normal life I was going to have to crawl out of my shell and interact with people. Normal people.

Relief washed over me as I saw that there were only five other people in the room. It was best to start off slow and work my way out of the lonely hole I had dug for myself.

I remembered seeing the flyer for a new yoga class that was starting up when I was in town last. I had given it next to no thought at the time but it seemed the perfect way to ease my way back into normal society. I could be around people but not have any pressure to have to talk as we would all be focusing on relaxing and building flexibility.

Dressing for the class had taken some careful consideration. I knew the normal attire that was to be worn to practice yoga, but the small strappy tops wouldn't do in covering my scars. Instead I had opted for a tee-shirt until I could find something that would work better. I knew it was going to drive me crazy but I had little choice but to leave most of my mane of hair down and loose. I would just have to deal with it being in my face.

Most everyone stood around, not meeting each other in the eye, experiencing that first awkwardness that came with this type of thing. There were four women, two of which seemed to have come together, and one man who was as thin as a twig.

A woman walked in from a side room and I couldn't help but stare at the way in which she moved. She seemed to glide over the floor rather than walk and she held a certain air about herself that said she knew exactly who she was and knew exactly the direction she wanted her life to be moving in. Her facial features were strong and sure. Her hair was a nearly white color of blond and hung in perfectly styled curls down to the middle of her back. She couldn't have been more than a few years older than me.

"Good morning," she said cheerily as she observed us all. "My name is Emily Lewis. I'm so glad all of you came today."

She asked for our names and we each gave them in turn. I knew it was going to take me a few more classes before I was going to remember any of the other student's names.

It took me longer than I would have hoped to figure out the breathing techniques she taught us. Each of the poses was indeed a challenge to keep up the endurance to hold them. Flexibility wasn't ever an issue, I was abnormally flexible. But by the end of the class I was surprised at how relaxed I felt and the energy that refreshed me.

"Jessica." I stopped as I had turned for the door when I heard Emily call my name after the class was over.

She walked up to me with a bright smile on her face. "I wanted to ask you. Have you ever done yoga before?"

I shook my head.

"You're a natural at it. Quite flexible, I must say. I think once you can get the breathing down it won't be long before you'll be a master."

I felt myself blush slightly at her compliments. "Thanks," I managed. "I'm glad I came today."

Emily only nodded before she walked away to put the mats back in their bins.

I smiled as I walked out the door, knowing that what I said was indeed the truth. I was glad I had made the decision to come today.

As I left the building, I now confronted a new uncertainty. I had been quite proud of myself that I had made it safely into town without causing a wreck in Alex's monster of a vehicle. As I had driven, I realized it was in fact a fairly normal sized truck, but I had certainly never had to maneuver something so big. I wasn't sure if I was ready to pick up the challenge again. But having no choice but to drive the thing again, I carefully made my way further into town and pulled into to the parking lot of the mall.

Making the decision to be around other people made me realize just how pathetic my wardrobe had gotten. And I was becoming embarrassingly aware of how sad my excuse for pajamas was. If Alex really did come back I didn't want to be caught in my old threadbare ones again. And besides that, I realized I was starting to dress like a sixty-year-old hermit.

I spent longer than I had meant to at the mall, taking way more care in picking a few new items of clothing than I cared to admit to myself. It felt good to spoil myself though. I didn't do it often.

After picking a few things up from the grocery store, I started the drive home. Even though the snow had been slightly inconvenient it had been beautiful to look at. Snow wasn't common in western Washington so it was nice to see it, as long as it didn't stay long. But with the rise in temperature it had melted and left the world looking water-logged and mushy. With the temperature remaining low and the sad absence of the sun, everything was just cold and damp.

I was tempted to pull straight into Sal's driveway so I could unload everything I had gotten for her easily, but an enormous moving truck was blocking the way. Several men scurried in and out of it and into the house next to Sal's. Strange, I hadn't noticed it was for sale.

Very, very carefully I eased the truck into the garage. It took me longer than it should have to unload my things. I had spent more than I should have but somehow could not feel completely guilty about it.

With Sal's three bags in hand, I took the ninety-one steps to her house, silently cursing at my returned habit of counting.

For once, I did not have to look for her as I entered. She stood at the window next to the front door, her hands twisting into nervous knots as she stared anxiously at the men as they worked.

"Is everything okay?" I asked her as I set the bags on the counter. I should have realized a change like this would set her on edge.

"Where did Henry go?" Her voice came out as a whispered hiss.

It took me a moment to remember Henry was Sal's other neighbor. He was a quiet man who seemed incredibly shy, but would always smile and wave.

"I guess he sold the house," I said as I glanced out the window. Five movers were carrying a baby grand piano into the house. "I never saw a for sale sign though. Did you?"

"Why would Henry leave?" she said as she started to bounce on the balls of her feet. "Where did he go?"

"I don't know," I sighed as I put the last of the food away. I wiped my hands on my stretch yoga pants before walking over to where Sal fidgeted.

I placed my hands cautiously on her shoulders, so as not to upset her further. "I'm sure Henry's fine, Sal. Remember, his wife passed away last year. Maybe he just needed a change."

She was still anxious, but this seemed to placate her for the moment as she followed me to the couch. I cleared a stack of worn looking books from it to make room for her to sit down.

"Do you think Alex would come over tonight?" Sal asked as I stacked the books back on the shelf.

"Alex had to go away for a little while," I called over my shoulder, remembering that I had not told her yet. "He said he would be back in a week or so."

"Oh," I heard her whisper. "Alex is a nice boy."

Even though it sounded terrible, it delighted me to hear her sound sad at this news. Sal didn't trust many people, especially men. She had let Alex get behind her defenses so easily I was still in slight shock over it.

"I'm going to come back over tonight and make you dinner," I said as I walked back toward the door. "Would that be alright with you?"

I saw the wheels turn in Sal's head and she considered this. I generally preferred to be by myself in the evenings and had never offered to make her dinner before. But I needed to be around people more, even if the only person I had for company was slightly crazy.

"That would be fine," she answered finally. "I could help you."

I nodded my head even though I doubted the kind of help Sal might be able to offer. "I'll come over at five-thirty then."

The evening had passed uneventfully. I had made Sal stroganoff and she had managed to whip up a surprisingly delicious green salad. She seemed uneasy and not exactly up for company so I had not stayed long. I supposed she was still upset by the sudden change of her other neighbor.

Later that night, I sat with my arms wrapped around my knees, perched on the upper deck, rocking back and forth slightly. Even though it was only seven it had already been dark for almost two hours. A low mist had settled itself over the tops of the trees and it was slowly descending upon the tops of the houses. The towering evergreens that encircled the lake swayed in the slight breeze, tracing patterns in the silver mist, the moon invisible behind it. I loved the smell of the night here, like the earth was alive, like if you listened hard enough it might tell you its secrets.

A hand unconsciously rose to the back of my neck as it began to prickle. I wasn't sure if it was actually warm to the touch, but under my freezing hands it felt much hotter than the rest of my skin. The angels were calling.

I squeezed my eyes shut. Seven... eight...nine...ten... The numbers started flowing before I even allowed the thoughts to process.

Without realizing, I had reached for the phone at my side and I was staring at it intently. I wanted to dial the number I had already memorized but what was I going to say? I silently hoped Alex would call. The aching wish sat in the pit of my stomach like a festering ulcer.

Trying to distract myself, I reached for the envelope that I was half sitting on to keep from blowing away. I took a deep breath before tearing it open.

The letter was from my father. He said that he was doing fine and had just moved his orthodontic practice into a new building. My younger sister Amber was anxious for the last few months of her senior year to go by. She had a new boyfriend but this was the fourth one this school year so he didn't expect it to last long. He said he missed me and wished I would come home. There was no mention of my mother. There was never any mention of her.

"Careful, it's going to drip," my mom said as she handed me an ice cream cone.

A cold trail of mint ice cream ran down my six-year-old hand. I licked it off, smiling at my mom, the gap in my teeth felt weird against my lips. I'd been proud of myself for having pulled the loose one out myself.

My mom smiled back before she turned her attention to Amber, who was whining to be let out of the stroller. She unbuckled her and my two-year-old sister ran toward the playground.

I watched as she climbed up to the slide. "Watch me, mommy!" she shouted from the top.

"I'm watching!" mom called to her, blocking the sun from her eyes with her hand.

Amber squealed and went down the slide head first.

My mom clapped as she reached the bottom. She looked back at me. "Do you want to go play with her?"

I shook my head. "Not right now."

We sat in the quiet for a minute, licking our quickly melting ice cream cones. Mom watched the other kids, the sound of happy screams coming from the public pool that was fenced off on the opposite side of the park.

"Are you sure you don't want to take swimming lessons this year?" my mom asked as she looked back at me.

I shook my head, my pigtails flopping around my neck.

"How come?" she asked.

"I just don't," I said a little sharper than I had intended to.

Mom let it drop, running over to Amber to check her knees after she tripped.

I looked over to the pool, watching as two kids my age did a cannon ball into the water. I really did want to learn to swim. But I would never be able to put a swimming suit on. The scars on my back controlled my life.

I folded the letter and slid it back into the envelope. I hadn't actually spoken to any of my family members since I had run away four years ago. In a moment of weakness, I had written my father a letter a year ago, giving a return address to my post office box in Bellingham. I didn't want him to come looking for me. If he could find me so could my mother and as soon as she did she would haul me off to the loony bin.

Anger welled up in me as I thought of her. I balled up the letter and let it fall to the ground. Mothers were supposed to be kind, loving, and understanding. Instead, mine was disappointed in, irritated with, and afraid of me.

A movement caught my eye and my head whipped around to find the source. I had sworn I just saw someone standing in the window of the new neighbor's house, but it was dark and empty with no hint of life.

An odd sense of fear filled me as I waited for something to move again. Darkness may have been the enemy of trying to stay awake, but I had never been afraid of what might be hidden in it, other than the strange episode of me passing out. The sense of dread that filled me was foreign.

I quickly rose and walked back inside.

CHAPTER ELEVEN

I had just thrown a load of laundry in when I heard the screaming and shouting.

Panic rose in my blood. I knew in an instant where it was coming from. Without bothering to throw a jacket on and barely taking the time to slide on a pair of shoes, I hurtled myself out the door.

I heard a door slam shut as I came into view of Sal's front door and barely glanced at the man that stood on her step as I sprinted up the steps.

"All I did was try and introduce myself!" the man hurriedly tried to explain as I tested the door knob. Of course it was locked.

"I swear I didn't do anything!" he said, his voice raised and slightly panicked sounding.

"Sal?" I yelled. "Sal, it's me, Jessica."

I listened intently for any sounds within. Nothing.

"Sal? Are you alright?"

"Tell him to go away!" I heard her scream from just behind the door.

"Are you alright, Sal?" I demanded again.

"Tell him to go away!" she shrieked again.

"I didn't do anything!" the man behind me insisted again.

"I know," I said over my shoulder. "Sal, it's ok. Everything's fine. Do you want me to come back later?"

"Both of you, go away!" she screamed, her voice sounding further away as if she had walked toward the back of the house.

Realizing there was nothing more I could do at the moment, I let out a frustrated sigh and turned from the door.

I could do nothing but stop and stare when I finally actually looked at the man that stood there. He was tall and lean with the body of one of those half naked Abercrombie models. His skin was tanned and absolutely flawless, his strong chin covered with dark stubble, as if he hadn't shaved in two days. He looked to be around twenty-five. His hair fell slightly long and shaggy. It was dark and difficult to tell if it was black or simply a very dark brown. But it was the eyes that held my nearly open mouthed stare. The same dark color as his hair, like deep caverns beckoning me in to come and explore. The overall effect of his appearance was stunning. No one should be allowed to look that perfect. But as I stared at him, a strange sense of familiarity settled itself into the back of my mind.

"I promise I didn't mean to frighten her," his voice made me jump as the sound interrupted my thoughts. As if the rest of him wouldn't have enough effect to stun me into a stupor, he also had to have a buttery British accent. "Like I said, I just tried to introduce myself and she started screaming at me and telling me to get away."

My lips flapped open and shut a few times before I seemed to be able to make any sound come out. "She...uh...Sal has a hard time...uh...trusting new people." *Wow*, I sounded idiotic.

"I do hope she's alright," he said, a look of concern crossing his face as he looked back at her door.

"She'll be okay," I said as my brain started to recover. "Sal's just a little...different."

This seemed to satisfy him enough as he nodded his head. "I'm Cole Emerson, by the way," he said as he stepped forward to shake my hand. "I moved in yesterday."

The hand I grasped felt just as perfectly flawless as his face looked. A small shiver worked itself up my spine.

"Jessica," I managed to get out. "Jessica Bailey."

"Pleased to meet you Jessica," he said with a dazzling smile. I stopped breathing for several long seconds as he raised my hand and pressed his lips to it for the briefest moment before releasing it.

"So you must live on the other side of, did you say her name was Sal?" he questioned as he stuffed his hands into rather expensive looking jeans.

"Yeah, Sal. Well, it's Sally Thomas but she doesn't like to be called Sally usually. And yes, I care take the house on the other side of hers."

Cole flashed another brilliant smile as he nodded. He seemed to be gauging me for a moment, almost as if he was looking for some sort of reaction he wasn't getting. "Would you like to come over for a bit? Can I offer you something to drink?"

Again I struggled for words and coherency. "Uh...sure."

"Fantastic," he said as he flashed that smile again and motioned for me to follow him toward the house.

I didn't mean to, but I couldn't help but stare at the way Cole walked. I had never seen anyone move so gracefully, almost as if he were walking on a sheet of glass and was being very gentle to not crack it. And yet I had never seen anyone so graceful look so masculine or confident in the way he moved.

"You coming?" he called after he had walked a few steps away and I still had not moved. A different kind of smile crossed his face as if that reaction he had been looking for had now crossed my face. I could only nod and shuffle forward.

The house Cole had just bought was even newer than Sal's. That was part of the reason it seemed so strange Henry had sold it. He and his wife built it just four years ago. It seemed fantastically modern for a couple of their age. Sadly, his wife had contracted breast cancer just months after it was completed and had passed away a year later.

Cole opened the door wide and let me in. I had expected to see boxes stacked in every corner and to see furniture scattered about, not quite in their permanent places. To my surprise Cole's home looked as if he'd lived in the house for months, not less than twenty-four hours. Everything was neatly in its place, the couches and tables looking perfectly natural in their positions.

"Wow," I breathed as I took it in. "You sure didn't waste any time in settling in."

He let out a lighthearted chuckle as he walked into the immaculate gourmet kitchen. "I did have a bit of help," he said as he opened the refrigerator.

I then remembered all the men that were moving things in and out all day. I had a hard time imagining all those gruff guys had helped him place everything in such perfect order though.

"Coffee?" he called as he turned to a pot on the counter.

"Um..." I scrambled, not wanting to sound rude. "I'll pass."

"I've got some juice if you'd like that instead," he said, turning those eyes on me again.

My breath caught in my throat for a second as my eyes met his. "Juice would be great."

He smoothly poured me a glass before pouring himself a large mug of the coffee. I noticed he left it completely black, ignoring any sugar or cream. He handed me the glass and sat at the large cherry wood table.

"Will you apologize to Sal for me?" he started. "I feel terrible for frightening her like that."

"Don't worry about it," I answered, glad my vocal chords seemed to have finally recovered. "She'll be fine."

Cole only smiled and nodded.

"So where did you move from?" I blurted out, instantly realizing it was a stupid question. The accent should have given that away. I could feel the blood rush to my cheeks.

"Well," he said as he sat forward, resting his elbows on the table. "I grew up in a small town in England, I'd tell you the name but I'm quite sure you won't have heard of it." He said this with one of his blinding smiles. "I've been helping in the family business all my life and decided it was time to get out on my own and see a bit more of the world."

"And what is the family business?" I asked, sounding incredibly awkward.

"Real estate," he said with a slight smile. "My family owns quite a bit of land." I could tell he was done explaining, leaving it at that. From his tone I got the impression Cole had money, rather unlimited amounts of it would have been my guess. He wasn't going to try and flaunt it however.

"So tell me where you are from, Jessica," he said, blinding me with that smile again.

It took me a moment before I could speak; that smile should be illegal.

"I'm afraid it's going to bore you," I said with an uneasy chuckle. "I was born in and grew up in a tiny town in Idaho. I don't think the population has broken 1500 yet."

"It seems tiny was the appropriate description," he said with a chuckle as smooth as honey.

"You have no idea," I said with a sigh. "Anyway, I moved to California for a while and then moved up here. There's not much to tell," I said. At least not much I could tell him without him thinking I was crazy.

"I'm sure there are many more interesting things that have happened in your life," he said with a slightly sly smile tugging at the corners of his mouth. "Everyone has an interesting story to tell."

I couldn't help but feel momentarily uncomfortable under his intense eyes but it was soon washed away by his smile. I self-consciously brought my glass to my lips and took a long draw.

"That is a very beautiful bracelet you have there," he said as he reached for my hand and examined it. "Rather expensive, I'm sure. It must have been given by someone who cares a great deal for you."

I had to admit that I had almost forgotten the delicate thing that wound around my wrist. Was I imagining the look of anger that crossed Cole's face for the briefest moment?

"Um…" I struggled, unsure of how to answer his unstated question. "A friend gave it to me?" I hadn't meant it to come out as a question but I wasn't sure of what exactly to call Alex.

"You don't sound too sure about that," he said as he dropped my hand, his gaze intense again.

"It's kind of a weird situation. Complicated I guess."

"Uh-huh," he said, encouraging me to continue.

I wondered briefly why it seemed so important to him, but couldn't help but feel a little flattered that he seemed interested in this matter.

"I told you how I house keep the home next to Sal's. Alex is the grandson of the owners and they just died. He came to the house the other day in the middle of the night and scared the crap out of me." I paused there, unsure of how to continue.

"And this guy that just showed up on your doorstep just decided to give you this ten-thousand dollar bracelet?" Cole pressed doubtfully.

"Like I said, it's complicated," I said shyly, suddenly wanting very badly to not have to try and explain the relationship between Alex and I. I still had no idea what he was thinking after my revelation of the truth and I especially did not want to think about what my feelings still were for him in the presence of the most magnificent male specimen I had ever lain eyes upon.

"Not trying to buy something out of you, is he?"

"No!" I nearly shouted. "It's nothing like that at all."

Cole looked at me for another intense moment. "Are you sure you don't want some coffee?" He took me off guard with his sudden change in conversation. "You look tired."

My eyes dropped to my lap and I let some of my hair fall into my face. "No, thank you. I'm fine."

"You sure? To be honest it looks like you haven't slept in days."

At first I thought he was intentionally being rude, but when I looked up I could see what looked like genuine concern in his eyes. I silently calculated in my head just exactly how long it had been since I had last slept and realized it had been the night Alex had heard me screaming and later held me in his arms. A sudden pang of longing struck me in the chest.

"I should probably get going," I said as I glanced at the clock that hung over the kitchen sink. Shock crossed my face as I realized I had been there for nearly an hour and it was already nine. I had barely noticed that darkness had blanketed the earth. "I didn't realize how late it was getting."

"You're welcome to stay," Cole said, and from reading his expression I could tell he meant it.

"Thank you," I said as I stood and pushed my chair under the table. "But it really is late."

I thought I heard him sigh slightly but he stood and carried both the cups to the sink, dumping them both in, although his was still completely full. I didn't think he had even touched it. "Alright. I'll see you later then?"

I nodded stiffly. "Thank you for the drink."

"Anytime."

Without waiting for any more of a response I walked to and out the door.

I wasn't exactly sure why I had felt such a sudden need to leave and go home. I hadn't exactly liked the way the direction of our conversation had turned I suppose. I did, however, feel terrible for how rude I had been at my departure.

When I made it back through the door, I saw the answering machine flashing. That seemed strange; no one really knew my number. I figured it was probably just a solicitation but pressed the play button anyway.

I immediately understood why I wanted to leave when I heard the recorded voice.

"Hi Jessica. It's Alex. Um... I just wanted to call and make sure everything was ok. I checked the weather report for up there and it's supposed to be clear until Saturday, there's a chance of snow again." He chuckled a little here. *"I sound pathetic, giving you the weather report on the answering machine.*

"Anyway, give me a call, if you want. Um...take care of yourself. Tell Sal I said hi. Talk to you later."

I realized when the message was finished playing a comically huge grin was plastered on my face. I couldn't bring myself to feel pathetic however, I felt too good inside. It was amazing how just hearing the sound of his voice could calm and reassure me so completely. Perhaps all was not as lost as I had feared before.

I played the message one more time, this time listening for what time he had left the message. Just after I had run out the door. I debated for a moment whether or not to call him back but in the end chickened out, unsure of what to say to him and afraid I might say something I shouldn't. And besides, he might be asleep already. I tried to convince myself of that, although it seemed quite unlikely.

I walked down the stairs to the dark basement and into my apartment. I closed the door behind me, leaning against it for a moment, not caring about the blissful smile that was spread on my face. The moment was temporary as the back of my neck prickled, goose bumps flashing across my skin. I started shivering even when the brand flashed with heat. The sound of distant twisted laughter haunted me.

Rubbing my arms, I walked to the kitchen and quickly downed a soda. I wasn't sure if I could make it all the way through the night but I was sure going to try.

It took only a moment for the water to steam as I turned the shower on. I shot a quick glance over my shoulder into the mirror before I stepped in. I looked every time even though I knew the marks were never going to disappear. They were always there. Permanent in the deepest sense of the word.

The water burned my skin as I stepped in, turning it pink almost instantly but I didn't care. Hopefully it would help me wake up.

I shaved my legs, taking more time than was necessary, but I had a full ten hours at least before the sun was going to come back up. It was a lot of time to kill. I did not admit to myself that I had shaved them almost every day since Alex had shown up. I didn't want to admit that I was that pathetic.

After being in the shower for at least thirty minutes, I realized that I was becoming too relaxed. Without a second's hesitation, I switched the hot water completely off and gasped as the icy liquid drenched me. I closed my eyes and let it pour over my face.

Another gasp escaped my lips when I opened my eyes again only to find my surroundings pitch black. At the same time I heard a few loud beeps and realized the power had gone out again.

I had just shut the water off when I thought I heard whispering. I held my breath and listened for a moment, frozen in fear and unwilling to move.

It sounded like a low buzz and my brain started to sort out the sound of hundreds of voices whispering excitedly. One rose just above the others and I was barely able to make out the individual words. They sounded far too real and all too close, as if the words had been whispered right into my ear.

You shall be mine.

The horrible vision or nightmare of when I passed out suddenly engulfed me and I could recall all too clearly the feeling of the dozens of cold clammy hands covering my body, the arms that had encircled me just before those words were whispered into my ear.

The lights suddenly flashed back on, followed by a few more beeping sounds. I realized I had crumpled to the bottom of the tub and was lying on my side, my arms wrapped around my knees as tightly as I could manage. My knuckles were turning white as they grasped at my elbows.

With violently shaking hands, I crawled out of the tub and wrapped myself in a towel. I climbed straight into my bed, wrapping my quilt around myself to try and stop the tremors that ripped through my body.

I had never heard *voices* when I had been awake. Occasionally I heard the demented laughter of the condemned ones but *never* distinct voices.

CHAPTER TWELVE

Morning could not come soon enough; I had never spent a night so long. Though my eyes seemed to grow heavier by the moment, I had managed to keep them open. I had been terrified to leave the safety of my bed even though I knew this was ridiculous. Angels were people who were dead, they didn't exist in the same way I did anymore. It wasn't like I was going to find any of them hiding under my bed. The most reasonable explanation was that I had had a paranoid auditory hallucination. That was what I was trying to tell myself anyway.

After a quick look in the mirror, I realized just how scary I looked. My eyes were blood shot and the bags under them looked as if they would never return to normal. I was going to have to sleep tonight. I tried futilely to cover it all up with makeup but the damage was too severe. I still looked frightening.

I dressed comfortably, excitement building in my system despite the previous night's terrifying experience, whatever it was that happened. I was looking forward to going to yoga and hopefully it would help relax the nerves that had been eating at me since the shower incident.

My spirits climbed further as I climbed into the truck and breathed deeply. I couldn't help but start to associate its smell with Alex. I was ridiculously comforted by it. I closed my eyes for a moment, my hands resting on the steering wheel, fighting the urge to run inside and call him. It was too early in the morning for that.

I was grateful for Alex's logic in leaving the truck with me as I pulled out onto the road that led to the freeway entrance. The normal morning dew had turned to a thin sheet of ice as the temperature hovered just below freezing. A light on the dash indicated more than once that the automatic four-wheel drive had kicked on. A sigh of relief escaped my chest as I finally reached the freeway and saw it was in better shape.

Despite the white-knuckled drive, I was the first of the students to arrive. As I walked into the blissfully heated building, I caught a glimpse of Emily as she walked into a small side room. She must have seen me as she whipped her head back for a moment and flashed a perfect smile.

"Good morning, Jessica!" she said as she stepped back into the room. "Care to help me out for a second?"

"Sure," I answered as I set my purse on a chair against the wall and quickly walked over to join her in the other room.

The room we entered was fairly large but seemed much smaller than it actually was due to the myriad of sporting equipment that lined the walls. I recalled that this building was used for karate, aerobics, gymnastics, and several other sports as well.

"Can you carry this out for me?" she asked as she dragged a green bin out.

"Yep," I said as I bent and picked it up, noting it was filled with the straps and blocks I had noticed most everyone using on Monday during our session.

Just as we walked back into the main part of the building, four students filed in through the door. Two women and two men. I stopped in my tracks as I saw who the second male was.

"Cole?" I choked.

"Jessica!" he said as a broad smile washed over his perfect face and he walked over to me. "What a coincidence. I didn't know you practiced yoga."

"I didn't know you did either," I said with a confused expression. Not so much over the coincidence but over the feelings that were going on inside me. Part of me couldn't help but swoon over his absolute perfection and be delighted to have him near again but the other part was still remembering how he had seemed almost possessive before. I also briefly recalled the strange chills what worked their way up my spine when he had touched me and the odd sense of not exactly fear, but unease.

"Yes," he said as I saw a flash of confusion and almost frustration cross his face. In an instant it was replaced by a warm smile. "I was very glad to hear there was a class not far away."

I couldn't help but let my eyes wander over his frame. He was wearing one of those tight, black workout shirts with long sleeves and a mock neck. His bottom half was covered with a pair of light and breezy looking track pants. The effect shouldn't have been so stunning.

I realized I hadn't moved from my spot since I had first seen Cole enter and that I was still holding the bin like a frozen idiot. Clearing my throat, I turned to look for Emily and ask her where she wanted it. I was surprised to find her standing just a few feet behind me, frozen as I had been, staring at Cole. Her expression was difficult to read. Was it anger, fear, interest, curiosity? I couldn't tell. Perhaps it was a mix of all of the above, but I couldn't understand it.

My looking in her direction seemed to unfreeze her and she glanced at me for a second. "Just put those at the front," she said as her eyes went back to Cole's face.

I didn't hesitate as I put the bin where she told me and couldn't help but listen as she addressed Cole finally.

"Have you been to this class before?" she asked.

"I can't say I have," he said, his accent smooth and even. "I just moved here."

Emily was silent for a moment as she seemed to be thinking of something. "Huh... you seem... really familiar."

"I guess I just have one of those faces."

I almost snorted out loud at this. Cole definitely did not have "one of those faces." *Anyone* would be able to remember his face anywhere. I didn't know how anyone could possibly forget *that* face.

Emily simply nodded and walked to the front of the class, carrying the bin of mats with her. She instructed each of us to choose one and the class quickly got underway.

I felt self-conscious having Cole in the class. That was part of what made this transition back into society not quite so scary was the fact that I didn't know anyone that would be there. I could start fresh. Even though I did not know Cole really at all, he was still my neighbor now and I couldn't help but feel how intimate our one conversation had been.

Throughout the class I thought I could feel his eyes on me, watching, but every time I checked he looked utterly focused on whatever position we were in.

Emily walked slowly around the room, giving quiet, personal instructions on how to adjust positions. She neared me as we came out of a downward facing dog into a standing position when I noticed the slightly wide-eyed expression she directed toward me. As her eyes met mine they narrowed slightly as if she were contemplating something. The moment passed just as quickly as it happened and she moved on, giving further instructions.

As she walked away, I realized the position I had been in as she walked toward me would have drawn my hair away from my neck, quite possibly exposing my brand. Had she been looking at just the right spot, it was quite likely she would have seen it. It would look pretty frightening and gruesome to most people but it was nothing to panic about. It wasn't like the truth behind it was written on my forehead. At worst she would just think I was into some extreme skin art.

Class passed quickly despite not learning much of anything different from Monday. This was surprising considering how uncomfortable the entire thing had been. Everyone was still getting used to the breathing techniques and trying to get unwilling muscles to move in new ways. The general sense of well-being seemed to be widespread as class came to a close.

Part of me wanted to leave class as soon as it was dismissed to avoid possible questions about what Emily might have seen. Another part of me was willing to take questions if only to have some more normal human contact. And I could not help but feel drawn to Emily. Something within me felt we would get along well if given the chance.

The other students left the room quickly, leaving me alone with Emily again.

"I'll help you clean up," I said and didn't wait as I finished gathering the few straps that had been left out.

"Thanks," Emily huffed as she dropped the last mat into the other bin. "You really have some natural talent in yoga."

"I don't feel like it sometimes," I said with a little chuckle. "The flexibility isn't a problem but I have a hard time relaxing sometimes."

"I can tell," she laughed as we set the bins down. I followed her out and she locked the storage room behind her. "Try working on the breathing techniques at home. It will help. I think you'll be surprised how energized and awake they can make you feel."

As we grabbed our purses I doubted she realized just how helpful that would come in my life.

I was surprised to see that Cole was still in the parking lot, leaning against a very new and very expensive looking black sports car. He flashed that dazzling smile again as he saw us.

"Emily," he said as he nodded to her. "Jessica, I was wondering if you would care to join me for a play tonight. I have heard some really amazing reviews about it."

I was momentarily stunned as his eyes locked on mine and I tried to form a coherent thought to answer him. Without really thinking, the word yes was forming on my lips when I realized what day of the week it was.

"I can't" I sputtered. "I've got something I have to do." I wasn't sure if I was glad for the excuse of movie night with Sal or not.

"Some other time then," he said and before I could tell if a flash of irritation crossed his face or not, he slipped into his car. The engine roared to life and he peeled out of the parking lot.

"*Wow*," Emily exaggerated the word.

"What?" I questioned as I turned to face her.

"That guy is too perfect," she said, her voice sounding like a swoon but her expression looking almost accusing.

I gave a slight chuckle that came out as more of a snort. "Cole is my new neighbor. He just sort of showed up Monday. I didn't even know the previous owner was selling."

That strange accusing look on her face deepened. "That's weird."

"Yeah," I said as I walked to the giant truck and threw my stuff on the passenger seat.

Emily walked to her tiny compact car and opened the door. She put the key in the ignition and went to start it. The only noise it made was a click.

"Ah crap," she said as she rested her forehead on the steering wheel. "I forgot to turn the headlights off again this morning. You wouldn't happen to have any jumper cables on you?"

"Um..." I fumbled. "I'm not sure. I'm kind of borrowing this car. Let's take a look."

Emily jumped out and joined me in the search. It took us only a moment to find them tucked behind the back seat.

"Thank goodness!" she said as she grabbed them and went to her car, throwing the hood up.

Emily seemed to know what she was doing as she hooked the two cars up so I stayed out of her way. I had always been glad my GTO ran without any trouble, I wasn't the most mechanically inclined.

We both leaned against the glossy surface of the truck, our arms hugged tight to ourselves to keep warm.

"I was wondering if you wanted to catch a movie tomorrow and maybe get some lunch if you're not busy," Emily suddenly blurted out. "I know it sounds kind of weird since we don't exactly know each other but, well, I could kind of use a friend and you seem like the kind of person I'd get along with."

"Yeah," I said with a smile. "I'd really like that actually." I was a little more than glad Emily had made the first move toward forming the friendship. Social normality was still feeling a little long gone to me.

"I heard the new chick-flick was pretty good if you're into that kind of thing."

"That sounds great actually. I can't remember when I just went out and had a girl's day," I said with a little laugh. Actually, I couldn't recall *ever* having one.

"Me neither," she laughed. "Here," she said as she pulled her purse out and pulled out a piece of paper and a pen. She scribbled something down and handed it to me. "That's my cell."

I quickly told her my number, feeling a little out of touch with modern technology that I still didn't have a cell phone.

"K, I'll give you a call tonight when I check the show times," she said as she pulled the cables off.

"Sounds good."

I put the cables back where I had found them, waved a quick good-bye and we both pulled out of the parking lot.

CHAPTER THIRTEEN

The day seemed to be confused on what type of weather it wanted to have. One would never know there had been ice on the roads this morning through all the beautiful sunshine and rising temperatures. As I got on the freeway I actually turned the heater completely off. Strange weather for February.

I gently eased the truck into the garage and walked back out to the road to check the mailbox. I softly hummed to myself as I sorted through the Wrights mail and walked back to the house, wondering what you were supposed to do with it all when the intended recipients were deceased. Well, that was up to Alex now I supposed.

"Hey."

I jumped nearly a foot into the air, dropping several envelopes, when I heard the voice just a few feet in front of me.

Cole had seated himself on the bottom step leading up to the doorway. Had he not said anything, I would have walked right into him. He had his arms crossed over his knees, looking up at me with that too perfect smile.

"I thought since you were busy tonight we could go for a little excursion," he said with hopeful eyes that no one could have said no to.

My mouth opened and closed more than once before I could make any sound come out. "Uh…yeah. I guess."

"Great," he said as he stood. I then noticed that he had already changed into a pair of jeans and a light sweater. He was also the only male I had ever seen wear a scarf and not look in the least bit gay.

"I'll, uh…just go in and change," I said as I opened the door slightly.

"Mind if I come in?"

My vocal chords were still unwilling to work so I only shook my head and let him come in behind me. I set the mail on the dining room table before turning to the fridge.

"Would you like something to drink?" I called. "There's milk, orange juice, or water." I did feel a little guilty for looking through Alex's food but I didn't want to be rude.

"I'm fine, thank you," Cole said, making himself comfortable on one of the couches. "So this Alex guy isn't going to storm in here any second and shoot me for entering his house is he?"

I struggled for a second to answer, not sure how I felt about his comment. "No," I finally replied. "Alex had to go to California. He'll be gone till, well, for a while."

Cole only nodded as he looked around the house, taking his surroundings in.

"I hope you don't mind waiting for a little bit. I'd kind of like to shower."

"Of course," he said with a nod and a grin.

I didn't wait to look any more like an idiot and ran downstairs, trying hard to not trip over myself.

The water hadn't even completely gotten hot before I shut it off, hoping I had managed to get all the shampoo out. I threw on the first sweater and pair of jeans I came across and yanked a brush through my hair before resurfacing; a whole ten minutes had maybe passed.

"Ok," I huffed as I came back into the main room. "So, where are we going?"

Cole's eyes wandered very non-subtly from my head to foot, not bothering to cover up the grin that tugged in one corner of his lips. I could feel the blood rush into my cheeks and couldn't help but feel flattered and embarrassed at the same time.

"I noticed the canoe tucked under the deck and thought maybe we could go out in that, if that would be okay with Alex?"

The fleeting moment of flattery passed as slight irritation filled me. I didn't really understand why it flustered me so to have him talk about Alex. "Alex won't mind," I said as I walked out onto the deck and led Cole down the stairs to the lower deck of my apartment.

It only took us a moment to pull the large canoe out, maneuver it down to the dock, and roll it off the side into the water. I accepted the hand Cole offered as I stepped shakily into the canoe.

We each took a paddle and slowly started making our way out into the water. A sudden rush of embarrassment washed over me, realizing we were definitely going to be the only ones out on the water. No one went out in the middle of

February. I felt embarrassingly on display and too obviously in everyone's view.

"Is this good?" I asked as we got about a third of the way across.

"Sure," Cole said from behind me. I slid my paddle into the bottom. Carefully bracing my hands on either side I turned around to face Cole.

"Are you alright?" he said, his expression both amused and anxious at the same time. "You look a bit flushed."

"I'm fine," I said with a huff, glad I had not fallen into the water. I couldn't help but return the playful grin Cole shined at me.

I felt momentarily uncomfortable as I wondered if his plan was to simply sit out here on the lake and float around for an unknown amount of time. Luckily I was saved from wondering in silence for too long.

"There don't seem to be a whole lot of people living here. What do you do for fun around here?" he asked, waiting as though my answer would be the most interesting thing he would ever hear.

"Um..." I struggled to answer, not exactly willing to divulge to this glorious being how pathetic I truly was. "Yeah, it's pretty quiet until around Memorial Day. Believe me, there will be plenty of people here after then. As for fun around here... let's just say I don't get around or out much. I'm kind of pathetic like that I guess." There, I told the truth.

A small smile tugged at the corners of his mouth. "We will have to try our best to change that now that I am here. I will do some checking around and find us something very entertaining to do next week."

I couldn't help but chuckle at Cole's enthusiasm. There were other feelings going on at the same time though. Cole almost seemed to be sending electric currents through his intense gaze as his eyes locked with mine. Strange emotions ran though me as I couldn't help but stare back into the perfection of his face. There was a sense of familiarity about Cole and yet at the same time, I knew he was like no one I had ever met before.

Conversation seemed to come naturally for Cole as he kept up a constant flow of it. It wasn't easy diverting attention away from myself, telling about my past was difficult without letting on that something was very wrong with me. Cole brushed lightly on his childhood in England. He had grown up in a fairly small town but from the sound of it, the population was made up of fairly wealthy people and apparently, the Emerson's were no exception.

"So how old are you, Jessica?" he asked as he leaned forward, resting his forearms on his knees.

"Twenty," I answered, meeting his intense eyes, daring him to make a comment back about me being young. "How old are you?" I asked as I raised an eyebrow.

Cole chuckled. "I just turned twenty-six." I almost missed how he seemed to have to think about his answer.

"Aren't you a too old, you know, for this?" I teased as I made a circle with my fingers, indicating us and the situation we were in.

"Come on!" he joked back. "Don't be like that!"

We both laughed, moving on to mundane questions about favorite books, colors, foods.

Perhaps I had been overly sensitive before. Cole had come off as judgmental and almost possessive at first. Maybe I was wrong. Cole was the perfect gentleman and I was beginning to feel perfectly at ease in his presence.

Two hours must have passed as I noticed the sun had already left the highest position in the sky and was heading west. We had slowly drifted back toward the shore and were not too far from the house. A slight lull in conversation settled and my mind reeled for something to fill the silence. I was, however, coming up blank.

"Can I be perfectly honest with you, Jessica?" I was momentarily relieved when he finally broke the silence, but once I registered his question, I couldn't help but feel incredibly uneasy.

"Of course," I stammered, twisting my hands together in my lap.

"I really enjoy spending time with you," he said, his eyes glowing with intensity. He sat forward, reaching for my hand, which I hesitantly gave him. "I'm not going to pretend otherwise. I like you very much, Jessica. I feel like I have a very strong connection to you."

My heart hammered in my chest and had my brain been functioning correctly, I would have been embarrassed by the possibility that he might be able to hear it. My mouth opened once but with no words for them to say I unconsciously closed it.

It was difficult to tell if Cole was waiting for me to say something. His expression seemed sincere as he continued

143

his unwavering gaze. He leaned forward ever so slowly until his face was less than a foot from mine.

As his smell drifted into my space I had a hard time remembering why I wasn't jumping headlong into the arms Cole seemed to have opened for me. It seemed the perfect male specimen had just walked into my life. Not only was his face and body absolutely perfect and flawless, he seemed to be flattering and considerate. Why was I been holding back again?

As these thoughts raced through my head, I had hardly noticed Cole had continued to move closer until something automatic within turned my head just as his lips were about to meet mine.

I heard him give a frustrated sounding chuckle before he planted a very soft and gentle kiss on my cheek. I very nearly shuddered as an unexpected cold current raced down my spine.

When he sat back there was no evidence of the frustration I'd heard or any signs of rejection. His face was simply calm and serene.

"Shall we head back?" he said smoothly.

I could only nod before I stiffly returned to my seat at the front of the canoe.

Cole said nothing as we cleaned up from our afternoon, for which I was glad, despite the awkwardness that hung in the air. I simply didn't know what to say. He didn't seem dejected in any way as most men probably would. He still held that air of absolute confidence about him, teetering on the edge of arrogance without being irritating. There was a certain look in his eyes as well, almost as if he knew he would eventually get his way. With everything.

"I will see you later then," he said with that smile. He gently tucked a lock of hair behind my ear, sending another tingling shiver rippling through my body as his skin brushed mine. He then turned and walked back up the hill to the road.

Despite the beautiful sunshine I was suddenly freezing. Another uncontrollable shiver shook me and I hurried inside and cranked the heater up past eighty degrees.

X

I sat with my arms wrapped around my legs, my chin resting on my knees, teetering on the edge of my tiny couch. I couldn't shake the cold that seemed to have seeped into my skin.

There was something strange about Cole. From the outside he seemed fine, more than fine. Perfect. He could be a perfect gentleman when he wanted to be but those glimpses I caught of underlying emotions frightened me. Like Mr. Hyde was waiting just under the surface, waiting for that weak moment in Dr. Jekyll to break loose.

While these feelings were strong, I could not deny that I felt *something* toward Cole. He had called it a connection. Maybe that was what it was. There was something that was strangely familiar about him, as if I should already know him and had known him for a long time. Or perhaps it was more just physical attraction than connection. Hormones reacting to a flawless face and body.

I rubbed my arms vigorously, trying to shake the cold and rising, festering feelings. I suddenly didn't want to think about Cole and longed for something comforting and secure feeling.

Before I even realized fully what I was doing, I had the phone in my hand and dialed the number I had memorized.

Oddly, I felt perfectly calm and steady as I listened to the phone ring. I did, however, feel a crushing disappointment when after three rings the voicemail kicked in. And even more disappointed when it was the standard female's voice telling me to leave a message, not the one I longed to hear.

I didn't leave a message as I was unsure of what to even say. He would know it was me who called anyway when he saw the number under his missed calls.

Not five seconds after I hung up the phone rang, sending my heart leaping up into my throat.

"Hello?" I answered, too much excitement in my voice.

"Hi Jessica, it's Emily!"

"Oh," I couldn't help but sound a little disappointed.

"Not who you were expecting?" she half laughed.

"Oh no, sorry," I tried to quickly recover. "I just hung up, he didn't answer."

"Don't worry about it," she rushed on and I was grateful I didn't have to keep trying to scramble. "I looked at the movie times and there's one at noon and another at two. I was kind of thinking the two. That would give us some time to get lunch and walk around the mall before."

"Yeah, that sounds great," I said and meant it.

"Okay, I'll just meet you at the food court in the mall around noon then?"

"I'll see you then."
Emily said a quick good-bye and hung up.

CHAPTER FOURTEEN

It felt like the amount of cleaning I had to catch up on should have taken longer. Sadly it didn't. When I found myself twiddling my thumbs in the evening, I headed to Sal's, trying to ignore the burn that blazed on the back of my neck.

I found Sal sitting next to the window that faced Cole's house, glaring through the blinds. From the looks of her, she hadn't changed her clothes or bathed in a few days.

"Is everything alright, Sal?" I said as I draped my coat over the back of a chair.

"Why is he here?" she hissed as she continued her intense glare out the window.

"Who? Cole?"

"That man shouldn't be here," she mumbled. "You shouldn't be spending time with him, Jessica." I realized then that Sal had probably been watching as Cole and I had gone out on the lake in the canoe.

I was taken aback by her comment. I had never heard her speak like this before. She was always so caring, crazy and unpredictable at times, but never hostile. Though I had heard her screaming her ex-husbands name in her sleep before.

"Cole is a nice guy," I said as I seated myself on the couch, tucking my legs under me. "He's really sorry about scaring you the other day. He told me to tell you that."

"I don't like him," she said as she went to the other couch. "He should leave."

I could only silently chuckle and shake my head. Sal was stubborn; she didn't often change her mind about things. I knew there wasn't going to be much I could do to change her opinion of Cole. But then again, I wasn't really sure what my own opinion of him was.

Sal never seemed to relax, even after she turned her show on. She sat in a tight ball, a blanket wrapped snuggly around her, muttering things under her breath. I hoped her strange hostility would wear off after a few days.

I knew I was going to have to sleep tonight, it was becoming harder and harder to fight. My eyes drooped every few minutes and I had to constantly rearrange the way I sat to keep from getting too comfortable. I could only imagine what would happen if I fell asleep at Sal's.

The credits finally ran and I stretched on the couch, trying to will my body to move.

"Do you want to watch another?" Sal asked hopefully. I was surprised by her eagerness as I didn't think she had gotten much out of the episode.

"I think I'd better get home and go to bed actually," I admitted solemnly. "I'm about to fall asleep right here on your couch."

"You're welcome to if you'd like," I could hear the enthusiasm in her voice. In the back of my mind I wondered if perhaps Sal didn't want to be alone tonight. This seemed unlikely, Sal almost always wanted to be alone.

I gave an uncomfortable chuckle. "Thanks Sal, but I really should get home."

"Alright," she said as she stood and moved back to her position at the window.

"Sal," I sighed. "Really, don't worry about Cole. He's not going to bother you. You should take a long hot shower and put on those new soft pajamas I just got you." I tried to make the suggestions without sounding rude.

She acted as if she didn't hear me as she parted the blinds wide and peered outside.

I sighed again, knowing there wasn't much more I could do. I wasn't going to force her into the shower or her bed. "I'll see you tomorrow. Sleep good."

She still said nothing and I slipped out.

As I stumbled through the door, I went to the phone and saw there had been a missed call from Alex. I was tempted for a short moment to call him back, but it was well after ten and I knew I was in no condition to think straight, much less have an intelligent conversation.

My neck seared and my ears started ringing as I nearly tripped down half the stairs. My breathing came in short intakes and I tried to calm myself before I hyperventilated. My hands shook violently as I dressed in my pajamas. It took me a second to realize why my new bottoms felt off, I had put them on backwards.

I stood staring at my bed for a long time. Even though I knew it was only in my head, I could hear the sound of demented laughter and felt as if thousands of eyes were watching me, just waiting for me to slip under. They were going to win tonight.

I refused to look up from my bare feet as I heard the rustle of wings and knew the council had arrived. My lips moved franticly as the numbers slipped silently over them. My hands were balled into tight fists, twisting around each other, causing the golden chain that bound me to dig into my skin.

"Alice Green," the leader of the exalted began. *My name is not Alice, my name is Jessica,* I hissed to myself as I squeezed my eyes shut. "The deeds of your life have been accounted for and judgment will be passed. Your actions must be made known."

The demonic laughter rose swiftly from below, nearly drowning out the beautiful voices that descended from above. I could feel the hundreds of eyes burning into me as they settled themselves along the staircase that wound around the cylinder.

"Alice Green, your deeds will now be revealed," the perfect man before me continued. I could not find the will to even look up to see which scroll was longer. The numbers continued to roll off my tongue, faster and faster.

I nearly breathed a sigh of relief as the items on the list were read aloud. One was much longer than the other and tonight I was fairly sure I would not get a branding.

I was about to find out though.

"Up," the leader of the exalted began.

"Up," said the second.

"Up," the third.

As each of the exalted sentenced, me to ascend I finally lifted my head. Their faces were so beautiful. How was it possible they could cause such terror in my life?

But as I observed each of their beautiful faces I stopped breathing. Something was different. Where the leader of the condemned usually sat was a lower member of the council. The leader was gone. Another angel I had never seen before had taken a seat on the council.

I had endured the torment of these trials for as long as I could remember and the council had *never* changed. So many things were changing lately. The terrifying experiences of my life were becoming all the more horrifying.

I did not even hear what the condemned members sentenced me to as I tried to rationalize why there could have possibly been a change. I was coming up empty handed.

Angry hisses broke from around me as I barely registered the last sentence of "up" spoken.

"Alice Green," the first of them spoke again. "Judgment has been placed."

My skin crawled, twisted and shivered. I could hear the tearing and pain filled me momentarily as my beautiful wings burst from my skin.

Being exalted was no less terrifying than being condemned. There was just less pain involved. Angry screams ripped through the throats of those with the black eyes as *everyone* leapt from their seats at once. Those with blue eyes clasped my hands and with beats of their powerful wings, tried to heave me upward toward the clear blue sky. The condemned were never willing to let anyone get away though. Clusters of them grabbed at my ankles, doing their best to drag me back down into their fiery hell. It is absolutely true when they say misery loves company.

A brutal tug-of-war began with my body serving as the rope. I screamed and kicked at the cold hands that tried to pull me downward but I could feel the grasps that held my hands slipping. After a moment I lost hold. I heard the heckling, victorious laughter as I freefell through the air, before blackness swallowed me graciously.

I almost called Emily and canceled. I had been a mess all morning, nearly in a vegetative state as I sat motionless on my couch. I just couldn't make sense of the most recent trial.

But somehow, after a few hours of not moving I found my will again and told myself I had to continue on my mission to gain some normalcy. A girls day out was very normal.

So I managed to drag myself into the shower and get dressed in some of the new clothes I had bought. I finally made it out to the truck. It took another five minutes or so of sitting there with my hands braced on the wheel to convince myself, but finally I backed the truck out of the garage and made it to the freeway.

It only took me a moment to find Emily once I reached the mall's food court. She was dressed in an almost too short skirt that showed off her mile long legs and a cute pink sweater. Her hair was worn down as always, but one could tell she had taken some time to get the perfect curls to stay. The whole effect drew quite a few unabashed stares from the male shoppers. I suddenly felt very plain and boring next to her.

"So are you hungry?" she said cheerily after we exchanged excited greetings.

"Sure," I lied. The thought of eating made my stomach churn slightly. Apparently I still wasn't over the effect last night had on me.

We each got some food from different places and I decided I was only safe with a smoothie and a bag of chips. Emily, practically bouncing like a giddy fifteen-year-old girl, led us to a table that wasn't surrounded by too many people.

"Thank you so much for coming with me today," she began as she forked a bit of salad into her mouth. "I know it must seem really weird, me asking you to come with me out of the blue like that, but I just really needed a friend and I don't know very many people here yet."

"Where are you from?" I asked, suddenly realizing I knew nothing about Emily other than her amazing flexibility.

"I grew up in Texas but I've moved around the west coast since I was eighteen. I'm twenty-two now."

I nodded as I took a long draw of my drink. We had that in common at least, leaving home at a young age.

"So tell me about yourself," she said as she looked up at me, excitement over our surroundings shining in her eyes. "Where'd you grow up?"

I chuckled uneasily. I should have guessed this wasn't going to be as easy as I might have hoped. "Um, I grew up in the amazing state of Idaho," I began sarcastically. "I finished high school in California and moved up here a year and a half ago." There. I kept it simple and easy.

Emily's eyes narrowed for just a moment as if she were considering asking something she possibly shouldn't. It only lasted a moment though before she showered me with questions about what I liked to do, what I did around here for fun, guys.

"So what's the deal with you and Cole?" she said as we dumped our now empty trays in the garbage and headed toward the stores.

It took me a second to say anything as I thought over my confused feelings for him. "I don't really know. Things are a little strange in that department."

"Well I can tell you now," she said as she led me into a clothing store. "Cole's feelings are plain and clear on his face. You didn't see the way he kept looking at you yesterday."

"What?"

"Oh yeah, girl. He definitely knows what he wants and that is you, my friend. I'd be careful. Not that he isn't absolutely perfect in every physical way, but there's something a little strange about him."

I felt a little relieved as she said this. So I wasn't just crazy and the only one who felt a little wary toward him. "Thanks," I said simply.

By this point we only had a moment to wander around the store before we needed to head to the theater.

I couldn't remember the last time I had gone to see a chick flick with a female friend. I decided as the movie started I was going to have to do this more often. It made me feel almost normal, like I actually fit into the world. It almost made me forget that I had a pair of wings embedded into the skin on my back and an X branded into the back of my neck.

"Oh my gosh," Emily squealed as we exited the darkened theater. "I cried so hard at the end there when he *finally* kissed her!"

I could only nod in agreement as I dabbed at my eyes again, grateful she'd had a pack of tissues in her purse. I hadn't expected the movie to be a tear jerker *and* a comedy.

"Do you mind if we stay around here a little longer?" she asked with hopeful eyes. "There's supposed to be a killer sale going on right now at my favorite store and I was hoping to get some serious shopping done."

Even if I had something going on it would have been hard to deny her with all the hope that shone in her eyes. "Sounds fabulous," I answered. She gave a delighted squeal and hooked her arm through mine as we marched down the hall.

Emily had meant it when she said she wanted to do some serious shopping. We were in one store for almost three hours. Not that I could blame her for taking her time, the sale had been amazing and I knew I was spending too much money as we both checked out. I could only hope it was true when Alex had said there was a fund to keep paying me.

CHAPTER FIFTEEN

It was almost completely dark outside by the time we made our way back to the cars, each bogged down with too many bags. I had offered to carry a few of Emily's as I had not gotten near the amount she had and so I helped her load them into her tiny car.

"Thanks," she huffed as she closed the back hatch. When she turned back to face me her face was suddenly very serious and very out of place, considering the day we just spent. "We need to talk," she said, her tone very matter-of-fact.

"We've been talking all day. Is everything ok?" I asked, feeling suddenly uncomfortable.

"I need to talk to you, now," she said, her tone far too serious. "You aren't going to be sleeping tonight, are you?"

I froze suddenly and felt a little light headed. How could she know to ask a question like that? "What are you talking about?"

Emily didn't say anything as she turned her back to me. She gathered her hair in one hand, lifting it clear of her neck.

My heart stopped for a moment and the world fell eerily silent as the all too familiar scar on the back of Emily's neck came into view.

I didn't remember Emily turning back around to face me nor did I remember the bags in my hands falling to the ground at my feet. I did, however, remember the not so gentle pats Emily gave me on either side of the face. Her eyes suddenly came back into view as the world started to focus again.

"We need to talk," she said simply again.

I think I nodded as Emily guided me back to the truck, grabbing my bags from off the ground and placing them in the back seat.

"Can you drive? I was thinking we could go back to your place and talk tonight."

It took me a moment to realize I wasn't breathing. As I took a sudden gasping breath the world came into sharper focus and my head cleared a little, though what I had just seen still wasn't making the slightest sense.

"Yeah, I think so," I said as my brow creased and I gave Emily a good hard look, reassessing everything I had ever learned or thought about her.

"Okay," she said, her own brow creased as she nodded. She seemed to be gauging if I was telling the truth about my state of mind. "I'll follow you there."

I could only nod as I watched her slide into her car. Numbly, I climbed into the truck.

The drive home seemed to flash by in an instant as I tried to make my mind comprehend what this meant. I couldn't make sense of any of it. The image of the X branded into the back of Emily's neck wouldn't leave my thoughts though.

I parked the truck in the garage and walked up the slight hill to the road as Emily parked her car on the narrow shoulder.

"I'll be back in just a second," I said as I approached cautiously. "I've got to check on something really quick. You can go ahead and go in. It's unlocked."

She gave me a long hard look as if trying to decide if I was going to suddenly run off and never come back. "I'll wait for you inside," she finally said before walking toward the house.

All the lights were off inside and I wondered briefly if Sal might be asleep. That would be very out of character. Sal was a night owl; it was rare she went to bed before midnight. I tried to make out any signs of life but it was too dark. I searched along the wall by the door and quickly found the light switch.

Sal was lying on the couch and I silently wondered how she could possibly sleep in the position she was in. She looked so uncomfortable. I crossed the room to try and rearrange her if not make her move into her bed.

I was about half way across the room when the orange bottle of pills came into view. I crossed to her side in two long bounds.

"Sal?" I nearly screamed as I shook her violently. She remained as still as she had been when I first saw her. "Sal!"

The bottle of pills looked as if they had fallen from her hand just before she crashed onto the couch, only a few of them seemed to be left to scatter across the floor.

"Sal!" I screamed again as I pushed her onto her side and felt around for a pulse. It took me a moment, but I finally found it. I timed it to the clock that hung above her sink; it was very faint and barely detectable.

"What did you do?" I muttered as I stumbled across the room to the phone.

My fingers shook violently as I dialed the three numbers.

"911, what is your emergency?"

"There is a woman unconscious here," I tried to keep my voice even as I spoke. "It looks like she's overdosed."

I tried to keep my head clear as I followed her few instructions and gave her the address.

"An ambulance will be there in just a moment," the woman's voice said comfortingly.

"Thank you," I managed as the first of the tears escaped down my face.

It seemed to take an eternity for the ambulance to arrive, though it could not have been more than a few minutes. As soon as I heard the wailing I ran to the front door to let them in.

They asked only a few questions as they loaded Sal onto a stretcher. I barely heard them tell me that they were taking her to Saint Joseph's Hospital as I thought how fragile and helpless Sal looked, laying completely limp there.

As I followed the paramedics into the driveway, I noticed several of the neighbors as well as Emily were standing on their front steps, looking to see what all the noise and flashing lights were about. I suddenly felt slightly hostile and wanted to shout at all of them to go back in their houses. Sal didn't need any more judgments being placed on her. Everyone thought she was insane enough; they didn't need to see this.

I walked swiftly back to Emily's side as the sirens wailed away.

"I'm guessing you need to go then?" she said as she followed me to the still open garage.

"Yeah," I said as I dug the keys out of my purse with shaky hands. "Um…" I struggled with words to say as I looked back up at her.

"I'll stay here," she said with surety in her voice. I was grateful for her ability to think clearly when I couldn't. "I'm sure you could use some moral support when you get back. That is if you want me to stay around. Though we do need to talk."

I could only nod as I wiped a single tear away.

"Hey," she cooed as she wrapped her arms around me. "I wish I could say everything is going to be okay but I don't exactly know. You can handle this though. Go be with your friend."

"Thanks," I whispered as I stepped away from her. I didn't wait for her to say anything more as I opened the truck door and climbed in.

Despite the fact that I had gotten some sleep last night, I felt drained as I got to the freeway. Too much had happened since then that didn't make any sense. First there was the council changing for the first time ever, then Emily showing me the brand on the back of her neck. I still couldn't understand what that meant exactly. And now Sal.

That was as strange as the rest of it all somehow, even though it should seem, well not normal, but well, at least not supernatural. Sal might have been slightly crazy but she wasn't suicidal. She had her times when she was completely

161

out of touch with reality, but there were times when she was with it, times she appeared content and happy. She understood what it meant for her to now be freed from her ex-husband and she absolutely appreciated that, so for her to try and kill herself like that made no sense.

I found the hospital with no trouble. I had been taken there once, just after I crashed my car into that ravine. I had, of course, come out of it unscratched. Not a bone in my body had been broken. But the paramedics still insisted on checking me out.

The emergency waiting room was quiet when I arrived. There was only one other man waiting inside.

The woman at the counter was friendly and answered my questions kindly. She said that the doctor would probably come out soon to talk with me when I told him Sal didn't have any family that I knew of.

I sat in one of the uncomfortable chairs that lined the wall, sitting as far across the room from the other man as possible. I suddenly wished that I had asked Emily to come with me. She was so level and clear-headed, it would have been nice to have her with me.

I waited for almost an hour, and asked the nurse twice if she had heard anything before the doctor finally came out to talk to me. He introduced himself as Dr. Ostler. I hesitantly asked if I could see Sal and he ushered me into a tiny private room.

The tears welled in my eyes and threatened to spill over as I saw Sal lying unconscious in her bed. They had changed her into a nightgown that drowned her tiny form. Tubes were stuck in her nose, a few were coming out of her arm, and I could see traces of black smudges around her mouth from when they pumped her stomach.

"You told the nurse Sal doesn't have any family that you know of?" Dr. Ostler asked kindly.

I nodded my head, not entirely trusting my voice.

"And can I ask what your relationship is to Miss Thomas?"

"I'm her neighbor," I whispered. "I help her out. I do her shopping and run her errands. I check up on her every day. I had been gone all day so I hadn't been over yet. That's when I found her."

He asked my name and I told him.

"Well, Miss Bailey, normally I wouldn't be able to tell you much but as there doesn't seem to be a nearest of kin we will say you are a caretaker of sorts to this woman." He motioned for me to take a seat in one of the two stiff looking chairs. I numbly sat. "As I'm sure you have already assumed this looks like a suicide attempt."

A few tears spilled over as he finally formed the words I could not will my head to think.

Dr. Ostler was very kind and patient as he asked me questions about Sal's mental status and medical history. I told him what I knew and gave him the name of Sal's doctor.

"She is stable and should be fine physically. We are, however, recommending she be placed under psychiatric observation for at least a week to determine if it is safe for her to be living on her own," he said after he showered me with questions, all the while making notes on his clipboard. "You are welcome to stay with her for as long as you like."

I nodded and thanked the Doctor before he quietly left the room.

It took me a few long minutes of simply staring at Sal's still form before I could find the will to drag my chair to her side. My hands still shaking, I took one of hers carefully in mine. It broke my heart as I looked at her face, seeing the almost anxious expression that was set into it. One would think at least in a medicated state of unconsciousness she should be able to find some peace and rest.

I couldn't hold back the flood of tears I had fought so hard for the last few hours. How could she have done this? How could she do this to me? Sal was as close as any family I had now. Despite how untraditional our relationship was, she was still the best friend I had. I needed her as much as she needed me. Perhaps more. She had gotten along without me for several years before I came along. I couldn't imagine what I would do if I were to lose her now.

My only sense of time as I sat at Sal's side was when a nurse came in to check on Sal's vitals. She told me everything looked fine and asked if she could get me anything. I told her no and thanked her. I glanced at the clock as she left and noted it was now just after midnight. I tried to press back any thoughts; everything was just getting to be too much.

CHAPTER SIXTEEN

I lay with my head resting on the side of the bed, Sal's hand still held securely in my own when I felt the warm hand touch my shoulder. Sleep had been threatening to pull me under but at the contact, a warm jolt of life and energy flooded through me.

"Alex!" I exclaimed as I lurched to my feet and launched myself into his arms.

He didn't say anything as he wrapped his arms around me tightly and pressed his face against mine, momentarily pressing his lips to my cheek. Tears flooded my eyes again and spilled onto his shoulder. Such a deep sense of relief and comfort washed through me, I felt as if I were physically melting into his embrace.

After several long moments of pure joy, I opened my eyes and saw Emily leaning in the door frame, a tiny half smile on her lips.

"Thank you," I mouthed to her. Despite the bomb she had dropped on me earlier, I would be eternally grateful to her for however she had magically made Alex appear. She simply smiled and nodded.

I stepped back just a bit, not releasing my arms from around his neck, so I could look at Alex's face, not caring how horrid my own must look. "How?" was all I managed to say.

He pushed the hair from my face as he looked seriously in my eyes, emotions playing intensely across his impossibly blue eyes. "Things got wrapped up in California more quickly than I expected and I just had this feeling that I needed to get home." My insides quivered slightly as he said the word *home*. "I got back to the house just a little bit ago and your friend here was there and told me where you were and that there had been an accident with Sal. We got up here as fast as we could."

A little sob escaped my lips as I buried my face in his chest, unbearably grateful he arrived when he did. It had been all I could bear to contain everything that had happened in the last twenty-four hours.

"I'm sorry I couldn't get here sooner," he whispered as he stroked my hair.

"Don't be ridiculous," I choked. "You couldn't have had better timing. I'm just so glad that you came back at all."

I regretted saying the last part almost as soon as I said it. Alex pulled me away from him just enough so he could look me in the face. He seemed to be searching my face for something for a long moment before he spoke. "It was much harder than it should have been for me to be gone as long as I was." He pulled me back into his firm embrace again and I thought I heard him mutter something like, "Don't you realize?" but I wasn't sure, nor did I have the energy to ask him what he had said.

After several minutes that passed all too quickly, I realized I was being very rude in not formally introducing Alex and Emily.

"Oh," I said as I stepped away from Alex. "I'm so sorry, Alex this is my friend Emily Lewis. Emily this is Alex Wright."

"Yeah, we did actually get to that part in the whirlwind of this evening," Emily said with a little smile from the doorway.

I blushed slightly, feeling a little stupid. Of course they would have at least gotten each other's names considering Alex most likely had found her in his house.

"Please, sit," I said as I wiped my tears on the sleeve of my jacket. Once everyone was settled I took a deep breath, preparing myself to say what I knew needed to be said.

"The doctor said it looks like Sal tried to commit suicide," my bottom lip quivered slightly as I spoke. "The hospital wants to keep her under observation for a while to make sure she really should be living by herself."

Everyone was quiet for several minutes after I spoke, each unsure of what to say. A few tears escaped down Alex's face, though he made no move to wipe them away.

"I'm so sorry Jessica. Alex told me how close you two were and that you took care of her," Emily said as she stood and wrapped her arms around my shoulders. "You are a good woman."

I accepted the embrace immediately. The raised skin of what I knew would be an intricate set of wings was barely detectable through the fabric of her sweater. She backed away after a moment, a knowing look on her face.

Just as Emily backed away, a nurse came into the room to check Sal's vitals. I realized they were checking her every hour.

"She's doing just fine," the dark-complexioned woman with motherly eyes said. "The medication we gave her should be wearing off soon so she could wake up at any time. We have her on the monitor down the hall but she's likely to be very confused when she wakes up and her throat is going to bother her from when we pumped her stomach. Just push this button here when she wakes and someone will be here in just a moment."

We nodded and thanked the woman and she left with a comforting smile.

"Do you want us to stay with you?" Alex whispered as if he were afraid to wake Sal.

"You don't have to," I said as I rubbed my eyes. "I'm sure you're tired after traveling all day. You should go and get some sleep."

Alex grabbed my hand in both of his and brought it up to his face, gently pressing his lips to my knuckles. "Do you want me to stay with you?" he asked earnestly.

"Yes," the words slipped out of my mouth before I could tactfully think of a way to say so without sounding so desperate.

"Then I'll stay."

I just nodded my head and tried to keep the thankful tears back.

"Um," Emily said, sounding slightly uncomfortable. "I don't want to make Sal uncomfortable when she wakes up since she doesn't know me. Maybe it would be best if I go back to your house and get my car?"

I considered this for a moment. She was right. Sal did have a hard time with new people, Cole was proof of that. "Yeah, that would probably be a good idea. Thank you for coming up though. I really appreciate it."

Emily stood and gave me an encouraging hug. As she stood, Alex dug around in his pocket and handed her the keys to my car.

"Can you drive a stick?" he asked. "You can take my truck if not."

"I think I can manage," she said as she gave us a wink. "I'll leave the keys on the table. I'll call you later, Jessica."

"Okay," I managed, my voice sounding hoarse.

She left with a quiet click of the door.

We sat in silence for a moment, simply staring at Sal's still form. I wondered what was going on in her mind right now, what could cause the perplexed expression she bore. It didn't seem fair that she should have to be so tortured in her sleep.

I stretched my legs out in front of me as a huge yawn escaped. I couldn't help it as I rubbed my eyes.

"Why don't you take a break for a minute," Alex said as he rubbed a hand in circles on my back. "I can sit with Sal for a bit. Why don't you go get something to drink? I saw a vending machine in the waiting room. I'm pretty sure they even had Dr. Pepper in it," he said with that half smile.

I let out a little chuckle. So apparently he had noticed my drink of choice.

"I think that would be a good idea at this point," I said as I stood, raising my arms above my head, trying to make my blood circulate again. "I'll be back in just a minute."

"Take as long as you need."

It was indeed a relief to be out of the tiny room that was beginning to feel stuffy. I was however not exactly anxious to leave Alex's side so quickly after he miraculously returned. But the halls were a welcome break and oddly, they lifted my fallen spirits a bit with their white walls and bright lights. It also helped me to feel more alert and awake.

My first stop was to the ladies' room that was just off the waiting room. I was glad to see it was empty as I stood at the counter and looked in the mirror. I looked like a nightmare. The bags under my eyes were frightening and I wondered if they would ever return to normal. My eyes were swollen and bloodshot; all evidence of the make-up I had worn earlier had been long washed away with the tears. My skin looked splotchy and unhealthy. The mane that was my hair was turning frizzy and looked disheveled. I suddenly wished I were the type of girl who kept a portable salon in her purse- anything to help the scary face that looked back at me in the mirror.

I splashed some water on my face and dried it. It felt refreshing and I wished I could take a shower. That was going to have to wait though.

I felt suddenly ashamed after I stood looking at myself for several long minutes. Sal had just been fighting for her life and I was worried about what I looked like. How could I be so shallow?

There was indeed a vending machine in the waiting room and I was grateful they did have my favorite drink. I bought two of them and quickly made my way back to Sal's room.

"Feel better?" Alex asked with a little smile as I closed the door behind me.

"Much," I said as I tried to force a smile onto my face unsuccessfully. I held one of the sodas out to him but he shook his head.

"I'm okay. I can't say I care too much for that stuff anyway. Thanks though."

"Well, I don't think I'll have any problem downing both of them," I chuckled as I unscrewed the lid to the first one. I downed half of it in less than thirty seconds.

"Whoa!" Alex laughed. "Slow down there."

"Sorry," I said as I wiped a tiny drop that had escaped onto my lips onto the back of my hand. "I'm tired."

The laughter that had just filled Alex's face suddenly died away. My heart sank into my stomach for a moment. I hadn't forgotten what I told Alex but up until this point I was pretending I could ignore that fact and just simply enjoy that he was here.

But rather than just look at me like I was a freak, he opened his arms and ushered me to him. My heart gave a little flutter as I settled myself into his lap and he wrapped his arms comfortingly around me. I let my head rest on his chest and his chin settled softly on the top of it. He began humming softly and after a few minutes I couldn't find the will to ask him what the tune was and break the near perfectness of the moment.

There was a not entirely small part in the back of my mind however that wondered if the closeness we were experiencing would last beyond this dramatic night and into tomorrow when things would return to a more normal state. I was trying hard not to think about that.

The clock ticked on, the second hand seemed to grow fractionally louder with each tick. Despite the setting and circumstances we were there under I couldn't help but be wonderfully happy.

Just before three, the magic was broken, though it was not an entirely heartbreaking experience.

Sal's eyes fluttered open and then shut once, her brow becoming all the more furrowed. Her lips quivered, almost as if she were trying to say something, but was unable to find the strength to make the words come out.

We both jumped to the side of her bed and I took one of her hands in mine as I sat on one side.

"Sal?" I whispered. "Can you hear me?"

Her eyes opened briefly again but they were unfocused and clouded looking. They slid heavily closed again. Her lips began to move a little more deliberately and small hissing sounds escaped them as she tried to force air up her throat to speak.

"It's Jessica," I whispered as I touched her face, pushing her wild hair out of her eyes. "Alex is here too. He got home this morning."

"Where?" the raspy word made its way out of her throat.

"You're at Saint John's Hospital, Sal." I had to try very hard to keep my voice steady as the tears threatened to spill over again. I didn't think I could handle telling Sal what had happened as I knew it was likely she wouldn't remember the incident at all.

"He told me…" her voice quivered as her eyes remained closed, the furrow between her brows continued to deepen. "Make me forget. Forget what happened."

I looked up at Alex with a worried and confused expression. His own face reflected how I felt.

"Let him in. Black eyes said trust him. Face tricked me." Sal's eyes slid open and she found my face, suddenly able to focus. Her eyes stared intently into my own and I saw fear spread through them. "Wasn't what he seemed. Tricked me. Don't trust him."

"Sal, I…" I stumbled for words as I kept the intense stare she was giving me. "Who are you talking about?"

"Don't trust him, Jessica," she wheezed as she squeezed my hand with much more force than I thought she would be able to muster.

Just then the nurse came in the door with a quiet tap.

"I thought she must be awake," she said. "The monitors suddenly started jumping all around."

She walked to Sal's side and began checking things and Alex and I had to move to get out of the way.

"Dr. Ostler is going to want to check her out again and talk to Sal in private," the nurse said, turning to us. "I suggest the both of you head home and get some sleep. It's been a long night I'm sure. The hospital will give you a call, Miss Bailey, to let you know what is happening."

I simply nodded my head, which suddenly felt like it was spinning with the possibility of leaving Sal in this hospital full of strangers by herself.

"We'll be back soon, Sal," Alex mercifully spoke when I couldn't. She stared at him blankly before her eyes slid shut once again.

I grabbed my things from the room and we left silently.

CHAPTER SEVENTEEN

I quietly explained to Alex what had happened prior to his sudden arrival as he drove us back home. I was tempted to lie down on the seat but knew if I did I was likely to fall asleep. So instead I propped myself against the door, letting my forehead rest against the frigid window.

"I can't believe it," Alex said softly as he stared at the dark road before us. "I don't know Sal very well but I just can't believe she did this."

I could only nod my head slightly. I was trying to push the whole incident from my mind. It was too much to think about.

"Emily must have left some lights on when she left," Alex observed as he pulled into the garage. I barely even glimpsed to see if my car was returned to the garage, which it was. He offered a hand and helped me climb out into the dark. My legs felt shaky and wobbly and I was glad that Alex held on for a few moments longer than necessary, maybe for more than just that simple reason.

Alex held the door open for me as we went in through the garage door that led into the side of the kitchen. I nearly jumped a foot in the air when I saw a figure rise from the dining table and take a few steps forward.

"Cole?" I nearly screamed, my pulse hammering in my ears.

"Jessica, I'm so…" his buttery voice trailed away when he saw Alex enter behind me.

A rather tense moment passed as Cole's expression turned strangely hard. I wasn't sure what to expect if I were to turn around and look at Alex's face. I suddenly felt very uncomfortable standing between them.

"Uh, Alex, this is Cole Emerson. He bought the house next to Sal's a few days ago," I stammered. "Cole, this is Alex Wright, the one I told you about."

I heard Alex's breathing relax slightly behind me but Cole's expression stayed tense and hard, his dark eyes seeming to turn flat black. I felt a cold shiver run down my spine.

Alex stepped around me, his hand extended toward Cole. "Nice to meet you, Mr. Emerson."

After a moment's hesitation Cole's face relaxed just slightly as he shook Alex's hand. "Please, just Cole."

Alex only nodded before he motioned toward the couches next to the fireplace. They each took a seat on a different couch. I chose to stand.

By now Cole seemed to have regained some of his composure, his face now looking more relaxed but concern now filled it instead. "I got home just as Emily was leaving. She told me what happened. I'm so sorry, Jessica. That must have been a terrible ordeal for you."

I could only nod my head as I hugged my sides. I really didn't want to talk about it anymore tonight. It was all just too overwhelming.

"You know you can call me anytime if you need to talk," he continued, his eyes were intense, still that chilling black color. "Or come over. Anytime."

"Thank you," I managed to get out, my voice sounding terribly hoarse.

Cole continued his intense gaze for just a moment longer. Different emotions seemed to be rolling in his eyes as if he were struggling with some internal debate. Finally he nodded once before he stood. He took the four steps toward me before wrapping his arms around me in an embrace which I returned stiffly. I fought off a shiver as he stepped away.

"I'll see you later then," he said as he quickly crossed the room and left without another word or backward glance.

As soon as the door closed I collapsed onto the couch, knowing my legs wouldn't support me much longer. I leaned my head on the back of the couch and let my eyes slide closed.

"I'm sorry about that," I murmured, not really wanting to talk about it but knowing there was need for some sort of explanation. "That must have been really awkward for you, coming home and finding someone who wasn't supposed to be there in your house."

"Well, it wasn't the first time," Alex replied, his voice just a little too serious for the joke I knew he was making. I opened one eye and peeked over at him just to make sure he really was joking. He was looking back at me, a small tired smile on his lips.

"You should get some sleep," I said. "I'm sure it's been a long day for you."

"Longer for you," he said matter-of-factly.

"I'm used to long days," I replied feeling slightly uncomfortable.

Alex looked into my face for a moment, his expression soft and nonjudgmental. "Jessica, you should get some sleep if you need. Don't worry about me being here. Really."

I tried to manage a small smile and hoped the tears that suddenly sprang to my eyes didn't show. "Thank you. I still haven't decided if it's worth it or not tonight."

He gave another small smile before getting to his feet. He extended a hand to me and helped me to my own.

"Whatever you decide is just fine. I do think I need to get some rest though."

I simply nodded as I followed him down the stairs. We didn't say any good-nights as we each went into our separate rooms.

I changed into the new pajamas I had bought earlier. They were surprisingly comfortable, silky slick blue bottoms and a tank. It felt surprisingly wonderful as I brushed my teeth furiously and scrubbed my face till it felt raw. It felt as if the events of the past few days and weeks were covering me in grime and filth that would never come off.

My bedroom felt suddenly incredibly empty and cold as I perched on the edge of my bed. While I knew I should take time to think about everything that was happening I couldn't bring myself to do it. Unreality was calling to me and I knew I couldn't think straight through it. The brand on the back of my neck prickled, reminding me of the ever constant human need for sleep.

I was knocking on the door before I had even allowed myself to make the decision to walk out of my own. I opened the door when I heard a muffled invitation from within.

My eyes swept the darkened room as I closed the door behind me and leaned against it. Alex was already in his bed, watching me where I stood.

It was a strange moment as we both simply stared at each other through the dark. I saw the same emotions playing across his face that ran though my own head; uncertainty, nervousness, longing, confusion, hope.

"Would I be terribly out of place if I didn't want to be alone tonight? If I asked if I could stay with you?" I finally whispered, not entirely ready to break that strange silence.

"Not at all," he whispered back as he slid over under the covers.

Surprisingly I didn't shake with nervousness as I crossed the room. I knew I was being very uncharacteristically presumptuous here. A very big part of me knew exactly what I wanted and needed in this moment though.

He pulled the covers down for me and I slid in beside him, not sure if I was glad or not he had a bigger bed than I did, if I was being honest with myself. He extended an arm and I snuggled myself into it without hesitation. My heart gave a strange little sputter as I couldn't help but notice he wasn't wearing a shirt. Even in the darkness it was easy to make out the chiseled chest muscles and perfectly shaped abs.

I felt myself relax more than I had since he left, as the scent of him flooded through me. It felt like I had finally found home.

"I have to warn you," I whispered. "I will probably fall asleep. You really can tell me to leave. I won't blame you."

He said nothing as he nuzzled his face into my hair, his hand coming up to stroke the side of my face, trailing across my eyelids. "Please don't leave."

I took a deep breath again, letting his comforting scent fill my senses. He continued to stroke the side of my face for a moment but soon his hand came to rest on the side of my neck, his fingers dangerously close to my scar, and his breathing turned slow and even.

As I fought off sleep, a few deeply important thoughts occurred to me, perhaps life changing realizations. Cole's feelings were becoming quite clear over the last few days and he obviously wasn't going to waste any time in trying to get what he wanted. I couldn't deny the attraction I felt to him but that was something I was quite sure every woman who laid eyes on him felt. I also couldn't ignore the warning bells that went off in my body every time he was near me. Cole was something I was going to have to address quickly. He wasn't the one I wanted.

If I ever were to believe that angels were as books and movies depicted, I knew that I lay in the arms of one now. He may not be perfect; he was a bit presumptuous and knew basically no boundaries. His face may not have been as flawless as Cole's but in my eyes that made him all the more wonderful. He was so human and real. And the most wonderful fact of all: he seemed to be able to handle the bizarreness that was my reality. I hadn't scared him away and while he hadn't exactly come out and said it, he didn't seem to think I was completely crazy.

The third, final, and most important realization: I wasn't falling in love with Alex Wright. I was already there.

I bolted upright as the screams erupted from my lips. Confusion immediately flooded my thoughts when I realized I wasn't in my room. The emotion deepened when I realized it was getting light outside. I never woke from my nightmares as it was getting light unless I fell asleep during the day. My bleary eyes found a clock and I was stunned to see that it was nearly seven. As I remembered where I was and what had happened the night before I was shocked to realize I had slept for nearly five hours. I couldn't remember the last time I slept that long.

All these thoughts raced through my head with a dull throb that didn't recede as I stifled the screams. But of course I had woken Alex. His eyes looked wide and alarmed as he jerked awake. As soon as he looked upon my shamed face his expression calmed and became soft.

I couldn't hold his gaze for long as I sat with my legs hanging off the edge of the bed. I felt so ashamed of who I was. I was so abnormal. Normal people didn't have such tormenting dreams. Normal people didn't wake every time screaming.

I heard him shifting in the bed and a moment later felt his fingers trace softly up my arm. They drifted across my shoulder, brushing my hair slowly over my other shoulder.

My heart pounded and every nerve screamed at me to make him stop. It was natural for me to never, ever let anyone see my scars. But there was such a deep part of me what wanted him to see them, for him to know every part and detail of me. I wanted him to know the true and whole me.

I listened intently for his reaction as the branded X came into full view. There was no sharp intake of breath, no hiss of disgust, nothing to indicate that it revolted or disgusted him. His fingers traced the pattern slowly, leaving it feeling pleasantly warm and tingly. Goosebumps rushed to cover my skin.

After lingering on the X for a while, his fingers slowly drifted down toward the tip of the raised wings, just barely visible under the top I wore.

Heat rushed to my cheeks as I brought my hands to the hem of my tank top; though I was overwhelmingly grateful I had left my bra on last night, and pulled it over my head. Alex could now see every detail of the wings imprinted there and I knew with the light that was coming through the window now he would be able to catch glimpses of that strange metallic glint in them.

Again his fingers traced over the feathered patterns, slowly trailing from the tops to the very tips of the wings at the bottom. I suppressed a shiver of pleasure, nervous anticipation, and uncertainty.

"They are beautiful," he breathed.

I rested my chin on my shoulder, not quite fully looking at his face. "They don't disgust you?" I whispered, my voice shaking obviously.

He rested one hand on my other shoulder and the other on my arm and leaned forward, gently pressing his lips into the center of the brand.

"Nothing about you could disgust me," he whispered against my neck.

I finally turned around and faced him, getting the first full look of his face. His impossibly blue eyes burned with an intensity and sincerity that sent my heart fluttering in an almost painful way.

"Alex, I…" I hesitated as I looked down for a moment at my hands where they sat in my lap. "I want you to know everything about me, about the truth of my life but I'm afraid. I'm afraid it will scare you and make you run from me."

Alex placed his hand under my chin, lifting it until I had to look him back in the eye again. "I haven't been able to stop thinking about you since the moment I first saw you in the stair well with that bat. I just about went crazy those few days I was gone. And it drove me nearly mad when I kept missing you on the phone. All of these intense feelings got so much worse after you told me the truth about what was going on. I'm not going anywhere and I plan on being around as long as you can stand me."

As he spoke these last words I couldn't hold myself back any longer. I leaned forward, wrapping my arms around his neck as my lips found his. Alex's arms wrapped tightly around my waist as he half pulled me back and half fell back onto the bed.

My pulse raced and my breathing became ragged as the kiss deepened and our lips parted. His hands again traced the raised skin on my back, caressing and touching in a way that was almost overwhelming with its acceptance and need.

I felt as if a match had been lit and held to my blood that had suddenly turned into lighter fluid. Even as I breathed in his already familiar scent I felt as if I could not get close enough. As if I could never get enough of him to satisfy my need and burning desire. And yet at the same time it felt like the most natural thing in the world, as if his lips and body had been made to fit against mine and mine to his.

After a few heated minutes Alex pulled away, his eyes holding mine in a wonderfully burning gaze, as if there was so much more he wanted to do, yet he knew he couldn't. He wasn't alone in those thoughts.

We lay on our sides, Alex lightly trailing his fingers along my arm. Our breathing slowly returned to normal and the heat rush that filled my body slowly ebbed back toward normal.

"How is it possible to have such strong feelings," I whispered as I stared softly into his content looking face. "When I've only known you for such a short time?"

"I always used to think love at first sight was such a ridiculous idea," he breathed. "And while I can't say that I totally believe in it now, I realize love can develop much, much more quickly than I ever thought possible."

I couldn't suppress the smile that spread on my lips as I leaned toward him just slightly and pressed my lips lightly to his. When I pulled away the same smile was reflected on his face but his eyes held a new emotion. Was that curiosity now?

"Tell me more about it," he asked softly as he played with the bracelet he had given me. I still had yet to take it off for longer than it took me to shower. "I want to understand better what it is that happens. You didn't tell me much detail before."

I bit my lip as I stared hard into his face, hesitating for too long. "Are you sure? It is going to sound completely crazy."

"Please," he whispered, his eyes sincere. "I want to understand."

I hesitated for a long moment again. I reminded myself though that I had basically declared my feelings to him. Wasn't he worth the risk of telling the truth?

Yes. Yes he was.

It was difficult to decide where exactly to start, what aspect of this messed up life to try and explain. I decided to start with what seemed the most simple to explain, just exactly what happened in my dreams. I told him of how Adam, with those strange grey eyes, would take me to the narrow catwalk. I explained how each of the council members was devastatingly beautiful yet I could never seem to remember the details of their faces when I woke. It was difficult to describe the terror I felt as I stood there, listening to the demented laughter as sentencing would be given and how my blood pounded painfully through my system as the brand was raised to be pressed into the back of my neck. I finally ended with how I was always graciously saved as I would fall off the catwalk and slip back into the darkness. I decided it was best to leave out the details of how everything seemed to be changing concerning the nightmares.

There was silence for a few moments after I finished. I knew I couldn't tell him any more this morning, it was too overwhelming. It had been difficult enough to say what I already had. It went against the nature I had built up in myself my entire life.

I caught a glimpse of the clock sitting on his nightstand and jumped to my feet.

"Oh crap," I hissed as I grabbed my tank from off the floor. "I have to go."

"Where?" Alex questioned as he sat up in the bed, his voice hinting just a fraction of alarm.

"I've started this class this week. That's where I met Emily," I said as I raced into my bedroom, Alex following me. I went into my closet, pulling on the first comfortable looking clothes I found. Alex graciously kept where he couldn't see me. "Under normal circumstances I would probably skip it today, considering what happened last night, but I really need to talk to her."

I stepped out of the closet and started pulling on some socks. "She knows something about my nightmares. She has the same scars I do."

"What?" Alex gaped. "How?"

"I don't know," I said as I stood, heading out back into my tiny kitchen. "We were supposed to talk last night and then I found Sal. So I really need to talk to her today."

Alex didn't seem to know what to say as he nodded his head.

I grabbed my purse and headed out the door and up the stairs, Alex still trailing behind me. I found my keys on the kitchen table, just where Emily said she would leave them.

"I'm going to see how Sal is doing when I'm done," I said as I rested my hand on the door knob leading out into the garage. "I'll call you from the hospital."

"If you can let me know when you're done with Emily, I'll go to the hospital with you if you want."

A small smile spread on my lips again. "Thanks," I said as I leaned toward him and pressed a quick kiss to his lips. He smiled back. He covered my hand with his and opened the door for me. I smiled back again before going down the stairs to my car.

I stopped in my tracks, just two steps from what I thought was my car. But surely the glossy, very tough and fast looking beast before me couldn't be my rusty GTO.

"I thought it would be a shame if it never got restored to its full glory." I could hear the smile on his face as Alex came to stand beside me.

"Alex," I breathed as I continued to stare at the flawless new black paint job. "It looks amazing. I don't know what to say. Thank you."

"You're very welcome," he said as he pressed a quick kiss to my cheek. "Now, I believe you were running late?"

"Right," I said as I snapped out of my shock. "I'll call you when I'm done with Emily," I called as I slid into the driver's seat. He waved once as I pulled out, and I could clearly see the goose bumps that were spread across his arms and still gloriously bare chest.

It baffled my mind and I still couldn't allow myself to fully comprehend that this nearly perfect man could be mine.

CHAPTER EIGHTEEN

I walked into the studio just as everyone had finished their breathing exercises. Emily barely glanced up at me as she moved into down dog, but Cole stopped and stared for a few long moments before moving into the position. I tried to draw as little attention as possible and quickly slipped my shoes off and joined the small group.

It was difficult to concentrate on the session, much less let myself really get into the breathing and stretches as I tried to figure out what I was going to say to Emily, which of the million questions to ask first. I was coming up blank and was feeling slightly panicky.

The session passed all too quickly of course and seemed to speed by in a quarter of the time it should have taken. I knew I was stalling as I took far more time than necessary to roll my mat perfectly on the floor.

"How are you, Jessica?" I glanced up when I heard the perfectly smooth voice from above me.

I stood, fumbling with the mat. Cole stood only a foot away, just slightly too close for comfort. I took a slight step backward. "I'm okay," I stuttered. "It was a long night."

"I'm sure," he said, his eyes boring into my own. It was difficult to find the will to look away, despite the feeling of recoil spreading through my entire body. "I wanted to invite you to come over tonight, maybe watch a movie or something. I thought you could use a little break from everything."

"Um..." I scrambled to know what to answer. "I'm not really sure what I have going on today. We'll see how things pan out, you know, considering what happened yesterday. I'll have to call you later and let you know."

Within those infinitely deep and captivating eyes I caught that glimpse of Mr. Hyde. A flash of irritation and perhaps impatience. This time however he did not work to swiftly change it to that perfect smile and gentle expression. He simply slipped into a neutral look. "Let me know then," he said as he pulled a piece of paper out of his jacket, quickly scribbling something on it. As I reached out for it he maneuvered himself and wrapped his arms around me.

"Things will work out the way they should, trust me," he whispered.

I couldn't suppress the shiver that ran down my back nor did I fail to notice how my scar prickled as I felt his breath brush the side of my neck.

As he stepped away, I could only nod and accept the paper he had written his number on. My hands rose to my temples and rubbed at the dull throb that started there as I watched him walk out the door.

"Dang girl," I heard Emily as she walked toward me. "Care to share one of the two Mr. McDreamies' you seem to have snagged?"

I tried to clear my head, which now seemed to be in a fog, and come back with something to her comment but could only manage half a smile.

"You okay?" she said as she eyed me.

"Yeah," I lied, and followed her to the low bench in front of a huge window looking out at the parking lot. I barely caught a glimpse of Cole's black car peeling out.

"Did everything go alright last night after I left?" Emily probed, her eyes looking concerned.

"Yeah, I guess. Sal woke up and started spouting off some gibberish about not trusting him and how he tricked her. Who 'he' is I have no idea," I added as she started to ask the question. "They asked us to leave after that and said they would be in touch with me soon. I'm going up to the hospital in just a bit."

After this explanation there wasn't much more avoiding the conversation we both knew loomed before us. "We um...never got to talk last night."

Emily stared at a certain point on the floor and nodded. She was quiet for nearly a full minute before she seemed to find the words.

"What did you do to bring on the nightmares?" she finally asked, meeting my eyes with a probing stare.

"Bring them on?" I questioned, wondering what on Earth she was talking about. "I don't know that anything brought them on, I've just had them as long as I can remember."

A deep furrow formed between Emily's eyes as she seemed to consider this. After a moment she finally spoke again. "I was twelve when they started for me. I always thought I was cursed with them as some kind of cruel punishment."

I waited silently for her to go on, assuming she would explain further and make some kind of sense.

"My father died when I was three in an industrial accident. My mother remarried way too fast to a man she shouldn't have. He abused me sexually for years and my mother refused to believe it.

"Finally, when I was twelve, I couldn't take it anymore. I didn't think I could live through another one of his assaults. So, I went into my mother's medicine cabinet and found some of her sleeping pills. I counted out what was left. There were ten of them. I figured that would be enough to do the job.

"It didn't take long for the drugs to start to kick in. I got so tired and crawled into our tree house in the backyard. I wanted to die somewhere I felt safe and my stepdad had never touched me there.

"That was the first time I had a nightmare. The first time I had the X branded into the back of my neck and the wings appeared. The drugs didn't work and instead of escaping the hell I was trying to get out of, I was thrust into one that was just as terrifying. Like I said, I have always assumed it happened to me as some kind of cruel and unjust punishment for trying to kill myself.

"Darren tried to rape me one more time after the nightmares started but as soon as he saw the scars he was so terrified he never touched me again. So for that I was grateful for them."

This seemed to be the end of Emily's story as she stared into empty space, as if remembering the feel of having her step-father touch her in a way no man should touch a twelve-year-old girl.

"And they happen every time you sleep?" I whispered, hoping she might give me an answer to give me hope.

"They did," she said as she squeezed her eyes closed.

"Did?" I breathed, sliding a little closer on the bench to her. My heart began to race painfully in my chest. "They've stopped?"

She nodded once.

"How?" I nearly shrieked as I stood, unable to control all the feelings that were now rushing though my system. "Emily, you have to tell me how to make them stop?!"

With her eyes still shut she simply shook her head. "I can't. I'm so sorry"

"Why not?" I demanded, finally coming to a standstill before her.

"It won't be worth it to you to make them stop. I can't let you do that to yourself."

I dropped to my knees before her and took one of her hands in mine. "Emily, please," I whispered, feeling tears spring into my eyes.

She shook her head again, still refusing to open her eyes. "You will hate me."

I pleaded for several minutes but Emily wouldn't give. Finally she stood, announced she had to go, and literally ran out the door.

Feeling totally flustered, confused, and angry, I rubbed the sides of my head again. The throbbing I had felt earlier had definitely gotten worse.

After taking a few minutes to calm myself down, I picked up the courtesy phone and called Alex, telling him to meet me at the hospital in a few minutes.

I was waiting in the lobby when Alex walked through the doors and despite my flustered and anxious state, my pulse quickened and a smile spread on my lips. He returned the smile and reached for my hand as we approached the front desk. I had never had a feeling as right as when my fingers were intertwined with Alex's.

"We're here to see Miss Sally Thomas," I said quietly to the young looking receptionist.

"Your name?" she asked, sounding absolutely bored.

"Jessica Bailey."

It took the girl a few moments to look something up on a computer. I noticed she chewed on the inside of her cheek as she worked.

"Okay," she said with a slight sigh, not bothering to look up and meet my eye. "Miss. Thomas was moved from her room in the E.R. this morning into another room. Go up to the second floor and check in at the front desk there and they will give you her room number."

I thanked her quickly and made my way across the large room to the elevator.

"How'd things go with Emily?" Alex asked as the doors slid closed.

"Um," I struggled to know how to answer. "I'm not sure. I'll tell you about it when we get home. I'm still trying to make sense of it all but I'd like to just be able to focus on Sal right now."

Alex only nodded before wrapping an arm around my shoulders and gave a tight squeeze.

The voices talking over the intercom sounded strange, like they couldn't have originated from a human's mouth. Everyone in the hospital seemed so somber as they stood in hallways, sat in waiting rooms.

My mom ushered Amber and I down a hallway of wide wooden doors. I glanced up at her face. Her eyes were red and swollen. I had heard her crying in the night. She took a tissue out of her pocket and wiped at her nose.

We stopped at room 325 and knocked softly. Not getting any answer, we let ourselves in.

My nine-year-old eyes had never seen a dying person until that point. My mother's mother was dying from some infection that I didn't understand. I just knew it was making my mom hurt too.

"Go give Nana a kiss," mom said as she hung her purse on the hook secured to the back of the door.

I hesitated at the foot of the bed, eying the wrinkled sleeping woman. Her eyes looked like they were sinking into her head, her white hair thin and flayed around her head. Five-year-old Amber rushed up to her and softly pressed a kiss to her forehead. I didn't want to, Nana smelled strange. It frightened me.

"You don't have to, Jessica," my mother said softly as she sat in a seat by the bed. She gave me a sad little smile. Her eyes were pooled with tears that hadn't left since she got that call.

"Mommy, I have to go to the bathroom," Amber said as she squirmed on her chair next to Nana.

"Can you hold it sweetie? Daddy should get here in just a few minutes."

Amber shook her head and hopped up from the chair.

My mom gave a sigh. "Okay, come on. Jessica, wait here with Nana. Dad should be here any time."

They left, leaving me alone.

I felt anxious, sitting with the woman I didn't really know. Nana had only recently moved to Idaho from Arizona. She complained how the cold made her bones hurt and made her skin dry. Now her skin just smelled strange. I didn't remember her smelling that way before.

Not sure what to do with myself, I sat in Amber's chair and watched the monitor with the green and red lines and lights. The beeping started slowing down, the peeks rising in the green line coming more infrequently. Nana's smell got stronger.

The machine suddenly let out a flat, loud wail that didn't stop. Before I knew what to do, the door had burst open and a few nurses filled the room. Thirty seconds later my mom stood in the doorway, her hand pressed over her mouth, Amber holding her hand.

My breath came in painful shallow gasps. Nana was dead. I knew where dead people went. The angels thought I was those dead people.

The doors opened with a soft ding and we made our way down more comfortable looking halls than the ones in the E.R. to the reception desk. A woman with friendly brown eyes and short graying hair actually met my eyes.

"We're here to see Sally Thomas," I repeated to this woman.

The woman only nodded before turning to the computer and keying in a few things. "She's in room 254," she said with a kind smile.

"Now might not be the best time to see Miss Thomas," a nurse said with a huff as she walked behind the counter of the reception area. "She just threw quite the screaming fit. She was throwing everything she could get her hands on at the door and anyone that moved. Kept screaming at everyone, asking why we let him in. She kept going off about how he tried to kill her. He tricked her. We finally had to sedate her."

My brow creased as I listened to the nurse's account. "Has anyone been in to see Sal?"

"No one signed in this morning and our security system is tight in this area of the hospital. The only people who have been in her room are a few nurses and Dr. Stanton. She's the doctor who was assigned to her when she was discharged from the E.R."

I glanced at Alex and saw that he wore the same confused expression I did. "Can we see her?"

"She's going to be pretty out of it right now, if she hasn't fallen asleep yet, but you're welcome to go back. Dr. Stanton said she wanted to talk to you today, since you're listed as her caretaker."

We thanked the two women and hurried down the hall. "What is all that supposed to mean?" Alex whispered. "She was going off about 'him' last night, or I guess this morning, as well. Who is this man she keeps talking about?"

I shook my head. "Is she maybe having flashbacks of her husband?" I mused aloud. It seemed unlikely. I hadn't heard her talk about her husband for a very long time other than in her sleep.

"I don't know," Alex said as he slowed and I realized we were already at Sal's room.

We let ourselves in and closed the door softly behind us. The lights were off and the drapes had been pulled closed, the only light coming from the few pieces of beeping and flashing equipment. I noticed everything possible had been pulled well out of her reach.

Sal's hair was disheveled and her clothes looked askew, but she seemed to be asleep as her head sagged toward her shoulder in an uncomfortable looking way.

"Poor Sal," I said as I moved to her bedside. I found a few pillows on the floor, almost under her bed, and arranged them under her head to try and make her more comfortable. Sal gave a soft snore but did not stir.

We each took a seat next to her bed and watched her as she breathed quietly.

The door was perfectly silent as it swung open and a face that looked much too young to fit the title of doctor that was displayed on her badge appeared. Her face was narrow and as fragile looking as a porcelain doll's and her hair hung in soft brown waves. Her frame looked as breakable as her face.

"I'm Dr. Stanton," she said quietly as we each rose to shake the hand she extended. "I was about to call you when the nurses told me you came in."

She asked us to sit and joined us on a small rolling stool as she produced a very professional looking chart.

"I will keep this brief and to the point," she said, though her face remained kind. "I've spoken to Dr. Ostler who admitted Sally last night as well as her regular doctor. We each feel that it would be best if she were admitted on a semi-permanent basis into our psychiatric clinic for an extensive evaluation. As the doctor told you last night, it is apparent that Miss Thomas tried to commit suicide and we want to be absolutely certain she will not be a danger to herself. She also seems to be hallucinating. As the nurse told you, she seems to think there is a man who has visited her and she also seems to think it was this same man who told her to take the pills. So," she said as she flipped through a few papers and pulled one out, "We would like you to sign this if you consent to the treatment. Sally has extensive coverage that will cover everything, but since you are listed as her caretaker, we do need your permission first."

My head spun as I tried to comprehend everything this young doctor was telling me. "How long would she have to stay in the clinic?" I whispered, my voice sounding hoarse.

"It's difficult to say exactly, but we would like to keep her for at least two weeks and evaluate her as we go. It could possibly be shorter than, that but it may also be much longer."

I glanced at Alex and felt my hands start shaking. He put a comforting hand on my back and rubbed small circles into it.

I took a deep breath before I could answer. "If you think that is what is best then I guess that is what we should do."

The doctor nodded once before handing me the form and a pen. My writing was barely legible as I signed and dated on several different lines.

"We will be in touch as soon as we get Sally moved into the clinic. It will probably take a day or two to get everything filed and ready."

Dr. Stanton thanked each of us quietly, then rose and left the room quiet as a ghost.

"I don't even know what to say about this," I barely managed to whisper as I stared back at Sal's still form. "It all just seems so bizarre."

"I know," Alex said as he wrapped an arm around my shoulders reassuringly. "Did you want to stay with her longer?"

I thought about it for just a moment. "No," I replied. "It sounds like she will be out for a while so we could come back later."

"Let's go get some lunch before we head back home," Alex said as he rose and pulled me to my feet.

"Give me just a second," I said as I hesitated at Sal's side.

Alex nodded once before he stepped just outside the door.

I wasn't sure what to say or do as I stood by Sal's side. I felt so sorry for her, for how messed up her life had gotten and how none of what happened to her in the last ten years or so was her fault. And yet at the same time, I couldn't help but be a little angry with her. I still couldn't believe she would do this to herself, to me.

Trying to compose myself, I bent and pressed a light kiss to her forehead. Her skin felt clammy and ice cold. I pulled the blanket she seemed to have kicked down to her knees up to her chest.

Something white caught my attention as it fell from the blanket to the floor. When I crouched to pull it from under the bed I was confused at first, wondering how in the world it had gotten into a hospital room. It was a perfectly white feather, about five inches in length and perfectly shaped, with absolutely no flaws in it. I had never felt anything so soft and smooth.

I turned it over in my hands several times as I examined it in the dim light. It seemed strange that it ended up in a hospital room. I certainly hoped there were no birds in this hospital, much less any that were big enough to lose a feather this size.

"Jessica?" I heard Alex call from the door.

I silently slipped the feather into my purse. "Sorry," I whispered as I crossed the room and closed the door quietly behind me.

"Things will be okay," Alex said with a sad smile as we started back down the hall. "We'll all make it through this and things will work out."

"I sure hope so," I sighed as I pressed the button to call the elevator.

We ended up just getting something to go from my favorite burger place in town before heading back home. True to Washington winters, it started to pour just as we got onto the freeway.

CHAPTER NINETEEN

A bright flash of color caught my attention as we drove up to the house, though through the downpour of rain I couldn't tell what it was. As I ran back out from the garage to the front step, I stopped in momentary stunned silence.

"Wow," I heard Alex say as he came up behind me, just barely standing in the rain.

"Yeah," I said, sounding confused as I made the last few steps to the porch.

There were dozens of flowers set there, different bouquets made into beautiful and colorful arrangements. I could not even identify the majority of them.

After searching for a moment, I found an elegant and rather expensive looking card set in the middle of the largest arrangement.

When the day seems darkest,
Remember there is always a friend nearby,
A shoulder to cry on,
A warm hand to wipe away the tears.
Hope to see you tonight.

Yours always,
Cole

I had to read the note twice to finally deduce that the words must have in fact been Cole's actual handwriting and not a generic card or something he'd printed off. It seemed like it was from another century, very strange for a guy of the modern day.

After a moment I realized Alex had not said a word since I found the card. I could only imagine what he must have been thinking. I could feel my happiness from earlier come crashing down around me.

"This is, um...nice," I managed to squeak out. "Totally unnecessary, but nice."

I managed to look Alex in the eye. He tried to give that little half smile I loved but it didn't reach his eyes. I could tell this bothered him and I wasn't sure how to reassure him that despite whatever Cole might have been thinking was forming between us, I didn't want anyone other than Alex.

"I'll help you carry them in," Alex finally said after a few heavy moments.

Still not knowing what to say, I could only nod and grab one of the elegant looking vases.

After we ate our lunch, Alex seemed to return to his lighthearted self, though I didn't fail to notice that he kept his distance. His warm touches and looks of longing and understanding were limited to almost none the rest of the day. I tried to keep my face light and unworried but I couldn't help but feel a slight sense of panic. I had to let him know just how important he was to me, but I felt at a loss to know how to do so.

As evening blanketed the earth, I took the phone in my room for a moment of privacy and hoped Alex would not wander too close by to hear. I called Cole, telling him that I was not feeling very well and that I had to decline his offer from that morning. I had been almost afraid of what his reaction might be when I first started dialing but he seemed perfectly calm and at ease as I told him the partial truth. My head was throbbing but it wasn't so bad that I couldn't have gone out if I truly wanted to.

Alex pulled me into a brief embrace and pressed his lips to my forehead for a short moment and said goodnight just before ten o'clock. I shuffled my feet into my apartment feeling confused and slightly frustrated.

I closed the door behind me as quietly as I could, knowing it was for no reason, and sank to the floor right there. I felt conflicted as I thought of Alex's reaction to the flowers Cole gave me. I could see why he would worry. Anything could have happened last week while he was away and in truth he didn't know me well enough to know if I was the type of girl that went from guy to guy. I hoped he wouldn't think that of me.

Yet after the things I had told him that morning, after spending the night with him and being so open and honest with him about myself, I would hope he would realize exactly how I felt and know that there was room for no one else in my heart.

I could tell if I sat and thought about this for too long I was going to work myself up and possibly say something I shouldn't. So instead I raised myself from off the floor and determined that I just wasn't going to think about it. Alex was under a lot of stress, with coming home from a week of meetings with lawyers to a disaster at home. If he was still acting so strange in the morning I would talk to him and explain things. I would be more rational and balanced in the morning.

The wind howled and screeched as it tore through the trees that night, rain pounded on the windows, begging to be let in. In a strange way, I was grateful for the elemental disturbance outside. I was oddly tired for having slept less than twenty-four hours ago but there would have been no way I could have slept during that storm. I couldn't understand how Alex did it.

With little to pass the time, I pulled out my computer and pulled up the internet browser. I typed in the name from my last trial and hit search.

The man I stood trial for last night had not been branded and was granted blue irises. He had led a very good life it seemed and touched many people throughout it. As I scanned through hits, I was surprised to see his name pop up all over the place. He'd had a lot of money and was one of the few who spent it the way a person in that position should. There was already a death announcement available, quite beautifully written by his youngest daughter; it stated her name as well at the end.

I pulled out my leather volume and carefully printed his name on the page.

The morning started in a deep grey tone, reflective of the beating the Earth had gotten the night before. Branches were strewn everywhere, pine needles piled in every corner that stopped them from being blown away by the wind. Pieces of garbage that had not been secured properly in their bins were lodged in odd places. The sky was an angry sea, seemingly just waiting to unleash it's wrath upon us all again. I simply stared up at it as I stood before the window, feeling somehow enthralled and enchanted.

A pair of strong arms wrapped around my waist, cocooning me in the blanket I had wrapped around me. I normally would have been startled but the warmth that immediately spread though me left no doubt who my entrapper was.

Alex rested his chin on my shoulder and pressed his cheek to mine. He gave me a tight squeeze followed by a slight sigh.

"I'm sorry for how I reacted last night," he murmured. "I was being really immature and rude. I overreacted. I hope you can forgive me."

I turned to face him, maneuvering so as to not break his embrace. His expression was so sorrowful and so sincere it was almost funny. I couldn't help but crack a slight smile. As soon as I did this, that little half smile broke onto his face, though it remained slightly sheepish.

"I think I can manage to do that," I said as I stared into those perfectly clear blue eyes. "It'll cost you though."

"Name your price," he said as that smile played on his face. "If it takes an entire life of servitude, I'll gladly pay it."

"I think that might be a little extreme but it will cost you this," I said as I closed that small gap between his lips and my own.

Neither of us seemed to be in a rush to part, though there was not the mindless sense of well, senselessness, as we stood before the window wrapped in each other's arms. I could have died there a happy woman.

But like all moments that seem too perfect, this one was broken by the sound of Alex's phone ringing. With a soft chuckle he stepped back.

"Sorry," he said, and really did sound so. He pulled the phone out of his pocket and looked at the ID.

"I'd better take this," he said with that sheepish grin.

I only nodded and watched him walk out of my apartment and into the main family room.

My head spun violently as I tried to make my breathing more even and as I leaned my forehead against the cool glass, I realized I suddenly felt as if my skin were on fire. The feeling seemed strange considering the fact that I had thought I had kept my head fairly well.

Slowly, the spinning sensation ebbed, though it never went away. It was, however, replaced by a queasy feeling in the pit of my stomach.

"That was my lawyer again," Alex said solemnly as he walked back in the room. I quickly straightened, hoping I didn't look as terrible as I suddenly felt. It must have worked because he continued. "It seems there are just a few more things that need to get taken care of. He said they're urgent though and that I need to come in now. Unfortunately he's down at his office in Everett."

I calculated the time it would take him to get from here to Everett. It was roughly an hour drive one way.

"How long do you think you'll be gone?" I asked, not just because I would obviously miss him for any length of time but it would be nice to not have to be alone if I was going to get as sick as I felt I was going to be in just a short time.

"Hopefully not more than two or three hours once I get there but my lawyer is never exactly quick with anything once he gets me into his office. I think money might have something to do with that," he said this last part with that playful smile on his lips.

I hoped my expression did not match my sudden fallen spirits as I nodded my head. I could already tell it was going to be a long day and it was only just after eight.

"You're welcome to come with me if you want," he said, though I could tell he sensed what the answer to that was going to be.

Against my rolling stomach, I tried to pin a smile on my face. "I think I'll pass," I said as I shook my head slightly.

"'K," he said as he wrapped his arms around me in a quick embrace. He pressed a quick kiss to my lips and started for the door. "I'll be back as soon as I can."

I wanted to tell him that he didn't need to rush back on my account but a part of me did want him to hurry back. Another part was worried I might vomit if I opened my mouth. I was getting worse by the second.

Alex closed the door with a soft click and I hurtled for the bathroom, barely managing to get my face over the toilet bowl before a small amount of acidic tasting bile came up my throat. I wasn't sure if I was glad I hadn't eaten anything yet that day or not.

As soon as my stomach stopped heaving, I sat with my cheek pressed against the cool side of the tub ledge, trying to slow my breathing and praying the lurching was finished. I sensed it wasn't.

Great beads of sweat formed on my forehead and I went quickly from feeling like my skin was on fire to feeling as if I had been dumped in the frigid lake in front of the house. My muscles started a series of violent spasms and within a few minutes my entire body ached as the muscles cried at me.

With a moan, I rotated just enough so I could reach the faucet in the tub, turn the hot water on, and stop the drain. It was nearly full before I could will my body to move enough to strip down and drop myself into the scalding water. I still wasn't sure if hot or cold water sounded better. My temperature seemed to be changing too rapidly to make a comfortable decision.

I continued to shake violently in the steaming tub, though the water did feel good against my skin. Light started to shine through the tiny window above the walls of the tub, irritating my eyes and making my head throb all the worse. I was glad I had been in too much of a rush to get to the toilet to turn the bathroom light on. I didn't think I could stand more than the natural light that managed to find its way in.

Again I was faced with the dilemma of moving when the water slowly changed from hot, to lukewarm, to freezing cold. I even pulled the plug out with my toes and let the water drain from around me before I managed to get up. My muscles ached and groaned as I pulled a towel around myself and shuffled very slowly into my bedroom and pulled on my warmest pair of sweats and a sweater. I was glad I hadn't gotten my hair wet. I would have been ten times more miserable trying to brush my tangled birds nest and laying back down with wet hair.

It was only a slight relief when I crawled into my bed and totally collapsed. Every one of my muscles was screaming at me, I doubted I could move again, even if I had the will to do so. For once, sleeping seemed almost tempting if I knew it wouldn't bring further pain from the nightmare into reality when I woke up. My body already felt like it was on fire every other minute; I didn't need more burning sensations.

After lying on my bed for what felt like hours, suffering in agony, I realized how thirsty I was becoming. My lips felt ready to crack and bleed and my throat felt as if it were sticking together on the inside, making it almost hard to breathe. I also realized that if I could only get a big glass of water and some Tylenol, my condition should improve. I had never taken it before, as I couldn't recall ever needing it, but I knew that was what it was supposed to do.

I made two attempts to get myself up. They both resulted in immediate dry heaving followed quickly by even more violent tremors ripping through my body.

I knew then that there was no chance I was going to get myself off this bed, into the kitchen for the water and then upstairs into the medicine cabinet where I knew the Wright's had kept a small supply of the basics. It seemed like hundreds of miles and straight up a mountain.

While I wasn't used to being taken care of, my first thought was, of course, to call Alex. After only a fraction of a second of that thought, I knew this was impossible. He had probably just gotten down to Everett and what he needed to do was urgent. And besides, even if I convinced him to come home now, which I knew I could probably do, it would be at least another hour before he would be home.

My next thought was Sal. This thought was even more ridiculous than the first. Even if Sal hadn't just tried to commit suicide and was committed into a mental institution, she never left her house.

I next thought of Emily, but considering she had literally run away from me the last time I had seen her, that didn't seem like the best option.

With a slightly sinking feeling I realized the only person left for me to call was two doors down. Cole.

An internal battle raged inside as I fought this final option. Things were already strange and unpredictable with Cole. I didn't want to give him the wrong idea further by calling him to help me out when I was sick. I knew of the whole cliché of the doctor/nurse patient thing. I didn't even want to go there.

But what other choice did I have? Call an ambulance? I didn't think so. I had to do something though.

Though my body screamed against me, I rolled onto my side and grabbed the phone from the bedside table. It took me only a moment to recall the number Cole had written down for me last night and though my fingers were shaking violently, I managed to dial the number.

It only rang once.

"Hello?" his perfect, smooth voice answered.

"Hi Cole," I croaked, my dry throat protesting against use.

"Are you alright?" he questioned, though for some reason there was no surprise in his voice one might normally use when asking that kind of question.

"Not exactly," I said. "Um... I was kind of wondering if you could come over and help me out for a minute." I might as well not beat around the bush and get this humiliating and agonizing request over with.

"Where is Alex?" he questioned. I thought I detected a strange hint of, was that...smugness?

"He had to go down to Everett," I explained simply, trying to ignore the irritation that burned just under my skin, totally separate from the burn of the fever.

Cole was silent for just a second and I felt as if I could almost sense his satisfied smile through the phone. I hoped I was just being overly judgmental.

"I'll be over in just a minute," his smooth reply finally came.

"Thanks," I said and hung up without saying a formal good-bye.

I put the phone back on the dock and I rolled back onto my back with a huff. My head spun at the motion and I immediately regretted moving so quickly. I squeezed my eyes shut, though it didn't stop the spinning sensation.

When Cole said he would be over in just a minute I didn't expect him to mean that so literally. I wondered if it had even been that long when I heard the door that led out onto the deck open and quietly close.

My heart did a strange quiver as Cole's lean frame appeared in the door. I couldn't understand it and I had a hard time sorting out the emotions. Of course there was a sense of relief at my rescue, but there were other odd emotions. Hesitancy, fear, attraction, it was difficult to tell which emotion was strongest, but the most confusing one- an odd sense of trust washed over me. I had been so wary of him, but why? There had been no question in his reply when he agreed to come and help me. It was all so confusing...

"Thanks for coming over," I found myself saying before I could really take a second to clear my head.

"Of course," he said as he took a few hesitant steps forward. As my eyes took him in I noticed that while he was dressed casually, he wore all white. A white turtleneck disappeared into his long, almost black hair and he wore a pair of rather expensive looking slacks. The entire look, while undeniably attractive, was also intimidating in a strange way.

"I hate to say it but you look just inches away from death," he said, though a smile was starting to crack on his lips.

"I feel like it," I croaked as I rubbed my eyes. The toll this sickness was taking on my body was draining and I knew it wouldn't be long before I had to sleep. If I could work it right, I could get rid of Cole and wake up before Alex got home. He didn't need to witness that experience any more than necessary.

Cole crossed the room and was soon standing at my bedside, looking down on me with those intensely dark eyes. He raised a hand and softly stroked my brow, pushing a few locks of stray hair away. "What can I get you?" he said softly, for which I was grateful for. Every sound sent another throbbing shot of pain through my brain.

"Some water would be wonderful," I said, suddenly finding my head much more clear as he touched me. I nearly violently wished he wouldn't. "And there is some Tylenol upstairs, in the master bathroom. Hopefully that will help."

"Okay," he said softly as he turned for the doorway and left. He was only gone for a few short moments before he returned with a towering glass and two pills in his hand. I accepted these greedily and downed them much faster than I should have, considering there was someone watching.

"Have you eaten anything today?" he asked as he watched me contently, perched on the side of my bed like some sort of mythical god.

I shook my head as I finished the last drops of my water. "I threw up a few times this morning, even though there wasn't anything in my stomach." I thought for a moment though and realized that my stomach was suddenly feeling much better. "Actually, I'm kind of hungry now," I blurted before I realized saying so was an invitation to have Cole cook something for me.

"Just give me a few minutes. I'll find something to make for you," he said with a hesitant smile and I suddenly wondered if Cole really knew how to cook. From the look on his face the answer was no.

"You don't have to," I tried to quickly recover. Cole just shook his head with that slightly arrogant smile. "I could try to make something for myself. Just give me a minute."

"I'll give you the whole day," Cole said as he reached the door. "Just relax. I'll take care of you."

"That's the problem," I muttered when I was sure he was out of earshot.

I listened intently for any sounds coming from my tiny kitchen but they were very minimal for which I was grateful, only the occasional note that fluttered in from a tune Cole was humming. I tried to place it but was unable.

As I waited to see what Cole could come up with, I thought of the dilemma that now faced me. What was I going to tell Alex when he got back tonight? The thought of how he might react to the fact that Cole had taken care of me when I was sick made my stomach clench up. Despite how he reacted earlier to Cole's flowers, it hadn't exactly seemed like possessiveness or jealousy. I wasn't sure what exactly the emotion was. Perhaps he was just feeling insecure, or maybe even hurt? It was difficult to say. Either way, it was absolutely unnecessary.

I'd had my eyes closed and feeling rather lost in thought when the bed jostled just slightly. My eyes flew open and I saw Cole sitting on the edge of it. In his hands he bore a silver platter with a bowl of something steamy, several saltine crackers, and a large glass of orange juice.

"I really hope it tastes okay," he said, his face looking genuinely concerned that it might not. "I have to admit, I'm not much of a cook."

"No," I crooned as I strained to pull myself up into a sitting position. "I'm sure it will be fine."

215

Once I was sat up, Cole carefully placed the tray on my lap. I took one small spoonful of the soup, seriously hoping my stomach was going to cooperate.

It was about the blandest soup I had ever had in my life and probably had fewer than four ingredients. It was also in desperate need of some salt. But I shoveled it into my mouth and kept a gracious expression. It was probably better that it tasted bland. My stomach should be able to handle bland.

"How is it?" Cole questioned, his face looking slightly pained.

"It's great," I lied as I shoved more into my mouth. It was at least helping to fill my empty stomach.

I quickly downed the crackers and the orange juice and Cole cleared the dirty dishes away. When he came back into my room he did not go back to his seat on my bed, for which I was grateful, but sat on the floor by the door, his back resting against the wall.

"Thank you," I sighed as I lay back into my comfortable bed. "I'm starting to feel a little better."

"You should probably try to get some sleep," he suggested casually.

Even though my mind protested the idea, my eyelids slid closed. "Maybe," I said as I tried to stifle a yawn. "Later."

I heard slight movement, like maybe Cole had shrugged his shoulders. I didn't bother to open my eyes and check.

"You've seemed a little distant recently," Cole said, his voice clear and while not sharp, very to the point. "I hope it has only been because of Sal's accident."

I didn't miss the implication behind his words. My stomach suddenly clenched up again. I squeezed my eyes closed tightly, already regretting my decision to call Cole over.

"Yeah," I tried to think quickly and avoid an uncomfortable conversation. "Things have been really busy and stressful since that."

"You seem to be rather happy that Alex is back," he stated. I could feel his intense, almost accusing stare burning through my eyelids.

"It's nice to have him back," I said honestly. I really didn't want to expound beyond that. I shouldn't have to explain anything to Cole. As grateful as I was for his help, he had no claim on me.

It was silent for a moment, each passing second growing unbearably uncomfortable.

"I hope I feel better this afternoon," I finally blurted, knowing I was babbling. "I really should go see Sal again. I wanted to ask her doctor when she is going to be moved."

"Moved?" Cole questioned.

I then realized Cole hadn't heard anything about Sal's condition. I wished I hadn't said anything suddenly. It seemed like an invasion of Sal's privacy to have told him.

"To a more permanent facility. It's supposed to just be temporary though. Just for some observation," I scrambled.

"Hum," he said simply, as if considering my hurried explanation. After a moment he spoke again. "You worry too much about other people. You should worry about yourself a little more often. Maybe then you would have seen this sickness coming up."

"Sal needs my help," I replied simply, still refusing to open my eyes. "If I don't help her, who will?"

He didn't seem to have an answer to this and remained silent.

An odd sense of triumph settled on me as the silence grew. He knew I was right and he had nothing else to say about it.

"You're a good person, Jessica," he finally said, and I heard him climb to his feet. I finally opened my eyes to see if he was going to approach me. He didn't. He placed his hand on the door knob. "Is there anything else you need?"

I felt momentarily panicked when I realized he intended to leave. He may have been irritating me and being far too presumptuous but it was comforting to know he was just a few steps away if I needed him.

I finally shook my head.

Cole seemed to sense my sudden distress. "If you need me again just call. I'll be at home all day."

I nodded my head. "Thanks," I managed to croak out, letting my eyes slide close again.

I didn't hear the door close but there was no more sound after that.

Frustration at myself flooded through me as silence settled back on my familiar room. That had been a very stupid move to call Cole. It could only give the wrong impressions, no matter what we had talked about. And now, what was I going to tell Alex? I should have just suffered through it all. I was feeling much better now; maybe it had nothing to do with the food and water that was in my stomach and the pills to calm my fever.

Just as these thoughts passed through my head, I lurched to my feet and bounded across the room in three steps. I barely made it to the toilet before Cole's bland lunch made a second appearance.

Strangely, after emptying my stomach, I felt slightly better. The throbbing in my head subsided some and the chills eased a bit. I was just left feeling incredibly drained.

Grateful for the good timing, if becoming sick ever had such, I climbed back into bed. I glanced at my clock next to my bed, noting it was just after one o'clock. That should give me plenty of time to sleep and wake up before Alex got home. Hopefully I would be feeling better by then. At least I knew if I wasn't, Alex would be a whole lot more pleasant to deal with should I need him to care for me. I sincerely hoped that wouldn't be necessary.

A light rain began to fall outside and I found soothing comfort in it. A lot of tension had built up in my system for how early in the day it still was and the sound of the drops on the roof helped to ease some of it away. Slowly, I felt my muscles begin to relax and soften.

A new fear began though. I knew I was exhausted and as nice as it was to relax a bit, too much relaxation would lead to sleep. I had been able to face the nightmares with Alex by my side before, he somehow made them seem almost bearable but I felt the all too familiar panic and fear seeping into my system. The sound of twisted laughter echoed through my memory.

Fourteen...fifteen...sixteen... I couldn't help it as the numbers rattled off in my head. It was the first time I could recall counting in a few days. Perhaps that had something to do with the amazing man that was now in my life. Despite all the terrifying changes that had happened with my impossible reality, Alex made me feel incredibly safe. I had always supposed that counting just made me feel safe. Numbers made sense and there was always a certain order they could be arranged in. I hadn't needed them as much lately. But Alex wasn't here right now.

With this last wistful thought of longing, I closed my eyes and allowed unconsciousness to claim me.

CHAPTER TWENTY

I knew something was different as soon as Adam came down the tunnel to get me. Everything looked just slightly off, as if all these years I had experienced the nightmares, a thin veil had been placed over my eyes. Everything seemed painfully clear and sharp now. And I was noticing things I had never bothered to consciously process before.

Adam was tall and built of pure muscle. I had never noticed before how his chest was always bare and exposed, the only clothing he wore were soft, loose white pants. His feet were bare.

It seemed strange now how the flames from the torches that lined the wall danced across his flesh. Considering he didn't have a gleam of sweat across his skin this seemed like it should have been impossible. Yet it was enchanting as it cast a strange glow all over him. The reflection of the fire danced dangerous and wild in his grey eyes.

The normal terror that filled me was still undeniably there as he bound my hands with the golden cord, but I was so distracted by the odd clarity that surrounded me it was lessened. I could only stare at everything in wonder.

Our footsteps echoed almost maddeningly off the walls of the low tunnel as we proceeded down it. The glow of light at the end of it was almost blinding. The faint rushing of air as it flowed around us seemed like the very breath and hissing of the stones that encased us, sending violent shudders of fear down my spine.

As Adam walked me out onto the catwalk, I took in a choking breath, feeling as if my throat was suddenly closing up. I had never noticed before how suffocatingly hot it was in the cylinder. The heat coated my skin along with the moisture that hung in the air and threatened to suffocate the life out of me right then and there.

In the few moments before I knew the council would arrive, I took in the detail of the ten stone chairs mounted onto the wall before me. They were amazing works of art. Tiny figures were carved into elaborate scenes, encased with symbols and swirls that made no sense to me. Perhaps there was no actual meaning. They were simply meant to look as beautiful as they were.

The rustle of wings began and I noticed the fierce sound of the power behind them. My eyes refocused from the amazing thrones and took in the graceful movements of the angels as they settled themselves into their seats.

I did not hear their words as they spoke. I knew what they would say; the only difference would be the name of the person I stood trial for. I did not even notice when the demented laughter rose from below me. I could not help but marvel at the beautiful faces.

They were each so flawless it made me want to cry. Not for jealousy, that I myself could not look like that. But for the pure fact that I knew this kind of perfection existed. Every detail and every line was flawless and flowed perfectly into the next. I found myself suddenly wishing I could lay my hand on one of their cheeks, just to see if it felt as amazingly wonderful as it looked. This desire was strongly contradicted though with a fear of what it might feel like as well. That kind of perfection was intimidating and alien.

There was an obvious difference between the condemned council members and the exalted. The latter each held a serene look on their faces. Perfectly calm and content, despite the horrific scene that surrounded them. The condemned however, held an excited gleam in their black eyes that chilled me where I stood and made my breath catch in my throat. Wicked smiles twisted in the corners of their mouths as anticipation boiled.

The men that surrounded us everywhere were dressed the same as Adam, each of their bodies as perfect as his. The women were dressed in simple white dresses. They reminded me of something one might see on a sculpture of a Greek goddess. The dresses swooped down remarkably low in the back, their beautiful white and metallic wings remaining free.

That was another detail I stared in wonder at. It was only in certain light you could see the metallic glint in their wings. It boggled my mind that this seemed to work in the same way my own imprint of wings did. When the light did hit just right, the effect was stunning and impossibly beautiful.

My blissful state of observation was broken as I finally registered the word that escaped the beautiful lips of the new leader of the condemned.

"Down," his beautiful voice damned me.

Despite how wonderful it had been to be so detached from this trial it was not worth it as I stared horrified into the new leaders face. His eyes seemed to almost glaze over with demented glee as his wings coiled and then propelled him toward me on the catwalk. I could see my own reflection in his eyes. The merciful white bag was on my head but I could make out my terrified eyes through the small slits in it.

I could not look away from his twisted eyes as he landed beside me. I had never so deliberately looked either this man or the one before him in the eye. It was a strange feeling. The mix of horror and terror, combined with the oddest sense of trust. Something about his eyes called to a place deep within me, telling me everything was going to be alright, he would only do what was supposed to be done.

I dropped to my knees only because I knew that was what I was supposed to do. My head bowed and I swept the hair from my neck. I heard another set of beating wings and knew the rod with the brand had been presented.

My breathing sped and came in shallow, uneven gasps. My ears started ringing as my pulse beat in them and I felt lightheaded. The ground beneath me started tilting and spinning.

The white-hot rod was pressed into the back of my neck and my scream shocked even me. It wasn't that of a human and couldn't fully express the tortured pain of a human. I had never felt pain like this before. I had been branded hundreds of times before and had never felt the searing pain of the iron in my neck like this. It radiated throughout my entire body and I could not process any other thought than the desire to die, right there and then on the catwalk.

I was yanked to my feet but I still did not hear the words that were spoken to me. My head rolled back and forth across my chest, my eyes wide open but unable to comprehend anything I saw.

For the first time, I didn't have to wait for the condemned angels to pull me off the catwalk. As soon as their leader let go of me, I simply fell off the ledge.

My scream as I woke was different. It had always been out of terror that I screamed before. This time it was out of immeasurable pain. My hands flew to my neck but I immediately jerked them away. The slightest touch sent sharp, stabbing pains radiating through my entire neck and down my spine.

Glad the spinning in my head had ended with the dream, I staggered into the bathroom. It took great effort not to scream with each step I took. Any movement was torture.

The light seared my eyes as I flipped it on and I had to cover them for a few brief moments as they adjusted. When I finally did open my eyes I froze.

I had known the dream was off, I remembered this, every detail I took in during the nightmare. But that hadn't ended when I woke. The person who looked back at me in the mirror was all too clear to be natural.

Her large eyes stared back at me, made all the bigger by the shocked expression on her face. I could easily pick out the different streaks of green and brown in them. They were more brown on the outside edge, more green on the inside. Her nose was perfectly straight and her lips proportional to her face. While her skin could in no way compare to that of the angels', it was nearly flawless according to human standards.

I had to blink several times to realize this wasn't just some trick of the mirror and that the person staring back at me was truly me. As I quickly glanced around the bathroom I realized *everything* had become much sharper, as if I'd had terrible vision all my life and had just barely gotten prescription glasses.

The slight movement of my head reminded me of the reason I had flown to the bathroom and I quickly pulled out my little round mirror from under the sink. Pulling my heap of hair off my neck, I looked into the small mirror, looking at the back of my neck in the other mirror.

The scar was all too familiar, but today it looked almost blistered in a terrible and fierce way. And instead of its normal angry red it was almost white, as if more heat than normal had indeed been applied.

As I looked into the mirror, I noticed something else that seemed odd. I had been sleeping in a plain white tee-shirt and it seemed the pattern of my wings was far more visible through it than normal. I could make out faint evidence of it along my shoulder blades, where the shirt met my skin the tightest.

I pealed my shirt off, stifling my screams at the same time as pain ripped through my body. I turned my back to the mirror and peaked over my shoulder, back at my reflection.

Anyone else would not have noticed much of a difference in them, but it drew my attention immediately. In the center, where, had they been real, the wings sprouted from the skin, it was more raised, spreading out towards my shoulder blades. I wished I could reach that far and tell if the feathery details were as soft as they looked. The metallic sheen was far more obvious there as well. It was not often I actually saw the metallic color come through in my bathroom but it was not difficult to spot now.

"Jessica?" I jumped violently when I heard the voice from the door.

I met Alex's shocked and questioning look for only a moment before a flood of heat rushed to my face. I was horrifyingly grateful I had been twisted in a way he could not actually see anything, my mane of hair providing a good enough cover. I twisted away, my back facing him and grabbed my shirt off the counter to cover myself. I whimpered slightly at the sudden movement as pain stabbed through my neck.

I started to yank my shirt back on over my head but before I could pull it down, Alex's hands stopped me. His hands hovered hesitantly over my scar and traced lightly over the changed portion of my wings.

"They've changed," he whispered as his fingers ran over the center portion. "The brand, it looks...painful."

"It is," I hissed as I finished pulling my shirt all the way down, the movement taking my breath away. "Would you mind getting me some ice?" I panted as I turned toward him, taking note of his shocked and slightly fearful expression. Alex's face too was unmistakably clearer. It froze me in my tracks for a moment and I simply stared at him. He may not have the skin of an angel but I couldn't resist as I placed my hand on his cheek.

"Of course," he said, his voice low. I could see the concern in his eyes, the questions he was dying to ask. But he held off and turned to go and do as I asked.

I went to my closet and quickly exchanged the tee-shirt for a tank top that would allow easy access to my neck. Being careful of how I moved, I walked out into the tiny living room and saw Alex wrapping a bag of ice in a towel. I gingerly made my way to the table and sat down.

Alex came to my side and looked hesitant if he should apply the ice himself or just give it to me. I saved him the trouble and reached for it. I couldn't help wincing and inhaling sharply as the cool towel met the brand.

The clock caught my eyes as I opened them. "Is that clock right?" I gasped. It read just after seven.

"Yeah," Alex said, sounding confused as he checked it to his cell phone.

I shook my head as much as allowed for minimal pain. "I've been asleep for six hours then," I hissed. "I don't know if I've ever slept for six hours."

"Is something wrong, Jessica?" Alex questioned, his expression still that of deep concern. "I hate to say it but you look...well terrible, to be honest."

"I feel terrible. Though I actually feel better than I did before." There was going to be no getting around it. I was going to have to tell Alex everything that had happened. "I got really sick right after you left. I threw up and right after that I got this terrible fever and chills. I've never felt so awful in my life."

Before I could continue Alex spoke. "You could have called me. I would have come back to help you."

I closed my eyes and nodded. "I know," I breathed. I opened my eyes again, meeting his gaze. "I thought about it but I knew what you were doing was important. And besides, when it got to the worst of it you would have still been more than an hour away." I took a deep breath, continuing to lock eyes with Alex. "I called Cole. He came over and helped me for a while."

I had prepared for Alex to be upset about this all day so when he didn't get angry, didn't hold his breath, didn't react in any way I expected, I wasn't sure how to respond. His face remained calm, the same concern it held before was still there.

"I'm so sorry. I wish I had known," he said soothingly.

The shock of his reaction clouded my thoughts and all I could do was nod my head.

"Why don't you come over to the couch?" he said, no hesitation in his voice like he was trying to hold back some frustration. "You'll be more comfortable."

Again I only nodded my head and followed him silently to my tiny couch.

"So what changed?" he questioned once we were settled, my head resting on his chest. He held the ice pack gingerly on the back of my neck for me, his other arm wrapped securely around my shoulders. "Why are the scars so different today?"

I knew that it was wrong, the way I had dragged him into this whole mess of things, a mess that was becoming more messy and tangled by the day. But I was selfish. I wanted someone to talk to about all of this. I needed him to know everything.

"There is more to this whole mess than I told you before," I began. My heart raced in my chest as I feared what his reaction might be to what I had to tell him. Again, fear of rejection and fear of him thinking I was crazy filled my head. "Things have been changing a lot recently with the nightmares."

Alex gave no negative reaction as I carefully explained the things that had been changing. I confessed what had actually happened the morning of Valentines when I mysteriously passed out at the sight of him with the angel wings in the snow. I still couldn't explain the dozens of hands that had covered me nor the voice that had spoken to me in the darkness.

I explained how my one defense of the sack over my head during the trials had been ripped away and how their leader had seen my face clearly. I told him of how the council had changed and the leader of the condemned was missing. I still couldn't understand why my vision was so bizarrely clear and enhanced ever since I had woken up from this last nightmare.

And I finally wrapped everything up by explaining how I had gotten so violently sick today. I didn't get sick. I had never been sick a day of my life. It was the same as how I had never broken a bone, never gotten a scratch or bruise. I couldn't explain any of it.

While Alex seemed concerned and confused over the things I told him, he took this the same way he had taken everything else. In stride and appearing to be unruffled by it. He didn't call me crazy, didn't pull away, or loosen his hold on me.

"Something big is happening, Alex," I whispered into his chest. "I don't understand what is going on."

I felt him press his lips into my hair as he gave me a soft squeeze. "We will figure this out," he whispered. "I will do whatever I have to to help you figure this thing out. And I will be here no matter what happens."

CHAPTER TWENTY-ONE

Things were about the same for the next nine days. One minute I felt fine and the next my world was spinning and my body would shake with violent chills, despite the high temperature I was running. I tried to eat but was managing to keep nothing down for more than an hour at a time. My body was starting to feel the toll of it all. Every joint in my body ached and all curves and padding were quickly disappearing from my body.

Sleep was unavoidable for more than about fifty-two hours. In all my life it had never been too much of a struggle to get to at least the seventy hour mark. I was also sleeping for longer amounts of time than I ever had in my life. Three, maybe four hours was the norm, now six and seven hours seemed consistent.

Things remained bizarrely clear. My vision did not return to normal and it was disorienting. Another strange thing it took me a while to notice was that I could hear everything. The same bizarre sharpness that had altered my vision seemed to have done the same to my hearing.

Alex wanted to take me the doctor the second day I was sick. I quickly pointed out that this was impossible. There was obviously something beyond normal scientific reason going on. Besides, how was I supposed to explain where my scars came from? They would likely assume I was into extreme body marking and assume I was on some sort of drugs. Alex quickly saw my reasoning but did not exactly like it.

I had been right in my thinking that should Alex have to take care of me, he would be much more pleasant to deal with than Cole had been. Alex never left my side for more time than it took me to shower, though after the fourth day, he insisted on waiting in the bathroom for me when I had become too dizzy and crashed to the floor. He was patient, never seeming to mind that I was becoming the absolute center of his attention.

Despite how terrible the entire scenario was, I couldn't be completely ungrateful for this unique time we were given. With so much time spent just one on one, it provided a very intimate opportunity to get to know one another better.

It started just as light conversation. As I would lie on the bed, usually with my eyes closed so the world would not spin so crazily, I would drill Alex with simple questions about himself. His favorite color was green, though blue was a close contender. Classic guy answer. His favorite holiday was Thanksgiving, no surprise there. He didn't really have a favorite kind of music, he liked just about everything. His favorite season was fall. His favorite movies were of course anything comedy. He shamefully admitted he preferred science fiction books, though I didn't understand why he was so ashamed of this fact.

When I finally ran out of simple questions I moved on to asking about his high school years. He told me how in his sophomore year his grandmother had gotten very sick and since his grandfather knew nothing of cooking, Alex had taken over the kitchen. That was when his obsession with food began. He claimed it was a miracle he didn't weigh four hundred pounds.

With his grandfather's encouragement, Alex had tried out for the high school basketball team and found he was quite talented at it. He was on his way to earning a college scholarship for it when he broke his leg his senior year, crushing that possibility. He didn't seem saddened by this and I got the impression that basketball had never been that important to him. It was simply something fun to do.

From the way he talked, it sounded as if Alex had been friends with every single kid in school and was one of the most popular kids. I couldn't help but wonder had we gone to school together, if Alex would have ever noticed me. I wanted to say that of course he would have, but I wasn't so sure. I felt so plain and simple next to this extraordinary man.

Without my prompting, Alex told me of his past relationships, which were surprisingly few. He'd had one girlfriend his senior year of high school, who he quickly broke up with when he found her making out with the athletic director of the school. He had dated another woman for only a few months while he was in school in England, but it had never developed into anything very serious. When Alex decided he needed to do some more traveling, she decided she didn't want to go with him and that easily ended the relationship.

I hadn't realized Alex could play the guitar until he picked mine up one day and started to play. He was skilled in many different genres and at times it was hard to believe that just one set of hands and one guitar were playing. He didn't have too bad of a voice either as he sang me songs both familiar and not. Some of them I felt quite sure he had made up, either from how specific to the two of us they sounded or by how silly and nonsensical they were.

If I had to spend so much time feeling like my body was being put through hell, this certainly wasn't a bad way to spend it.

I received a call from the hospital the day after my episode with Cole. They informed me that Sal had been moved into the more permanent facility and that she was doing well. She wasn't talking much to anyone, but her psychiatrist felt she could make some real progress with Sal. Unfortunately, they thought it unwise for Sal to have any visitors for a while, as they were afraid it might hinder her progress.

Despite how persistent and forward Cole had been thus far, he remained oddly distant. He called once, the day after he had come over, just to make sure I was doing alright and to see if I needed anything else but I had not heard anything from him since. I could only hope he had given up on the idea that there ever might be something between us in the future. I did however truly wish that someday we might be able to be friends. I could always use more of those.

Due to the fact that I could barely walk across the room most days, I missed an entire week of yoga. I longed to talk to Emily, to demand that she explain herself further, but I did not want to push her completely away. Finally, Monday morning, I was feeling almost my normal self and insisted that Alex take me to my class. He wasn't thrilled about the idea but seemed to realize that I needed to get out of the house and get some fresh air.

He dropped me off at the doors and waved as he pulled out of the parking lot. He was on a mission to get groceries and some basic supplies. Just as soon as he was clear of the parking lot, Cole's shiny black sports car rolled in. I tried to keep a cheerful expression on my face as he pulled into a spot and stepped out of his car.

No man should look that perfect in sweats and a muscle shirt.

"Good to see you, Jessica," he said as he flashed a dazzling smile that stopped the breath in my chest for a moment. "I'm glad to see you are feeling well enough to get out and about."

"Thank you, Cole," I said as I tried to make my smile seem normal. "I...feel...better?" I hadn't meant the last part to come out as a question but I suddenly wasn't so sure.

Cole hesitated for a moment as if gauging what I said. "Well, let's get inside," he said with another blinding smile. "No need to stand out in the cold."

He held the door open for me and I was indeed grateful to get in out of the wind that was picking up. I quickly scanned the room and realized we were the last two to arrive. Emily was just pulling out the bin of mats. When she laid eyes on me she froze for a moment before she started handing them out to everyone.

She met my eyes and I tried to gauge what her reaction to me was going to be as I reached for my mat. Her expression looked surprised, almost concerned.

"Are you ok?" she whispered. "Cole told me you've been sick. You look like you've lost at least fifteen pounds."

I glanced down at myself absentmindedly. She was right, I looked almost scary. My skin clung to my bones in an unhealthy looking way.

"Um," I hesitated. "I'm not sure. I really need to talk to you. Something's wrong. With the whole...well you know. Something's happening."

Emily stared up at me wide eyed and I saw a million questions flash across her face. After a few moments she finally nodded her head. "After class. I can't promise I will give you any more answers though."

"I know," I said, my voice obviously depressed.

She tried to manage a half smile then broke her gaze as she walked back to the front of the room. "Alright, everyone get into a seated position."

I was certainly feeling the effects of next to no food and being sick as we got into the routine. I frequently had to stop and rest, feeling like I was spending half of the time in child's pose. I had luckily chosen a spot at the far back of the room so the only person who saw my weakness was Emily. Mercifully, despite the fatigue, my body cooperated the entire session. No fever ate me up and even though my stomach was empty, the dry heaves that constantly attacked me stayed subdued.

I heard the dull roar of Alex's truck pull into the parking lot just seconds before the class ended. He walked in just as everyone was rolling up their mats. A few of the younger women in the class gave obvious drooling stares as they left the building. I didn't miss the cold, hard expression Cole kept on his face as he walked out without saying a word to anyone.

"You feeling okay?" he asked, his voice low as he gently placed his hands on either side of my waist.

I nodded my head and rested my forehead against his. "Tired, but okay."

It was so strange, the effect Alex had upon me. Like he was the sun and I was a solar panel, anxious to soak up the warmth and comfort that came from him. Like he made me work, brought life back into me. I couldn't imagine how I would survive this traumatizing time without him. He was a drug I couldn't live without now.

Realizing Emily was watching and waiting for me, I stepped away from Alex, though keeping a firm grip on his hand.

Emily gave Alex a firm look before turning a questioning glance on me.

"It's okay," I explained, realizing what her expression meant. "Alex knows everything. He should know anything you can tell us, too."

She gave him a slight look of surprise that quickly changed into an impressed look. "Wow, you really are Mr. Right for our girl here."

I blushed as I did not miss the double meaning behind her words.

"So you said something is happening. What exactly is going on?" Emily got right to the point.

"A lot has been changing with this whole messed up situation," I began. It was difficult to even know where to begin and it took me a moment to sort out everything I needed to say. I began by telling her about the time the bag had been ripped off my head during a trial and how the leader of the condemned had looked at me so intently. I considered telling her about the time I had passed out and the terrifying experience of the voice in the darkness saying "you shall be mine" but I couldn't bring myself to admit it out loud. That seemed too crazy, even if Emily had gone through the same experiences I had.

Next, I proceeded to tell her how the council changed, how the leader of the condemned was replaced by a lesser council member and someone new had been appointed. Emily's expression was beyond shocked at this.

"How is that even possible?" she demanded. "I suffered through those nightmares for almost ten years and the council *never* changed."

"I know," I said with a sigh. "I've dealt with them for even longer than that and it's always been the same."

"What could that mean?" she mused, almost to herself. "I mean, they're dead. It's not like they are going to really be going anywhere. Although, outside of the trials I have no idea what angels do."

I nodded my head. That was an interesting point. What did the angels do when they were not at trials? I didn't want to think about that too much.

"And then I've been really sick," I said, finally catching up to the present. "I mean sick, throwing up, fever of like 103, chills, sick. My brand has been much more painful lately and something's off with my vision and hearing. Everything is way stronger than it should be. So sharp."

Emily's brow creased as she considered this. "I kind of thought Cole was making it up that you were sick at first. You know, telling him you weren't feeling good, just to avoid Cole, or me more likely. And then I saw you today and I had to believe him. No matter how impossible it is."

"We don't get sick," I stated as I stared intently into her face.

"Even though they've stopped, I still don't get sick. I haven't been sick since I was twelve."

"Like I said, something's wrong."

At this Alex clutched my hand a bit tighter and took a step closer to my side.

We were all quiet for a moment as I let them process what all had been said.

"I don't know what to tell you," Emily finally spoke. "As terrifying as the dreams were they were always consistent. I can at least be grateful for that. I...I don't even know what to think could be happening. You're the only other person I've met who has the nightmares."

I simply nodded. I had a feeling this was all she was going to be able to give me. "And you still won't tell me how to make them stop?" I already knew what her answer was going to be.

"No," she said firmly. "Jessica, it's not worth it. I can't let you do that to yourself. You're too good. You're such a good person." With that she suddenly stopped talking, as if she felt she had said more than she should have already. I hadn't gotten anything out of that, whatever it was she felt she divulged.

Frustration flowed through me, giving my stomach an uncomfortable lurch. I could feel that exhaustion was not far off from completely consuming me. "Okay then," I sighed, taking a step closer toward Alex, closing the gap between us and resting lightly against him for support. "Call me if you think of anything."

Turmoil churned in Emily's eyes but she simply nodded her head. She was going to give away no secrets today. "I will, I promise. And call me if anything else happens or changes."

We said quick good-byes as the group of Pilates women who followed our class started coming in. I felt embarrassed and weak that I had to lean on Alex for so much support just to make it back out to the truck.

"Well that was frustrating," I huffed as he closed his door and started the engine.

"I'm not exactly surprised," he said as he looked over his shoulder and backed out of the parking space. "This isn't exactly a normal thing. You can't really blame her for not knowing what to tell you."

"I can blame her though for not telling me how to make the nightmares stop," I hissed. I could feel the frustration boiling just under my skin.

"It sounds like she has a good reason for not telling you," he said quietly, keeping his eyes on the road.

For a brief moment I wanted to be angry with Alex for siding with Emily, but the emotion was gone as quickly as it surfaced. "I'm sorry," I quickly apologized. "I shouldn't judge her like that." I still felt frustrated though.

Alex only glanced in my direction with a sad smile and reached for my hand, wrapping my rather frail looking fingers in his giant ones.

CHAPTER TWENTY-TWO

I tried insisting that I help Alex unload everything when we got home, but part of me was relieved when he demanded that I go lay down. I was pathetically exhausted and my head was starting to spin again. I suspected that had something to do with how everything was so shockingly clear; the effect was beyond disorienting.

A hot bath was calling to my aching body and even though I knew it probably wouldn't help my spinning head, I filled the tub with hot water and poured a good helping of bubble bath in. With how the light had been bothering my eyes lately, sending throbbing shots of pain through my brain, I lit a few small candles and set them on the counter and turned the light out. I quickly stripped down and dropped carefully into the steaming water. Only moments later I heard a faint knocking on the door to the bathroom.

"Jessica?" Alex's voice called quietly.

"Yeah," I answered, though it came out almost as a pained moan.

"You've got a letter here. The return address is from Idaho."

I gave a frustrated sigh and rolled my eyes. Great, just what I needed. A letter from my dad.

"Come in, it's not locked," I called when I realized it wasn't.

He poked his head in, not looking directly at me. I appreciated his respect for my privacy. He looked just a little more comfortable when he realized there was nothing he could see through the frothy bubbles.

I pulled a hand out of the water and shook the bubbles and water off it, reaching for the towel right next to the tub to dry it off.

"You want me to open it for you?"

"Please," I said as I tried to sit up a little better without showing anything embarrassing.

He tore the envelope open and unfolded the letter. "Would you like anything for lunch?" he asked hopefully as he handed me the single sheet of paper.

At his words my stomach gave a gurgling flop. My face must have reflected what my stomach felt.

"Guess that's a no?" he asked, his voice sounding downfallen.

His expression was so defeated it made my heart do a slight squeeze. "I'll try some toast. That should be safe enough for me to handle."

This seemed to brighten his mood a little and a small smile cracked on his face. "Okay," he whispered as he bent to press a kiss to my forehead and went out, closing the door behind him.

As his form retreated through the door, I couldn't help but smile just a little. I could not have found a more perfect person for me.

The smile quickly faded as I turned my attention back to the letter in my hand. It was quickly becoming limp and damp from the steam still rising off the surface of the water.

The letter was filled with a bunch of the usual. His business was going good, Amber had just broken up with her new boyfriend, and grandma was still hanging in there. He did, however, close the letter by saying he was going to be coming to Seattle in just a few days for my mother's birthday. She had always wanted to visit the huge city, well, huge to an Idahoan, and he was finally taking her for her forty-fifth birthday. He said he hoped and prayed I might tell them where I was or at least come to see them there. He said he missed me. He made no mention of what my mother thought about that scenario.

Despite my anger towards my parents, I did feel guilty for totally abandoning my father like I had. He had always been kind and, well, not exactly understanding, because how could one possibly understand what I was going through, but at least he was open and non-judgmental. He had always been there for me and made sure I had someone to talk to if I needed. Not that I had ever really taken him up on that offer. And I could always tell he had been ashamed of the way my mother constantly reacted to me. I knew it had been a source of strain on their marriage. I had heard the fights.

My mom seemed convinced that I was making everything up and that I was simply asking for attention. When she realized this wasn't just a phase, she got worried, becoming terrified about everything I said and did. When things still did not stop, she turned to anger and resentment. And then with the final step, she decided I needed to be committed. That was the end of my relationship with my mother. I doubted there was anything she could say or do to bridge that canyon she had blown between us.

I dropped the letter on the floor next to the tub and sank in as deep as I could manage. It was a strange thought; that my family would only be two hours away in just a few days. I knew there was no possibility of me actually telling them where to find me or of me going down to meet them, but it was still strange to know they would be so close. I had been so disconnected from them for so long; the thought of family seemed almost foreign.

It didn't take long for my head to start spinning and throbbing, forcing me to get out of the comforting water. With pleasant surprise, I found my pajamas folded on my bed, feeling delightfully warm as if they had just been pulled out of the dryer.

The days had been torturously slow since I had become sick, but finally the day came to a close. This was neither a sad nor a happy thing; there were mixed feelings. The end of a day brought the dim hope that the following day would bring an end to my mysterious sickness but at the same time it meant the never ending fight of sleep.

Alex didn't ever pressure me to sleep, but the last few nights he had asked me to stay with him as he slept. I was sure it had something to do with the fact that he felt he had to continually watch over me but I did not protest. I could think of no better heaven than being able to lie in his arms all night and stare into his beautiful face.

Tonight was different than other nights. Alex was normally perfectly peaceful as he slept but that night he tossed and turned. He muttered the same two words for hours. "No...stay." I debated waking him but could not bring myself to do so. It did eventually cease and he settled down, dropping off into a deep slumber. He even snored softly.

I had been ignoring it all night but I could feel the fever building back up. My hands were getting clammy and beads of sweat formed along my brow and along my upper lip. It felt as if there was a fire coursing just under my skin, threatening to scorch me to a crisp at any moment.

As reluctant as I was to leave Alex's side, I did not want to wake him. I was sure if he happened to touch my skin, the dangerous temperature would wake him instantly. With a stifled moan, I rolled out of the bed and wandered into my apartment. I retrieved a small, light blanket from my bedroom, then as quietly as I could, opened the door that led out onto the deck.

The air was crisp and cold. It felt refreshing on my burning skin. As I closed the door silently behind me, I took a deep breath, feeling the cleansing effect of Mother Nature. If only she could take away all the torment in my life. I was so tired of it all.

The deck was large, expanding along the entire backside of the house that overlooked the lake and on the bottom level it wrapped around the south side as well. I wandered to this side to my favorite seat. It seemed out of place, being on the side of the house that almost looked at the neighbor's house, the ones I had never met, but there was a slight nook that went into the side of the house. Right next to the built in seat was the window that looked into my bedroom.

I settled myself into the seat, resting my back against the wall, pulling my knees up under my chin. Dawn was not far off, I thought as I assessed the slight glow that hung in the perfectly clear sky. The clear sky also meant it was much colder than if it had stayed overcast. I wasn't about to complain though. This was exactly what I needed to help cool off the fever. None of the medications I had tried had any effect. The majority of the time they had made reappearances soon after ingestion.

A slight breeze picked up off the water, ruffling my wild curls. A faint movement caught my eye and I turned to investigate.

It took me a moment to realize what the movement was but as the breeze blew by again, I saw something wiggle in between the siding just under my window. The siding was coming loose and needed some attention that wasn't exactly my forte and I could see how it would be easy for something to get in it. I gingerly got to my feet and took a step toward it, wedging my fingers under it to pull the object out.

It was a feather. My fingers traced over its silky surface over and over again as I sat back in my seat. It was perfectly shaped, without a single flaw to its blindingly white surface, despite being wedged into the siding. It looked familiar for some reason but this made little sense to me. Why would a feather seem familiar? I quickly realized the reason. This feather was unmistakably just like the feather I had found in Sal's room at the hospital. The one that was still in my purse. I wondered for a brief moment if this was the same one but quickly dismissed that thought. The one I had found in Sal's room was much longer; this one was only about three inches long.

I couldn't help staring at the beautiful thing as I clasped it tightly between my fingers. I must have stared at it, memorizing its surface, for a good half hour as the sun finally managed to break over the tops of the trees before me.

My stomach gave a violent lurch and I just managed to spring to my feet in time to empty it over the side of the deck when I was blinded by the light that reflected in my eyes. A sharp metallic sheen had danced off the surface of the small feather I held in my hands. As I straightened back up, I held it as far from my body as possible, my hands shaking so violently I was afraid I would drop it.

It was undeniable and unexplainable as I stared at the glint that came off the feather. I had seen this before, hundreds of times, though never on just a single feather and never during waking hours. Where could this have possibly come from but the wing of an angel? It was obviously not from a bird and it in no way fit into the world of nature.

The world began to spin madly and everything tipped just slightly as the fear of what this actually meant sank in. I may have felt the physical effects of my nightmares and had the impossible scars on my neck and back but the angels stayed in the nightmares. I left them behind when I woke. But as I stared at this feather I realized I was never going to be free of this never-ending nightmare. They were somehow following me into the real world now.

Another horrifying realization hit me. I *had* seen this feather somewhere else, even if I hadn't realized what it actually was. I had found one in Sal's hospital room.

Hoping and praying that Alex was still asleep, I dashed into my tiny living room and rummaged through my purse. It had gotten a little buried but despite the abuse it had gone through, it still looked absolutely perfect and flawless. My hands continued to shake violently as I walked back to the window and held it up to the sunlight breaching over the tops of the trees.

The sharp glint that blinded me was undeniable.

I collapsed onto my couch, my knees no longer able to support my weight. I sat there numb with the two feathers clutched in my hands, unable to make my mind think.

I didn't know what to do or how to react to this. This wasn't anything I had dealt with before nor was it anything I had prepared myself to face. The possibility that the angels could follow me into waking hours never crossed my mind. It was too terrifying to consider.

But an angel had been outside my bedroom window. It had been watching me.

The sun had finally risen completely in the sky before I could pull myself slightly out of my numb state and with shock, I realized it was almost eight-thirty. I was amazed Alex had not woken up yet. Realizing I had only one hope, one lifeline to turn to for any chance of help, I grabbed the phone next to my bed and went back outside.

"Hello?" a cheerful voice answered.

"Emily?" I replied, my voice sounding frantic.

"Jessica, what's wrong?" she immediately questioned.

My nerves were too shot to beat around the bush or lead up to my question. I nearly vomited just asking it. "Can an angel escape?"

"Escape? What are you talking about?"

"Can they follow you into the real world? After you've woken up?" my voice trembled so horribly I was amazed she could even understand me.

"Follow you? I don't understand. They're dead, Jessica. How could they come into the real world?"

My breath holding painfully in my throat, I nodded my head. That was enough of an answer for me. Emily didn't know anything. She had never heard of them escaping.

"Never mind," I said quietly into the phone, keeping my voice carefully controlled. "Forget I said anything. I'll talk to you later."

I didn't wait for her to respond before I hung up the phone.

I returned the phone to its dock and climbed absentmindedly into the shower. I didn't even notice how the water was ice cold as it hit my skin, sending waves of goose bumps across my arms and legs.

A new fear spread through me as everything turned over and over in my head. A fear for those around me, those I cared deeply about. It was bad enough I had to deal with the angels but those around me did not know the true nature of them. They wouldn't be prepared for what they really were. Considering the things the condemned ones had done to earn their branding, they had their black eye color for a reason.

The faces that mattered most flashed through my head. Alex, Sal, my dad and my sister, who would be coming this way soon. I quivered at the realization that they would be coming to the place where an angel had escaped into.

As I closed my eyes and rested my forehead against the wall of the shower I heard the twisted laughter resounding in the back of my head. I couldn't help but wonder if this was just a crazy thing I subconsciously brought on myself or if it were a little more real than I had ever dared to consider. I couldn't bring myself to believe the latter was true. No, it had to just be something I was bringing on myself. It had to be.

CHAPTER TWENTY-THREE

The clatter of dishes being washed in my kitchen drew me from my thoughts. I quickly washed my hair, still not noticing the way the ice cold water was all too soothing to my scorching skin.

I dressed slowly, unsure of how I was going to do what I knew I had to do. I wasn't a good actress, but I knew I had to protect Alex from this. I had already put too much on him. I wouldn't let him bear the weight of knowing the possibility this whole nightmare was real. I cared for him enough to keep that away from him.

The face that stared back at me in the mirror looked calm and composed. I sat before it for a good full minute practicing before I felt I had really gotten it down. It may not have been my true and natural expression but hopefully the lie would be good enough.

I was going to have to pretend everything was perfectly fine.

Alex was indeed at the sink, just setting the last of the dishes on a towel to dry. When he heard my approach he turned, that dazzling smile that, to me, was more warming than the sun itself, spread on his face. I could see the concern in his eyes though, almost a permanent thing these days. A small crack broke across my heart, knowing I was the cause of so much worry and distress in his life. I was going to try my best to change that.

"Good morning," I said softly, making sure my voice sounded natural. I took the few steps to close the gap between us, wrapping my arms around his waist and resting my head on his chest.

"Morning," he breathed as he pressed a soft kiss into my still wet hair. "Sorry I slept so long."

"Don't worry about it. You were really restless in your sleep last night, I'm sure you needed it. Were you having nightmares?"

"Yeah," was all he said as took a step away and held me at arm's length, looking intently into my face. His expression was serious and deep but I couldn't discern the thoughts behind it. I didn't get a chance to question him about it though as he pressed a quick kiss to my lips then, taking my hand in his, started toward the door that led to the rest of the house.

"I'm making some breakfast, or maybe brunch I suppose," he said as he started up the stairs. "Is there any chance you will eat with me?"

My stomach gave the usual lurch at the thought of food but my will would have to be stronger than that today. I was pretending everything was normal after all. "I think I could use something to eat," I lied, hoping it sounded natural.

I took a seat at the bar and watched Alex as he went to work. He started some bacon and eggs before beginning work on French toast and what I could only guess was to become homemade syrup. It would have been enough food to feed four very hungry people. I hoped he was starving.

I was glad Alex seemed so focused on the work he was doing and didn't seem to feel the need for constant chatter. My mind reeled as I tried to come up with the next part of whatever I was going to do.

Alex set everything on the bar before me, apparently to be served buffet style. The smell was delicious despite how I had been feeling the last few weeks. But my strangely increased vision caught every little detail of the food, every speck of grease, every vein of fat that ran through the bacon, every tiny grain of sugar that hadn't been dissolved. Despite the strange details I couldn't help but see, I knew it would be delicious, of that I had no doubt. Alex had cooked it after all. If only my stomach would cooperate.

Trying to make sure Alex would be satisfied, I set two pieces of French toast on my plate and a small helping of the eggs. I didn't think I could trust myself to keep down the bacon. Alex quickly piled on large amounts of everything and dug in without a word. I couldn't help but smile. He may have been the most amazing and perfect man I had ever met but he was still a man. Men loved food.

We ate in silence for a few minutes and I was quite proud of myself for how well I was doing. Everything tasted wonderful and the homemade syrup was absolutely divine. Considering how my stomach tried to do small rolls the entire time and how my nerves were still so strung out, I thought I was doing amazingly well.

"I was wondering," I finally started, hoping I would be able to make this sound right without making myself sound just plain stupid. "It's been warming up the last little bit and it's getting close to spring. I would really like to get started on the gardens and hoped you could run into town and pick up some stuff I need."

"Sure," he replied through a mouthful of eggs, nodding his head. "Though I think maybe you should wait to start any work till you are feeling better. You shouldn't over do it."

I gave a little half smile, hoping my face looked almost back to its normal state. "I actually feel good today. No chills and look, I'm keeping everything down," I said as I indicated the small portion of food before me.

He considered this as he looked at my face, almost as if he was looking for the lie that truly was there. He finally gave a nod. "You do seem better today. I still think you should wait a few days though, just to make sure this isn't just some fluke this morning."

I gave an eager nod. I wasn't going to fight him about this. It didn't matter if he thought I should wait to do what I was pretending to be so suddenly interested in. I just needed him out of the house for a few hours.

"Deal," I agreed with a smile. "I'm going to try and get caught up on some of the laundry while you're out. I've got next to no clothes left to wear now."

He gave a little chuckle at this. "I may be able to do the cooking and the dishes while you're sick but I'm not going to touch your laundry. Believe me, that would be a huge mistake."

I couldn't help but laugh with him at this. I couldn't expect him to be perfect at everything.

While Alex worked on cleaning up after breakfast, I went downstairs and worked on sorting all the laundry that had been building up for the last two weeks. It was too bad I wasn't actually planning on doing it; it would take me at least a full day to get caught up.

When Alex finished upstairs he came back downstairs and waited on my tiny couch while I scrambled to come up with a list of things he could get. I hoped he wouldn't see through the lie. I had written down several things I knew I absolutely did not need. The weather also wouldn't be good enough to do anything for several more weeks. I knew that but hoped Alex didn't.

"I'll be back soon," he said as he put the list into his pocket and stood. He wrapped his arms around me briefly and pressed a kiss to my lips. They tingled where his skin met mine.

"No need to hurry," I tried to say casually. "Laundry days are never exciting."

He gave only a smile before he turned and walked out.

A huge sigh of relief escaped my lips when he closed the door upstairs and I heard the garage door open. I had done it. He didn't seem to suspect that anything was wrong, that anything had changed.

But everything had changed.

I knew that if Alex were to know the truth I had discovered this morning he would be incredibly upset I had not shared this information with him. He was far too supportive and was so eager to help me. He would have wanted to take some of the burden and help me find the answer. But I couldn't let him do this. I wouldn't let the angel's get to him. I had to protect those that mattered most. Alex mattered more than anyone else to me.

I waited ten or so minutes before I made my way to my bedroom, just to be sure that Alex wouldn't come back, forgetting something. It wasn't going to be hard to fall asleep. I was already exhausted. I just hoped I wouldn't sleep for hours again like I had been lately.

I knew it was a long shot and that this was likely to yield no answers but I didn't know what else to do. I had to return to sleep and see if anything was different, if anything had changed. I had nothing to gauge by and no exact time frame. I may have discovered the feather under my window this morning but how long had it been lodged there? And I had found the one in Sal's room two weeks ago now. I wasn't sure what I was searching for but I had to do something. This was the only place I could think to start.

Mercifully, I was not branded at the end of this trial. Despite the strangely enhanced vision, I did not notice anything different. Everything seemed the same as they had all been the last few weeks. No indicator that anyone had escaped. Not that I would have really been able to tell. There were hundreds, maybe even thousands of angels at the trials. But everything seemed the same.

The one difference, however, the enhanced, more raised parts of my wings grew while I was asleep. All the details that covered my shoulder blades had become more raised, more defined.

Alex returned that evening with the things I asked for, as well as a few groceries we were in need of and some exciting news. He had gotten a call from his best friend from when he was in southern California, saying he was in Washington for a few days. Alex said he was coming over for dinner later and that they would be going out all the next day. It seemed almost ridiculous how guilty Alex looked when he told me he would not be around the next day. I tried to reassure him that it was just fine if he went out.

Rod Gepper could have been Alex's more energetic twin if it weren't for the midnight dark color of his skin. He had Alex's laid back personality, mixed with a nonstop sense of humor. We both sat at the bar and watched Alex as he prepared dinner. While Rod was not rude at all to exclude me from conversation, I did not have to provide much of it. The two of them spent much of the night recalling old high school memories and telling stories of all the trouble they got into and all the detentions and suspensions they narrowly avoided.

It was nice to see Alex so light-hearted again and enjoying himself so much but I wore out long before they seemed they were going to be done. I politely excused myself, nearly giving Alex a heart attack which he did not outwardly show but I did not miss it in his eyes. I tried to silently reassure him as best I could without saying anything that might draw questions from Rod.

I sat on my bed, absentmindedly strumming at my guitar for the rest of the night. When three o'clock rolled around I realized it had been silent for a good half hour. I wandered quietly up the stairs. I found the two of them passed out on the leather couches. I couldn't help but smile as I pulled a blanket up around each of them. It was so nice to see Alex so relaxed again. This was the way things were supposed to be. He shouldn't have to worry so much about the supernatural. About things that shouldn't be real.

CHAPTER TWENTY-FOUR

Despite the late night, the boys took off just before seven in the morning. Alex came down to say good-bye before they left, his face looking all too guilty. He tried to offer to stay home with me but I didn't even let that conversation begin and insisted that he needed to go.

Even though I missed having Alex at home, it was nice to have the quiet slowness of being at home alone. Having a break from pretending things were fine and hiding just how horrible I constantly felt was nice. I needed some time to think and I desperately needed to get caught up on that laundry I was supposed to do the day before.

As I stuffed the first few loads into the washer I tried desperately to come up with a plan of action. I wasn't coming up with much. How was one supposed to handle something like this? I didn't know what to look for nor did I know exactly what this angel was after. It was terrifying to think that the feather had been just under my bedroom window. I felt violated and horrified that I had been being watched without knowing it.

After several hours the only solution I had come up with was to be on the lookout and had the silly temptation to install a security camera pointed at my window. This seemed like a ridiculous idea but it was all I had for now.

I had just switched my second to last load into the dryer when the phone rang. I dashed down the hall and picked it up on the fourth ring.

The woman announced herself as the case worker for Sal at the institution.

"We were wondering if you would be able to come in this afternoon and discuss the options for Miss Thomas? Maybe in about two hours?"

I couldn't see any reason I could not come up. I had been feeling pretty good that morning, almost back to normal except for the throbbing in my head that never seemed to fully go away. "Sure, that would be fine."

The woman gave me the address of the facility and the phone number in case I had any problems finding it.

As I gauged what time I needed to leave, I decided that perhaps I would head out early and pick up a few things I had been too embarrassed to ask Alex to grab for me. It would probably do me good to get out and about. I had practically become a hermit the last few weeks, despite the commitment I had made to do exactly the opposite and go back to normal social activities.

I dressed comfortably, wanting to make this as easy on myself as possible should I start to feel under the weather again. After checking that I had everything I needed, I headed out to the garage. I had to stop and admire my car again as the light hit it when the garage door creaked noisily up. It really was a nice looking car now.

Of course the time when I really needed to get out and Alex was not around for a backup, my GTO would decide not to start for me. It refused to turn over and immediately I realized the battery was dead.

With a frustrated sigh, I went back inside the deserted house and called Alex. It went straight to his voicemail.

Tears threatened to spill over as I dropped to the floor. I was so overwhelmed. There was just too much to deal with. An angel had escaped, I needed to take care of Sal, I was sick, and now my car was dead and Alex was gone.

I closed my eyes and counted backward from ten, feeling as if I were fighting off a panic attack. Perhaps I really was, I'd never had one before. It wasn't a fun emotion.

When I felt I had calmed down enough to think straight, I considered my options. I could call the institute and tell them that I couldn't make it today but that was about my last resort. I really needed to go see Sal. It had been a while.

If it had been summer, there might have been the option of catching a bus, but as it was just the beginning of March they wouldn't be running for at least another month.

My stomach gave another one of those sickening turns when I realized what my only other option was. Cole. Sometimes life was just plain spiteful. In both times of immense desperation he had been my only option.

I considered just calling and asking if he could jump my car but I realized it would be just as fast to walk over to his house and ask him in person. And it actually was a nice day outside.

Something I hadn't considered when I decided to walk was that outside was so open and exposed. I found myself constantly looking over my shoulder as I walked the short distance. For all I knew the angel could be lurking behind anything, just waiting to jump me and shove a red hot iron into the back of my neck.

Okay, my imagination was getting away with me. Maybe I really was going crazy.

Still, I couldn't help but breathe a slight sigh of relief when I got to Cole's doorstep.

I was surprised to see that there was no doorbell, considering the fact that the house was so new. There was only an antique looking door knocker. It was kind of charming. I found myself warming to the idea.

I soundly knocked on the door four times and waited, my palms sweating as they twisted around each other. This was about the last thing I wanted to do right now but I wasn't going to be a wuss and I wasn't going to hide from Cole when I shouldn't have to. He had to know how things were. We could still be friends though. He had no other choice.

As I waited, I could hear sounds coming from inside and after listening hard I realized what it was. Screamer rock music. I chuckled slightly at this. I wouldn't have pegged Cole as the type to listen to that kind of stuff.

I gave another five hard knocks on the door and waited for longer than it should have taken him to get to the door.

Feeling anxious to get out of the exposed outdoors but not anxious to walk back home and call Cole, I wandered to the window to the right of the door, standing on my tip-toes to look in. This window looked into the well-decorated living room but it seemed completely deserted. The windows practically shook from the vibrations of the music.

I crossed back in front of the door to the window to the left. This window was just slightly higher than the other because it was a little smaller and I had to climb up on a decorative rock that was placed just right to see into the window. This window shook even more dangerously than the other did and I saw the large and rather expensive looking stereo sitting on a stand next to it.

I had to cup my hands around my eyes to see through the glare and it took me a second to realize what the room was that I was looking into. It was not a large room and I figured it was an office. A large bookcase that was mostly empty spanned one wall and the wall opposite of the window had a large desk pushed up against it. Seated at it was Cole.

He was crouched over something and after a moment I realized it was a very old looking leather bound book. He seemed to be researching something, checking it against the computer that was set directly in front of him.

I paused in knocking on the window, not wanting to disturb him as he seemed to be working so intently on whatever it was that was in that book. I had to wonder how he could concentrate on anything when the music was blaring so loud. And beside the noise level, it all just sounded like angry screaming to me.

After a few moments, he sat up straight in his chair, lifting his arms high above his head to stretch. He then dropped his hands behind his head and leaned back as far as he could without tipping it. He stared at the computer screen for a moment then ruffled his hair as if to scratch an itch, or perhaps how a man might do when he is frustrated with the task at hand.

His hair was rather long and at the moment looked slightly shaggy. It was nearly as dark as if ink had been spilled on it and contrasted sharply with the white lines on the back of his neck.

My body froze as this last thought registered. If my vision hadn't been so bizarrely enhanced I probably would have missed the lines on the back of Cole's neck. I pressed my face against the glass and stared wide eyed as he brought his hair completely off his neck, pinning it with his hands against his head as if trying to cool it.

Cole's scar was the same design as my own but it was different in two ways. Mine was almost always an angry red but that was probably due to the constant re-branding I experienced. Cole's was a nearly white color as if the brand had been pressed into his skin long ago and had been given a long time to heal. The second difference was that it seemed to be almost shadowed. As if the iron had been pressed just briefly into his neck and he had pulled away before it had been pressed into it again, that time making its mark deep and sure.

I inched my face away from the glass slowly, my breath coming in shallow, short gasps. I knew I had seen this specific, unique mark before. A faint echo sounded in the back of my memory but I couldn't clearly recall where I had seen it.

One thing was for sure though. I knew Cole's brand was not the same as mine and Emily's for a reason. He had not come about his the same way we had.

Before I realized what I was doing, my feet were back on the ground, springing across the Earth as fast as my legs would allow me. Tears sprang from my eyes and leaked onto my cheeks but I didn't even notice. The panic that was rising in my system clouded my mind and the only thing I could think to do was to run and picture in my mind the spot I was running to.

I nearly tripped and rolled down the hill as I went directly to the door that led into my apartment. It took me longer than it should have to finally yank the door open. I made double sure to lock it when I was safely inside.

It took me maybe ten bounding steps to get from the back door and into my bedroom. I stood with my hand on the door knob to my closet for several long moments before I could work up the courage to open it.

The folder was buried in the back of my closet, along with several boxes of old memories I would have almost rather forgotten. I pulled it out and flipped on the light in the closet. The space was big enough that I could sit on the floor and set the folder in front of me.

My heart was racing in a scary way and my head throbbed with a greater speed than it had ever before as I opened the folder and stared at the drawings that gazed back up at me.

When I was younger I remembered the nightmares in much sharper detail. Nothing escaped the eyes of a child, though no child's eyes should ever have to see the things I saw. I had been a skilled drawer from a very young age and to help me cope with the fear it seemed to help if I drew the things I saw. I had hoped this would help my parents to understand the things I was going through, to make them believe. They had terrified my mother, these images of beautiful men and women with the powerful wings. She made me stop drawing them. And as I stopped drawing them my recollection of the details faded. They all became just a fuzzy recollection up until the last few trials.

I shuffled through the sheets of beautiful faces until I came to the one I was looking for. My body froze into stone and my ears started ringing till I could hear nothing else but the pulsing of the blood rushing all too fast through them.

On one side of the sheet was a perfect duplicate of the shadowed scar I had just seen. On the other side was an exact likeness of Cole's devastatingly beautiful face.

I knew that face well. It was the same face that had branded me hundreds, perhaps thousands of times. The missing leader of the condemned.

CHAPTER TWENTY-FIVE

As I walked through the front doors of the nearly brand-new facility, I marveled that I had made it there alive. In my desperation to get to Sal I remembered the shiny black and silver motorcycle that had sat long stashed in the corner of the garage. Amazingly, I had figured out how to start it and had somehow managed to get there without being pulled over. Considering it had tags that had been expired by two years and the fact that I most certainly did not have a motorcycle license, I was amazingly grateful I had not seen any cops on the road.

I made it to the institute just before the time my appointment had been made and the woman at the front desk politely directed me to the doctor I needed to speak with. The woman was a good four inches shorter than I was, with short cropped black hair and friendly eyes. She told me her name, which I immediately forgot. There were just too many other things racing through my head at the moment.

"Please have a seat," she said as she guided me into a tiny, well-kept office. I sat in the only available chair, startled by how uncomfortable it was.

"As you know, we have been observing Miss Thomas for a while now and I must say that I am quite impressed with the progress she has shown. I am sure you are aware she has her lucid times and these seem to be becoming more and more frequently. She has shown no signs of being a danger to herself and we believe she can be released. We believe that there is not much more we can do for her. We have made a few adjustments to her medication and she seems to be doing amazingly well.

"One of the reason's I wanted to speak to you though is we have talked to Sally about the possibility of releasing her and she is absolutely refusing. I wouldn't say she quite goes into a frenzy whenever we try and talk to her about it, but these are the times when she gets the worst. We were hoping that you could talk to her."

I had listened to the doctor, trying very hard to keep my head in our conversation. "Of course," I agreed. That wasn't the only thing I needed to talk to Sal about.

The doctor gave one short nod with a tight-lipped smile before she rose and led me down a long hallway. She stopped in front of a door that had the number eight on it in gold metal letters.

"Go ahead," she encouraged when I hesitated.

I only nodded as I grasped the door knob and opened it.

The room Sal was in was simple but comfortable. It had a double sized bed, a dresser, and a desk. There was a door that led off from the main part of the room and I caught a glimpse of a shower, indicating it was a bathroom. Sal, dressed in a pair of light green scrubs, her hair brushed nicely and pulled back, sat at the desk, a book laid open before her.

"Sal?" I called quietly as I closed the door behind me. I could already hear the sound of the doctors retreating footsteps in the hall thanks to my increased sense of hearing.

Sal turned in her seat to face me, a gentle smile on her face. "Jessica," she said, delight evident in her voice. "I'm glad you came. I missed you."

"I missed you too," I said, trying to reciprocate her smile as I sat on the edge of the bed, just two feet away from the desk. "The doctor told me you were doing much better. How do you feel?"

"Good," she said as she closed the book. "They are all very nice to me here and there are always lots of nice people to talk to."

I couldn't say anything for a while as I just stared back into Sal's eyes, unsure of how to approach what I needed to talk to her about. I most certainly did not want to set her off and destroy all the progress she had seemed to have made here.

"They said you don't want to come home," I started, keeping my voice as gentle as I possibly could. "How come?"

She took in a slight, sharp intake of breath before she looked from side to side, as if to make sure no one was listening to us. When she looked back at me her eyes were intense. "I can't. He knows where to find me there. He doesn't know I'm here so I'm safe. I can't go back."

I considered this for a moment and recalled the things she had ranted about in the hospital. "Is this the same man who came to visit you in the hospital?" I whispered, my voice shaking. In the pit of my stomach I knew exactly what had happened to Sal that dreadful night, though I still didn't understand why.

Sal's eyes grew large and she nodded her head enthusiastically. "They didn't believe me, Jessica. They told me there was no man and that he was just from my imagination."

"And this is the same man who told you to take the pills? That they would make you forget?" My heart pounded in my chest and the room threatened to start spinning.

Sal's eyes remained wide as she nodded her head again.

"What did this man look like, Sal?" I squeaked.

Sal looked at me for a moment as if trying to decide if I really believed her or if I was trying to continue the psychoanalysis she had been undergoing with the doctors and nurses. "His eyes were black as if there was nothing behind them but darkness. But they tried to tell me to trust him. His face though, I had never seen a face like it before. It doesn't belong here. He doesn't belong here. He needs to go back where he came from."

I closed my eyes and tried to hold back the tears that were welling there. I held my breath to try and keep back the sobs that were threatening to escape my chest. It was at least a solid minute before I felt I could ask what I needed to next without frightening Sal. When I opened my eyes finally Sal's met mine, filled with concern and confusion.

"Sal," I said, testing to see if my voice was stable enough to talk. It shook a little but I hoped I could cover it. "Do you remember your new neighbor that moved into the house next to yours?" I silently braced myself for what might be coming.

Sal's expression was blank for a moment then changed to thoughtful, as if she were trying to dig up a memory. After another moment it changed to outrage.

"That man!" she shrieked. "That man! He...he... I told you to stay away from him Jessica! He did this to me!"

Sal sprang to her feet and paced around the small space. Her hands twisted around each other, her knuckles turning white.

"It was Cole that told you to take those pills," I whispered, my body feeling numb. "Wasn't it?"

Sal slowed her pacing, her face looking almost enlightened. "Yes!" she nearly shouted. I hoped the nurses wouldn't come to investigate what all the sudden noise was about. "I forgot his name. I forgot who he was! You can't go back home Jessica! He might get you too!"

My mouth felt intensely dry as I tried to swallow. I wanted to do as she said, to never return to that house again and run away. But I couldn't do that. Alex was still there. I had to protect him and I couldn't simply just disappear. What would Cole do then?

Sal froze in place, her eyes staring intently down at my own. "Promise you won't go back there, Jessica. I don't want him to hurt you too."

My eyes dropped to the floor and I laced my fingers tightly together until they turned white. "Okay," I lied. I told myself I hadn't said yes nor did I agree to anything, knowing I was just trying to justify it to myself.

Sal sat back down in her chair and pulled the book into her arms. "I can't leave here, Jessica. You have to tell them that. I can't leave until he goes away."

I could only nod as I continued to stare at the floor. A soft knock on the door startled me and I looked up as a sun baked looking nurse poked her head through the cracked door.

"Is everything okay in here?" she questioned, looking around to make sure everything was in order.

"Yeah, it's fine," I said as I stood. "I think it's time for me to go."

The nurse nodded then closed the door. I turned to Sal, her eyes inquisitive on mine.

"I'll talk to the doctor and tell them you need to stay," I promised, knowing I could keep this one. "You take care of yourself. I'll come back to see you as soon as I can."

Sal nodded, still not breaking her stare.

I tried to give a half smile before I turned and left the room, heading back for the doctor's office. I was glad I found her there and did not have to go searching for her.

I stood in the doorway, not wanting to have to stay long. My composure wasn't going to last much longer. "Would it be alright if she stayed here for a while longer? She seems to be under the impression it isn't safe for her to go home. I want her to feel comfortable to go back to her house before she is discharged." I hoped I sounded convincing enough. After all, what I said was true.

The doctor nodded. "Her insurance will pay for up to four weeks so she can stay for that long if you feel she needs to."

I could only nod. "I think that would be best."

"Alright," she said as she opened a folder. "Thank you for coming up and talking to her. As always, we will be in touch."

"Thank you," I whispered as I walked back out into the main lobby. "May I use your phone?" I quietly asked the receptionist.

X

The motorcycle wobbled dangerously as I made it into the parking lot of the apartment complex. Yet again I had somehow managed to survive getting on the bike and still had avoided running into any cops.

It only took me a moment to find the apartment I needed; it was just on the second floor. As I knocked on the door, my stomach heaved as if some kind of storm was raging inside and I seriously hoped that I could keep it under control.

Emily's face was serious and immediately curious as she opened the door and ushered me inside. The interior was just as I should have expected from Emily. It was decorated in bright and sunny colors.

"Would you like anything to drink?" Emily asked, her voice unsure of how exactly to react to my strange phone call. I had not left her any option when I called her. I had demanded that we needed to talk and it had to be now.

"No," I said as I pursed my lips together, keeping back the bile that threatened to come up my throat.

Emily nodded and indicated a well-worn, but still in good shape, sofa. Debating whether or not I would be able to say everything better sitting or standing, I hesitated by the door.

"What happened?" Emily demanded, her voice sounding almost impatient. "You seem dazed and confused and you're as twitchy as a horse on Speed."

I realized then that I had been shuffling from side to side on her front rug, my fingers twisting around each other nervously. I stopped immediately, closed my eyes and took a deep breath. I slowly counted backward from fifteen in my head. When I opened my eyes again Emily was staring at me from her place on the couch with concern and confusion in her eyes.

"Cole looks familiar to you doesn't he?" I finally said as I slipped my shoes off and joined her on the couch.

Emily looked confused for a moment but her expression changed to thoughtful after a moment. "That's what I thought when I first saw him. He did seem really familiar and it was weird because he doesn't exactly have a face you could forget," Emily said with a slight smile.

"But he does look familiar to you?" I asked again, my voice slightly more demanding.

"Yeah, I suppose he does," she answered, her expression furrowed as if trying to dig up some old memory.

"What about his eyes?" I pressed. "How do you feel when you look into his eyes?"

Emily must have been on that train of thought because she didn't look at me like I was crazy when I asked my seemingly bizarre question. "They're... intriguing. They kind of...draw you in. But," she paused for a long while, her eyes closed as if trying to recall exactly how she felt. "He makes me afraid when he looks at me with those eyes. Like I

276

don't want him to look at me, as if I feel something bad is going to come soon."

At this she opened her eyes, confusion evident in them. "There's something wrong with Cole, isn't there?"

I nodded. "I was at his house this morning. He didn't know I was there. I saw something on the back of his neck. A shadowed brand."

Emily's face became frozen, her mouth hung open just slightly. Her expression became pale as the blood drained from her face and I saw realization slowly slip into her eyes.

"Cole's the leader of the condemned," I whispered. My voice seemed suddenly unwilling to work and I could hardly find the will to make it. "When I called you the other day and asked if they could escape, I had found a feather just outside my bedroom window. It had a certain metallic glint to it.

"A few weeks ago, in my nightmares, the leader of the condemned suddenly was gone and replaced by another member of the council. The same time Cole showed up." I shook my head as I said this. I had been so stupid before. How could I not have seen this? It was so obvious.

Emily remained frozen for several long minutes and I was in no hurry to say everything else I needed to.

"Jessica," she finally managed to whisper. "You've been so sick lately. We don't get sick. Has Cole got something to do with that?"

I could feel what little color was left in my face drain at her words. "I don't know," I breathed, fighting back tears that wanted to betray me. "I don't know what's going on at all anymore. Why I've been sick. What Cole wants.

"He was the one who told Sal to take those pills. She remembered today. Then he went after her again in the hospital but she put up such a fuss he must not have been able to finish her off. I...I found a feather in her room but didn't realize what it was then.

"Cole tried to kill Sal," I choked as the tears started to spill over. "And I'm sure it had something to do with me. I don't see how it could not have."

Neither of us said anything for a good long while as the horror of what was happening sank in further and further. Chills spread through my body and I had to try hard to not let my body shake violently.

Emily cleared her throat and sat up a little straighter. When I looked up at her she was staring at the floor, looking very determined that her eyes would stay glued there.

"Last year I had a realization. Maybe not a realization, that's not the right word. I developed a theory. If I could guarantee where I would be placed come my own judgment day then perhaps I no longer would be able to stand trial for all the others. That if I was no longer a neutral proxy I might be able to make it stop.

"It seemed so simple. It takes a lifetime of good living to not be condemned but it seemed there was one act, that if you committed this one action, you were guaranteed to be branded.

"I heard through an extended family member that my stepfather had slipped back into his old ways. He was abusing my two little sisters the same way he had abused me for years. It made me sick and perhaps a bit crazy but I

278

suddenly knew exactly what I was going to do. I was living in Oregon at the time and I drove all through the night back to Texas.

"I was so enraged and out of my mind it is amazing that I didn't get caught, that I managed to plan it out so carefully and flawlessly. Every detail fell into place perfectly when so much could have gone wrong. It wasn't like I really knew what I was doing. The cops never were able to even begin to guess who the murderer might be."

My heart seemed to have stopped beating as the realization of what she had done sank in.

"I got back home the next morning and I was so tired and probably more than a little in shock over what I had just done. I fell asleep as soon as I walked in the door. But there weren't any nightmares then. There weren't any more nightmares ever after that. My theory had been correct. In guaranteeing that I condemned myself I had stopped the nightmares and the brandings."

I didn't realize there were tears running down my cheeks until Emily lifted a shaky hand to wipe them away. She had tears of her own rolling down her face.

"You see why I couldn't tell you?" she whispered, her eyes full of shame. "I couldn't let you even consider doing that to yourself. I can live with myself, knowing what I have done, because it saved my sisters. But I can't let you do that to yourself. I couldn't live with myself if you went and did something like that because I was the one who told you how."

I couldn't make my head fully wrap around this information, around the fact that, despite how complicated things had gotten lately, the woman who was becoming one of my very best friends, was already condemned. Come her judgment day, her neck would be branded, her eyes would turn black and she would be pulled down into the fiery depths of the cylinder. She would become one of the angels who laughed dementedly at me from the walls.

"No," I whispered as my eyes grew wide with this thought. "No! It can't be too late! You...you could change that," my voice grew soft with this last sentence and trailed off. We both knew the likelihood of her being able to override what she had done. I could not recall anyone who had committed a murder not being branded.

Emily pursed her lips in a tight line and tried to smile unsuccessfully. She shook her head as she leaned forward and put her arms around me. "It's okay," she whispered into my hair as I started to sob into her shoulder. "I knew what I was doing. There's no going back now and I will live with the consequences of what I did. Right now I... I just have to enjoy the rest of my life. Thank goodness I'm still young, right?" she tried to say with a slight laugh which just sent more sobs escaping up my throat.

It took me a long time before the tears ran out and my face hurt so badly I did not think I could cry any longer. When I finally seemed to find my head again, it felt numb and I knew I could not take any more. I couldn't handle any more of the impossible today.

I had made two calls at the institute. The first had been to Emily and the second had been to Alex. He had told me that Rod wanted to go camping somewhere right along the Canadian border. He sounded ridiculously guilty about even bringing the possibility up and told me that if I needed him to come home he would do so immediately. Of course I told him he should go and was actually a bit relieved he would be gone. I wasn't sure if I could keep my composure and the façade that nothing was wrong around him. He had a way of getting under my skin too easily.

But even though I was glad Alex would be gone, that did not mean I necessarily wanted to be alone. Thankfully I did not even have to ask Emily if I could stay with her. She offered me her couch for as long as I needed it.

Oddly the rest of the night passed in a relaxed and comfortable way. Neither of us seemed to know what to do about the situation with Cole at the moment and I plain and simply did not want to talk or think about it anymore. The rest of the day and night was spent watching a few chick flicks, painting toe nails and eating take out Chinese food. For once, I just needed a night to be a normal twenty-year-old woman hanging out with her best girlfriend.

CHAPTER TWENTY-SIX

The morning dawned clear and with the promise of a beautiful day. Despite how my body ached, some from still being sick and some from Emily's not-as-comfortable-as-it-looks couch, I felt oddly good and clear. I still didn't know what to do about the situation with Cole but I didn't feel like my brain was so fogged I couldn't even think.

I may not have known what to do about Cole but I did have one plan of action.

As I had been lying on the couch that night, staving off sleep, I realized that today would be the day my family was supposed to be flying into Seattle. I had to call my dad and tell him not to come. It was too dangerous right now. Who knew what could happen. Cole had already gone after Sal. I couldn't imagine what he might do to my family.

Knowing my chances of catching him before they left were slim, I borrowed Emily's phone and called just after six, grateful for the time difference and that it wouldn't be so early there. Luck had not been with me however and it went straight to his voicemail. They must have already boarded the plane. Feeling frantic, I told him the name of a restaurant and a time to meet me. I made sure it was very clear that he was to come alone.

Emily was still asleep when I was ready to go. I couldn't help but feel both a pang of jealousy and fear mixed with pity, each in warring portions. I couldn't be angry at her any more for not telling me how to make the nightmares stop. While I was glad to finally know, she was right in not telling me what she had done. I left her a note thanking her for letting me stay and telling her that I would keep her updated.

I must have finally been getting the hang of the motorcycle as I made my way home. It felt almost exhilarating and if my mind had not been reeling I might have actually enjoyed it. The feeling of the wind whipping my hair around and feeling it part on the front of the helmet was a new feeling of freedom.

The fact that my father was on his way here jarred me from my momentary elation, encouraging me to push the bike all the faster.

"What are we doing here?" I asked my dad as we pulled into a car dealership. "Aren't you afraid of being attacked by the wolves?"

He chuckled as he stepped out of the car and closed the door. "Come take a look with me."

I didn't understand what was going on. After I had gotten home from school I was prepared to sulk around the house all day. No one had remembered it was my birthday all day. No one cared. But as soon as I got home my dad had dragged me out into his car and told me we were going for a drive. And here we were at the biggest car dealership Idaho Falls had to offer.

I followed behind my dad a few paces. He seemed certain where he was going. He walked to the end of an aisle and stopped in front of a shiny blue Toyota that looked nearly brand new.

"What do you think of this one?" he asked as he eyed it, his hands in his pockets.

"What's wrong with the Honda?" I asked as I stood next to him and folded my arms across my chest.

"Oh nothing," he said as a hint of a smile tugged at the corners of his mouth. "This just kind of screamed 'Jessica' at me when I saw it."

It took me a second to realize what he was saying. He had pulled a set of keys out of his pocket before it fully hit me.

"What? No... you...?" I stuttered.

"Happy birthday, Jessica," he said with a smile as he handed the keys over to me.

"Are you serious?" I squealed like the sixteen-year-old girl I was.

"Why don't we go for a drive? Give the new wheels a spin?"

"We can just take it? You already got it?"

"Technically you're not driving, since you don't have your license yet," my dad said as he glanced around to make sure no one was watching.

A few minutes later we had worked our way out of the city and switched.

"Dad, seriously, this is the best present. Ever," I cooed as I started down a quiet road.

"I knew you'd like it," he said as he settled back into his seat. He didn't even seem nervous that I was driving, without a license too. *"I wanted you to have something nice. I know life hasn't exactly been easy for you."*

"Thanks dad," I said feeling my throat tighten a little. *"It really does mean a lot to me."*

"I know you don't like to talk about it and I know your mother hasn't made it easy for you, but if you ever do want to, you know, talk, I'm always here."

"Thanks dad," I said as my eyes filled with moisture. *"I know."*

But no matter how bad I did want to tell him, to tell anyone how terrifying my life really was, I could never tell him. He would never understand.

Shaking off memories of the past that hurt me more than I cared to admit, I pulled into the driveway and got off the bike. I felt incredibly jumpy and scared as I keyed in the code to the garage and waited anxiously for it to open far enough to push the bike in. I felt only slightly better when the door closed again; sealing me inside what I hoped and didn't hope was an empty house. Considering Alex's truck was still gone I knew it should be silent.

The house that had been so familiar to me for the last year and a half now seemed foreign and intimidating with its dark corners and hidden spaces. I crept from room to room, turning on every light as I went along even though it didn't do much, the sun was streaming through the windows with wondrous glory.

Finally satisfied that the house was indeed empty, I climbed into the shower. The enclosed space seemed pathetically calming and safe. I could see every corner in the shower; nothing could be hiding in there. I did however keep the shower curtain open as wide as the water would allow. Just in case anything or anyone tried to sneak up on me.

Nervousness again settled upon me as I shut the water off, knowing I was going to have to go back out into the rest of the house. I took at least a tiny bit of comfort in the fact that I had locked all the doors as I checked the house earlier.

I pulled a towel around me and tried to relax a little as I started rummaging through a drawer, looking for a spring shirt I had bought last year. I heard the footsteps only a moment before a pair of strong but gentle arms wrapped around my waist. I barely even jumped at the unexpected touch. I knew this embrace well enough to know there were no sinister intentions behind it.

A pair of lips touched only briefly onto my bare shoulder before I twisted in his arms, my own lips searching for Alex's. My arms tightened securely behind his neck and as I strained to stand on my toes to reach his face, he placed his hands on my hips, hoisting me up and I wrapped my legs around his narrow waist.

Our lips parted and a soft moan of nothing but pleasure escaped them as Alex carried us to the bed. He half tripped as my back landed on my bed, his body a comfortable weight on top of me. His lips moved from my lips down to my neck, moving rhythmically as his hands slipped from my waist down my thigh all the way down to my ankle. I was glad I had taken the time to shave in the shower.

I couldn't think of anything else in the world as Alex's body pressed against mine. There was no such thing as condemned and exalted beings. There was no sinister more-than-man just two doors down. There were no such things as angels besides the one in my arms.

Alex rolled, pulling me on top of him. Somehow my towel managed to stay wrapped around me just enough to not show anything important. His fingers traced from the scar on my neck, down my spine to the wings, hesitating momentarily at the new raised portion. Graciously, he did not stop to ask any questions as his fingers continued their greedy inspection of my skin, a moan of both desire and slight frustration slipping out.

A few moments later we both seemed to realize we were going to go too far at any moment. With Alex's fingers still knotted in my hair, he pulled my face just slightly away from his own ever so gently.

He stared intently into my eyes and I was surprised at how serious and clear his expression was. He seemed to be considering something very important, as if trying to make some significant decision.

As I stared back, I marveled at the man who held me so tenderly. His miraculously blue eyes burned with sincerity and intensity. His gaze seemed to reach down into my soul and whisper every word I desired to hear into my very core.

"I love you, Jessica," he whispered as he continued his intense gaze. "I never have and I never will love another woman like I love you."

My pulse skyrocketed and my stomach fluttered in a wonderful way as his words spread through me. I realized then that it was the first time that he had said those words in that exact way. "And I love you, Alex. More than you could possibly imagine. And I will never stop loving you. I promise you that." As the words crossed my lips I knew they were true. The intensity of them should have frightened me but I had never felt so right saying any words in all my life.

A small, content smile spread on his lips just before he pressed them to mine briefly. "We should go do something special today. It's a beautiful day and I want to spend every second of it with you."

I couldn't help but smile as I thought of how ridiculously cheesy we sounded. And I couldn't have cared less. I loved it and couldn't have been happier to hear him say the things he did. I marveled at how it was possible to love someone so much. It seemed a miracle that my body didn't simply burst from the effort of trying to hold it all in.

"Actually," I said as I sat up, sliding off of him and adjusting to make sure I was decent enough. "I need to go down to Seattle today. Maybe we could spend the day down there?"

"That sounds great," he said with a wide smile. He pressed another quick kiss to my lips before he stood. "Why don't you pack an overnight bag? I have something in mind. I think you will really like it."

I smiled and nodded, feeling slightly relieved that he had not asked why I needed to go to Seattle. I hadn't really thought yet about what I was going to give him as the reason why I would need to disappear for a while today.

"I'll finish getting ready, you go shower," I said with a slight chuckle.

"Oh sorry," he said as he blushed and sniffed at his arm. "I bet I reek. We trekked straight through the woods to get to our camping spot."

I just shook my head and laughed. "Just go get ready," I said as I waved toward the door. "I need to get dressed before we do something stupid."

He gave a little impish grin. "Good idea." He then headed for the door and closed it behind him.

A girlish little squeal erupted from my throat as I jumped to my feet, pure joy and contentment flooding through my veins. I quickly stifled it when I heard a chuckle from somewhere outside my door.

I dressed with care, making sure everything looked perfect and just right and took the time to make sure my wild curls stayed in just the right place. It really could look nice if I took the time to try and tame it. I tried to pack light but ended up with twice what I would probably need. I had no idea what to prepare for. I was sure Alex would surprise me, he always did.

Just an hour later, we were loaded in the truck and on our way to the big city.

While I had no desire whatsoever to live in Seattle, I loved to visit the city. I felt so small there with its towering skyscrapers, and it was so easy to blend in and get lost with the thousands of people walking the streets. It was a nice change from the quiet secluded life of living on Lake Samish.

The day could not have been more perfect with the flawlessly blue skies and temperatures that had to have been pushing seventy. A perfect spring day. It was made all the more perfect having the man I loved more than I could have possibly imagined by my side, his fingers intertwined with mine.

Despite all the horror and chaos that had been revealed in the last day and a half or so, I somehow managed to keep all of that pushed out of my mind. I was bound and determined to enjoy the time with Alex that I had. No escaped angel was going to take that from me. Nothing would ever take Alex from me and I was willing to do *anything* to keep him.

I couldn't help but wonder at exactly how much money Alex had inherited when his grandparents died. Not that it mattered one little bit but the way he constantly tried to buy me things as we wandered from shop to shop and finally down to Pike's Place Market made me wonder. I had to be careful to limit the time I looked at anything or I would be in danger of having it gifted to me only a few minutes later. I actually felt proud of myself for having come out of our wanderings with only a few items of clothing, a pair of earrings, and a cheap ring that I was sure would turn my finger green in a few hours. Alex had insisted on the last one for some strange reason.

The time was approaching when I needed to head to the restaurant I had told my dad to meet me at. I had been trying not to think of how I was going to explain this to Alex all day and now the time had finally come. I decided to be as honest as I possibly could.

"Do you remember how I said I needed to go to Seattle this morning?" I started as we walked hand in hand up a pier.

Alex nodded as he licked at his ice cream cone. "You did say that. I didn't want to push you to tell me why if you didn't want to."

I gave a little half smile at this. "Um..."I scrambled to word what I needed to say. "My family is in Seattle today. Right now somewhere."

Alex suddenly paused mid-step and looked at me. "Really?" he said with surprise evident in his voice.

"Yeah," I said uncomfortably. "I'm supposed to be meeting my dad in twenty minutes to talk."

Alex considered this for a long moment. "And you want to do this?"

"Not exactly," I said honestly. "I haven't seen the man in over four years. But there are some things I need to say to him. It's been so long and I just think it's time I actually talk to him."

Alex looked as if he was debating asking me to explain what exactly I meant by that. I was glad when he didn't. "Is there a chance I could meet him?" he blurted out.

The color drained from my face as I thought of having him there when I talked to my dad. "No!" I said too quickly. "Um...I mean...I think I need to talk to him alone. Like I said, it's been four years since I've seen him. I have no idea how this is going to go. There's a good possibility this might not be such a pretty and lovey-dovey reunion."

"Okay," Alex said as he nodded his head and continued walking back up the pier.

A slight sigh of relief blew through my lips. I was so grateful Alex was so relaxed and willing to give me my space when I needed it. Thankfully he was also slightly clueless. Either that or I was a really great actress. I seriously doubted that.

We parted a few blocks from the restaurant with a quick kiss and plans to meet back up in an hour and a half at the same location. Finally I let go of his hand, feeling like I was leaving a part of me behind. Like a hand, or a leg. I didn't feel whole when he was away.

CHAPTER TWENTY-SEVEN

I stood in the half full lobby for a few minutes after checking to make sure my dad was not already there. My hands twisted around each other and my head started throbbing slightly again. My heart jumped in strange erratic patterns as my eyes stayed glued on the door. I'd already mapped out an escape route should I see any sign of my mother with him.

Thankfully, he was alone as he walked through the door. Our eyes found each other almost instantly and I rose to join him at his side. Not a word was spoken as we followed the hostess through the crowded building.

When we were finally seated, neither of us seemed exactly sure of what to say to the other. I was surprised at how much older he looked. His hair was the same dark brown color as mine when I left but it was now streaked with grey. Crinkles seemed to be permanent fixtures in the corners of his green eyes and his handsome face seemed softer all over. It seemed he had aged ten years in the four since I had seen him.

"It's so good to see you, Jessica," he finally broke the silence, his voice filled with emotion. As he spoke, moisture welled up in his eyes. He reached across the table and took one of my hands in his.

I tried to give a little half smile. "You too, Dad." My mind was drawing a blank on where to even try to begin.

"I can't believe you've become such a woman. You look so grown up now."

At this I did give a little bit of a smile. "Yeah, I guess there's a bit of a difference between how you look at sixteen and how you look at twenty."

He gave a little chuckle and a tear rolled down his cheek. He sighed as he continued to look at me. "I didn't tell your mother I was meeting you. I'm supposed to be getting her a special present while she and Amber go to a chick flick. Guess I have to do a little shopping when we're done."

"Thanks dad," I whispered. I should have known I could trust my dad to keep this a secret. He had always been the one whom I could trust.

The waitress then showed up to take our drink orders. I only asked for water and my dad asked for his usual Mountain Dew. Some things never change. The man had drunk at least one a day for as long as I could remember.

"So how have you been lately?" he asked, the pain of our long separation in his eyes. "You don't say much in your letters."

I debated on how to answer, wondering if I should pad the truth or if I should simply be honest. Honesty seemed the best route. I only had so much time.

"I've been really sick lately," I said simply as I looked in his face, wondering if he would see the meaning behind my words.

"You don't get sick," he said stiffly. Apparently he did.

"Well I have lately," I said, trying to keep my voice even. "Really sick. Headaches, chills, fever, I can't keep anything down. Something is happening dad."

My dad swallowed hard twice before he was able to talk. "The nightmares?"

"They've gotten worse lately. I have to sleep more often and I'm sleeping for much longer." I waited for a long moment, simply staring into his face before I could say the next part. "They aren't simply dreams dad. Do you remember the angels?"

He squeezed his eyes shut and nodded once before he opened them again.

"Do you remember that mark I used to draw all the time? The one that scared mom so bad?"

My dad looked from side to side as if to make sure no one was watching before he took a pen out of his front pocket. With shaking hands he drew a crude replica of the mirrored X on a napkin.

"The man who lives two doors down from me has this exact mark on the back of his neck. He is one of the one's from my dreams."

The space between my dad's eyebrows furrowed as he looked back at me. "I don't understand, Jessica."

I felt a sudden urge to hurry and tell him everything I needed to. I wanted to get this over with. "One of the angels has escaped, dad. He's the worst one of them all. He's

295

dangerous. You have to take mom and Amber and leave. I don't know what he's after exactly but it's too dangerous for you to be around here. He's the leader of the condemned for a reason."

He was quiet for a long time as he looked at me, as if debating once again if I was crazy or not. I knew that look all too well.

"I know how this all sounds, dad. I know I sound insane. But you have to promise me you will leave as soon as possible. You have to go back home."

There was another moment of silence as he looked at me long and hard. "Alright," he said with a nod. "We will leave tomorrow morning. But you have to promise me something in return."

I could feel the blood drain from my face at this. I wasn't sure how much I could promise in exchange for keeping my family safe. "What?"

"That you'll call every once in a while," he said as his voice quivered. "You can call from a payphone if you want it that way. But just promise me that you will call to talk to your old man every once in a while."

My heart gave a strange squeeze as moisture filled my own eyes. "Deal," I whispered.

After another long moment of silence our waitress returned with the drinks and we ordered our food.

"There's something I've never told you, Jessica, something you should know about," my dad said with a slight sigh, not meeting my eyes. "You were five, Amber had just turned a year old. You got really sick. You had a fever so high the doctors were concerned what it might do to your body. You would shake violently with chills and aches. You cried constantly as you held your head. You wouldn't eat anything and everything we managed to shove down your throat came right back up a few minutes later.

"The doctors didn't know what was wrong with you and they told us to prepare for the worst. You were declining rapidly and they told us they didn't know what else to do. They said your body would probably give out before the end of the week."

Tears were streaming down his cheeks at this point and he still did not look me in the eye. I could only stare at him blankly. This was the first time I had heard any of this.

"You were going to die and there was nothing I could do about it, it seemed," he choked. He took a moment as he tried to control his emotions. "I was alone in the hospital room with you. You were unconscious. You had been slipping in and out for a few days. I cried out to whoever would listen, begging them not to take you away from me. I said I would do anything to keep you. I begged whoever was out there to let you live, to give you some more time. You were too young to die and I couldn't bear to let you go.

"Not a half hour after I spoke those words aloud, the monitors started to show improvements. You were still asleep but your temperature started to fall and the sweat that had covered your body went away. The doctors all came in to check on you and they were baffled. They had all basically written you off as a lost cause, dead.

"A few hours later you woke up, screaming. Screaming at the top of your lungs. You were terrified. You kept saying 'angels', over and over. I had heard stories of people who were dying and saw angels while unconscious but you seemed to be terrified of them. Your grandma had brought a little porcelain angel to you in the hospital and set it next to your bed. As soon as you saw it you screamed, then threw it across the room, shattering it."

The waitress brought our food and my dad had to look away from her so she wouldn't see the way his eyes had turned bright red.

When she left he continued. "You were discharged from the hospital that night. We tried to get you to go to sleep when we got home but you were so scared. You refused. It was three nights before you finally couldn't fight it anymore. And then you woke up screaming again. It was the same every time you slept."

I shook my head when he paused. "Stop," I whispered, my throat feeling tight and suddenly dry. "I know how the rest went."

His lip quivered slightly at this but I could see the relief in his eyes that he didn't have to say any more.

Neither of us said anything for several long minutes as we started to pick at our food. What do you say after a conversation like that? I could now see how the pieces of the puzzle were fitting together.

Emily had asked me what I had done to bring the nightmares on. She had tried to commit suicide and said she felt she had to do trials as punishment for it. It seemed *I* had not actually done anything to bring them on. My father had asked for more time with me and so, in exchange for that time, I was forced to stand trial every time I slept. It was nothing that I did that brought them on.

As terrible as this realization was I couldn't bring myself to be angry with my father. How was he supposed to have known that was what the trade would be? And would I have rather died? Two months ago I might have said yes. I couldn't say that anymore.

"So who is the special guy?" my dad asked. I could tell he was trying hard to turn the conversation back to a normal subject.

I gave him a quizzical look, wondering how he had known that there even was anyone. With a slightly embarrassed chuckle he pointed to the side of his neck. It took me a second to realize what he must have been talking about.

Blood rushed to my cheeks as I put a hand on the side of my neck to cover the slight bruising that was apparently there. I hadn't even thought to check for anything after Alex and I's little wrestling match in the sheets. I wasn't exactly experienced in that area so the thought had never even crossed my mind.

"Wow," I said with a chuckle, looking sheepishly up to meet my dad's eyes. Thankfully he was smiling. "That's embarrassing."

He just gave a little shrug. "I'm not totally oblivious. You're twenty now, Jess. There's bound to be some guy that catches your eye at some point."

I gave a smile, glad that after all the heavy conversation we had just had we could still return back to something normal. "His name is Alex," I said. I couldn't help smiling at even just saying his name.

"I'd ask if he's a nice guy but that seems pointless. I may not have been around you in the last four years but I know you well enough to know that you wouldn't tolerate being with someone who didn't treat you right."

"He's amazing," I said, half to myself. "He knows, well, not exactly everything, but most everything. It doesn't scare him. He's trying to help in any way he can."

"Sounds like you more than just like him," he said with a smile as he forked some potato salad into his mouth.

"Dad," I said with a laugh and shook my head. "You really want to talk about my love life?"

"Believe me," he said as he rolled his eyes. "It's better than talking to Amber about hers."

The rest of our meal was spent in light conversation, keeping all supernatural and any discussion of my mother out of the picture. I had to admit to myself, I had missed my father. He may not have fully understood the horror of what I had experienced my whole life, apparently because of him, but he tried. He didn't think I was totally crazy like my mother did. He was non-judgmental and I knew he loved me no matter what.

My father was tearful again when we said good-bye in front of the restaurant but there was hope in his eyes. I had given my promise that I would indeed call every once in a while and that I would be better about staying in touch. I tried to feel the same hope he did. I didn't know how though, considering I had no idea what it was Cole wanted and why I was sick. I had a horrible feeling in the pit of my stomach that the two were related somehow. They just couldn't be coincidence.

I got done a few minutes before Alex and I had agreed to meet so I took the extra time to go into the chocolate shop I had discovered last time I had been in Seattle. I rarely could justify the astronomical cost of just a few pieces of chocolate but the stress of everything that was going on was too much. Chocolate is a stress reliever to any woman.

I returned to our meeting spot and downed the decadent pieces far faster than I should have. I couldn't help it though.

Alex's beaming smile was impossible to miss through the mass of people as he walked toward me. I couldn't help but return it. When he finally reached me he wrapped his arms around my waist and pressed a kiss to my lips that had a little more passion behind it than was appropriate for being out in public. When he backed away half a step I looked around to make sure no one was watching. Unfortunately, there were a few. They looked away, shaking their heads as soon as I met their eyes.

"So," he said as he took my hand in his and started heading back to where we had parked the truck. "How did the meeting with your dad go?"

"Better than expected," I said with a satisfied nod. "It was actually really good to see him. It wasn't easy but I'm glad I saw him."

"So…" he dragged out the word. "Any chance I might get to meet him?"

"Um…no," I scrambled. "He's actually going back home. Tonight," I lied. "There was an emergency back home so they've basically had to cancel their trip." I hated the fact that I was lying to him so blatantly. I didn't know what else to do though.

Alex's nearly radiant expression dimmed just slightly at my answer but he simply shook it off with a shrug. "I'm sorry to hear that. But would you like to see now the idea I had in mind and the reason I asked you to pack an overnight bag?"

I bit my lower lip and looked up at his glowing face, nervous as to what he had planned and why he was so ecstatic all the sudden. "Sure," I said, trying to keep my voice excited as well. I wished I could feel the same excitement about our time together; there was just too much going on with too many sinister motivations.

CHAPTER TWENTY-EIGHT

The yacht we boarded at Lake Union was massive. The shocking thing was that there were still a few around that were slightly bigger. I could only imagine the amount of money they must have cost.

Apparently *"The Reward"* belonged to an old business partner of Alex's grandpa. The man had been close to Alex as well and had given him permission to use it for the night. According to Alex, the man had only used it once since he had bought it four years ago. It seemed silly to me. Such a waste of money.

I had to admit though, the boat was beautiful. There were several bedrooms and bathrooms throughout it. There were two main decks and a kitchen that was four times bigger than the one in my apartment. I was afraid to touch anything, paranoid I might break something or smudge it with my fingerprints.

We had made one stop before we came to the lake located just north of downtown. Alex was making dinner for us tonight and I had high hopes that my stomach would continue to cooperate like it had all day.

Alex was incredibly focused when he was in the kitchen so I knew it was going to be difficult to try and keep up a conversation with him. I didn't mind as I found myself alone on the upper deck. There was so much running through my mind, it was nice to have some time alone to try and sort my thoughts out.

I took a deep breath in and closed my eyes to the fading light. I tried to clear my head of anything but my senses of what was around me. I could hear traffic moving constantly around me, the symphony of the city. It wasn't obnoxious though. It wasn't a sound I was entirely used to. Things got so quiet on Lake Samish that it was a welcome change. I could smell the salt of the water, how it clung to the sides of the boats. A faint breeze had picked up in the last half hour or so and I had grabbed a light jacket. The air felt crisp and refreshing on my face and as it flooded my lungs.

Just as I was opening my eyes it felt as if a pair of steel bands wrapped around my chest, pinning my arms at my sides. Another closed over my mouth, sealing in the scream that wanted to escape my lips and making it impossible to breathe. My eyes shot around, looking for the source of my captivity but I saw nothing but my arms frozen at my sides.

"Scream and I will kill you and then I will kill him," a cool, even voice whispered into my ear. I knew the voice instantly. The tone and accent were unmistakable. My body instantly went limp, but the steel bands of his arms held me upright.

"You've been doing some things lately that have not made me very happy, Jessica," he breathed into my neck. I could feel his nose touching the skin just behind my ear. I shivered violently. "It's not a very good idea to upset me. I do bad things when I get upset." His last words came out as an angry hiss. I felt hot tears spring to my eyes.

"I happened to overhear the conversation you had with your daddy this afternoon. I half expected you to figure out my little secret sooner. I don't exactly fit in this world anymore. And I was so afraid your crazy little friend was going to figure it out and tell you. She knew there was something wrong. I had to take care of her before she exposed me."

Black spots were forming on the edges of my vision and my head started spinning. I could feel the vying arms of unconsciousness pulling at me, trying to drag me into another form of hell. I suddenly wished for it. It couldn't be any worse than this.

"I will make you a deal," Cole's invisible voice sliced into the night. "If you do exactly as I say I will let them live, your family, your precious little Sal. Perhaps even *Alex*," he drew his name out in a morbid and twisted way. It sent chills racing through my bones.

"Do we have a deal?"

I instantly nodded my head.

"I am going to need you to be the best little actress you can manage for me tonight," he said, his voice smooth and even. "You are going to pretend that everything is just fine and that I am not here. If you give any indication that something is wrong I will kill you both without hesitation. Is that clear?"

I nodded again, the dark spots in my vision growing bigger.

"Now," he continued. "Alex has another special little surprise for you tonight. He did a little shopping while you were meeting with dear ole daddy. To a rather expensive little jewelry store. He wants to ask you a four word question tonight."

I had a hard time keeping my thoughts straight enough to understand what it was exactly Cole was saying. It hit me with sudden force though. Alex had bought a ring while I was with my father. He was planning on proposing tonight.

The huge smile on Alex's face that afternoon and the way he nearly glowed seemed so obvious now. He had insisted I get that stupid ring earlier so he could get my ring size. And the way he kept playing with something in his pocket all afternoon, there must have been a little black box in it. The way he insisted I wear something so nice when it was just the two of us alone. It all made sense now. I had been so blind. How could I not have guessed?

"You have to prevent him from asking that question," Cole hissed. "I can't expect you to be *that* great of an actress. And you will insist that you need to get to bed as soon as you can manage without his suspecting anything is wrong. And you will go to bed *alone* tonight."

When he paused I nodded once again. It wasn't going to be easy. Of course Alex would wonder what was wrong when I insisted I needed to go to bed. That was something I never wanted to do. He would ask what was wrong and what he could do to help.

It wasn't going to be easy to do what Cole insisted on. But to save Alex's life I could manage it.

"I am going to release you now but be assured; I will not be far away. Remember, any scream or any indication that I am here and I *will* kill you both."

I nodded my head once more and I felt the impossibly strong arms that bound me release. My legs threatened to collapse from underneath me but I forced them to do their job, knowing that at any moment Alex could walk out here and wonder what was wrong.

Knowing that I wasn't going to be able to make them cooperate for long, I took a seat at the table on the deck. I took two deep breaths, trying to clear the black spots from my vision. The effort it took left me feeling even dizzier than I had felt before. I wiped at my eyes, glad I had not worn any mascara that would leave evidence of the tears that still wanted to spill down my cheeks.

"That's better," I heard a cold voice whisper into my ear. I couldn't help but shy away in the other direction. At this he chuckled, his voice fading into the background.

I felt almost composed enough to appear normal except for my hands that shook so violently I wasn't sure if I would even be able to hold a glass. I folded them in my lap, hoping it would still be a while before Alex was done cooking.

Less than two minutes later, Alex came out onto the dock, wheeling a fancy looking serving trolley behind him. He only flashed me a smile before he turned his attention to setting the table. I was overwhelmingly grateful for how intent he got when he was doing his culinary thing. It would only buy me a few more minutes but hopefully that was all I would need. It was all I was going to get.

After wheeling the trolley back inside, Alex joined me again at the table and immediately set to serving the food. I couldn't even bring myself to look at what he had cooked. Even though I was trying not to look into his face, afraid he would see past the careful façade I was putting on, I couldn't help but marvel at him. He had never looked so stunning than he looked wearing black trousers and a black dress shirt. He had just shaved before he started making dinner, his face perfectly smooth and his skin as close to flawless as it could be and still be human.

But it wasn't just the amazing exterior of this man that made me love him so much. If he knew what was truly going on right now I could only imagine what he might do. And I knew he would do it in less than a heartbeat because it would be for me. No wonder I wanted to spend the rest of my life with this man.

My heart gave a shuttering crack, knowing that was exactly how it was supposed to go tonight and now knowing that it was never going to happen.

He finished filling two tall glasses with something bubbly and handed one to me. He lightly touched his glass to mine then raised it just slightly.

"To a perfect day," he said softly with a smile.

I raised my glass a fraction and could only manage a smile before taking a sip of the sparkling cider. Thankfully my hands had managed to stop shaking enough for Alex not to notice.

Still not fully realizing what I was eating, I forked something into my mouth. I didn't taste anything but the texture seemed leafy. Just as I swallowed I felt the light brush of invisible feathers against my left arm. It took everything I had in me to not scream and jump away.

Alex seemed content to stay quiet as we ate our meal but unfortunately he seemed to want to stare into my face all night long. Under normal circumstances I would have loved the fact that he would want to but tonight it simply meant that I could not slip even for a moment.

As the meal progressed, I could feel the pressure of what I knew was coming and what I had to stop. I could only assume Alex would try and propose soon after we finished eating and we were now about to start dessert. My breathing came in shorter, shallower gasps as the minutes ticked by and the world felt tippy and unsteady. I was sure it had nothing to do with the fact that we were on a boat.

"Are you alright, Jessica?" Alex asked quietly as he looked sincerely into my face. "You look a bit pale and you've seemed really quiet all through dinner."

Here we go, I thought to myself.

"Actually I'm feeling a little off again. I guess I haven't completely kicked this thing yet," I said, trying not to lie as much as I dared to.

Alex gave a half smile, as he set his spoon down. "Yeah, I guess we probably did a little too much today considering. I'm sorry. I should have thought about that a little more."

I shook my head, feeling a sheen of sweat breaking out on my forehead. My hands suddenly felt incredibly clammy. "No, it's fine."

Alex's brow furrowed a bit as he looked at me closely. "Maybe you should go lay down for a bit," he said, his voice full of concern.

I felt a pair of cold, inhumanly strong hands settle on my shoulders, much too close to my neck for comfort. I was going to have to be careful. Alex apparently could already see some change coming over me.

"I think that might be a good idea," I managed to whisper, not meeting his eyes.

Alex nodded and stood, grabbing two of the plates from the table. "Why don't you go ahead and lay down and I will be down as soon as I get everything cleaned up?"

"No!" I half squeaked as I felt Cole's hands tighten on my skin. "I mean, I think it might be best if I'm alone for a while. My head is kind of pounding so I think I'm just going to turn the lights off and lay in the quiet for a while."

I could see two flashes of disappointment cross Alex's face. The first I could tell was just because I was refusing the only kind of help he knew how to offer. The second was a deeper, resolved sense of disappointment. He was realizing that a proposal tonight was not how he wanted it to happen. He would want everything to be perfect, not with me feeling sick and acting distant.

"Alright," he said. I could tell he was trying to sound positive. "Let me know if you need anything."

"Thank you," was all I could say.

A slim feeling of relief washed through me as I walked down a set of incredibly narrow stairs to the bedroom. The task Cole had assigned me was completed. I had acted as normal as possible, prevented Alex from proposing, and was headed to bed alone.

I could bear whatever Cole might have in store for me now so long as Alex was safe.

My body felt numb as I walked into one of the luxurious, but tiny, bedrooms. The door closed quietly behind me but not by my hands. Beads of sweat formed on my brow as I stood frozen.

The still invisible hands rested on either side of my bare forearms, slowly sliding up till they rested on either side of my neck. I felt the air rustle slightly as he breathed into my hair and felt his lips trail lightly against my ear.

"What do you want?" I barely managed to whisper. "Why are you here?"

"The answer to that question is the same thing," he said in a low voice. His right hand trailed from my neck, down my arm again, all the way down to my hip where he paused. "You."

My blood seemed to chill and come to a standstill as his words penetrated into my system. Of course that was why he was here. In truth I had known that all along. I had simply been unwilling to see it. What else could the reason possibly have been?

"Now," he continued, his right hand returning to a less insistent spot on my arm. "It's been a long day for you. Why don't you lie down and get some rest?"

He didn't wait for a response from me as he started pushing me toward the king sized bed. But even as he did so I felt myself hit a wall. Everything I had been dealing with was falling before me like a pile of bricks and I couldn't move past it. I was exhausted and my body was going to refuse to deal with any more tonight. I was going to have no choice but to sleep. My body was shutting down.

I could tell I wasn't thinking straight when I didn't feel afraid as I lay down on the expensive feeling bed. There was so much to be afraid of. For simple starters, I was always afraid to sleep. Secondly, I had a demented angel lying down next to me and he had threatened my life multiple times tonight. And he had admitted the reason he was here was for me. And thirdly, I still had no guarantee that Alex would be safe while I slipped into hell.

No, I wasn't thinking straight. The fear that was so familiar as of lately wasn't coming. I only wanted to sleep.

I didn't have to wait for more than a few seconds.

The bars that held me captive felt like a welcoming home, but I could not figure out why they felt so safe at the moment. I knew there was something I needed to hide from, something out there waiting for me beyond the normal of the terror of the trials. It sat at the edge of my mind, looming like a shadow that refused to reveal its true ugliness.

Adam's face was a welcome sight when he started walking down the tunnel toward me. While his face was never friendly, it at least was not frightening. His steely gray eyes held my own and I suddenly wondered why he had yet to go through a trial of his own. Why did he have to wait so long? I couldn't imagine he would be granted black eyes once he did finally make that closing step.

As he opened my cage and wrapped the golden cord around my wrists the feelings of comfort were erased and replaced by a surge of panic. I couldn't go out into the cylinder. There was something out there that I could not face, something terrible.

Adam's face remained expressionless as he pulled me to my feet and started tugging me down the tunnel toward the light. A small whimper slipped from my lips as I tried to plant my feet and refuse to move. It took him only one tug to make me stumble forward and get my feet moving.

"Please," I begged, my voice sounding muffled through the bag that covered my head. "Please."

This yielded no reaction and no response. Again I tried to stop, to drag us in the opposite direction but Adam pulled again on the golden chain. This time as I was yanked back toward the exit of the tunnel the chain dug painfully into my wrists. I didn't care though. I couldn't go out into the cylinder.

My muffled sobs grew louder and more hysterical as we neared the end of the tunnel and I had struggled against Adam's sure strength so much my skin had turned raw where the chain dug into it. A few small slashes had formed around them; tiny drops of blood smearing on my skin.

I gave one final plea as we erupted from the end of the tunnel onto the catwalk and knew it was too late. I couldn't go back once I was out here. There was never any going back.

Once he was sure I was in my place in the center of the narrow stone bridge, Adam turned and walked back into the dark safety of the tunnel, leaving me to face what I knew was coming.

I stood frozen, tiny drops of blood dripping down to my feet, my eyes transfixed on one of the elegantly carved stone chairs. I didn't bother to look around when I heard the rustling of wings and felt the air stir. I could not look away from that one seat.

A few all too short moments later, a glorious and perfect form settled into that seat and eyes blacker than night stared back at me.

I could not force any air in or out of my lungs as I beheld Cole's glorious form. It was as if I'd had a veil over my eyes every time I had looked at him before and only now was I seeing him clearly. His face was so gloriously beautiful and perfect it brought tears to my eyes and I felt my body go numb. It was difficult to make my brain comprehend it fully, the perfect form of his bare chest, the defined lines of his arms, the strong set of his chin. But the intensity of those black eyes, they burned into me with unstoppable force.

It took me a moment to register the dark smile that spread on his lips as he too seemed unable to look away from my face.

Despite my inability to look at anything other than Cole, I could feel the agitated state that hung in the air. Something was upsetting the other council members, upsetting them enough to distract them from their one single task of the trials. I had no doubt the reason was the more-than-man staring back at me.

The trial began and only when I heard the heckling laughter from below me rising did I finally snap out of my state of numbness. The full realization of everything that had happened hit me in the gut with incredible force.

Cole was indeed the escaped angel. He was the leader of the condemned. There was no denying this as I now looked upon him, seated in his position of power. The council members held their positions for a reason. The exalted members had led lives of purity and goodness, far better than the average person could even attempt to lead. The condemned members had led lives of murder, deceit, adultery, and every other despicable act one could and could not think of. And Cole was their leader.

"What do you want?!" The scream erupted from my throat with a shrill force that would have surprised me if I hadn't been in such a fury. "Leave me alone! Make it stop!"

A look of shock crossed most of the council member's faces as they watched my eruption. They glanced around at each other, each seeming to wonder exactly what to do. Twisted laughter ricocheted off the walls and hundreds of fingers pointed at me as I struggled with the golden cord that bound my hands. Blood dripped faster and faster to the floor as I fought against the beautiful but deadly cord.

Two angels landed on either side of me and I barely even noticed one had blue eyes and the other black. They each took hold of one of my arms and forced me to straighten and face the council. I continued to scream and thrash but the leader of the exalted only proceeded with the trial.

The entire council seemed unsure of what exactly to do with themselves as they squirmed in their seats, looking anxiously back and forth occasionally from me to Cole.

When the trial started to come to a close I had no idea of what the outcome was going to be. I didn't care. I simply wanted to get out of there, to get away from Cole's smug smile and penetrating eyes.

"Down," said one council member.

"Up," said another.

The next few took quite a long time as they considered where whoever it was I stood trial for was to be sent. There were four up's and four downs. My screams turned to more of a whimper as I considered what would be coming if this person were to be condemned.

Cole and the other condemned council member gave their verdicts. It seemed it should have been impossible but the screams came out of me with a new intensity and ferocity as I fought with everything I had to get away from the grasps of my two captors.

With a powerful burst of his wings, Cole launched from his seat toward the catwalk. As he landed, I fought with every ounce of strength I had to fall off the catwalk but to no avail. Surprisingly though, Cole waved my captors away and they flew back to their positions on the stairwell.

Cole's black eyes locked with my own and my screaming and thrashing ceased. It was nearly impossible to look away. I felt as if my entire soul were being sucked out of my own eyes and drawn into his.

I did not even notice how Cole was standing only inches away from me or how the council squirmed all the more, a few quiet protests coming from their direction.

"This is all going to end soon you know," Cole whispered, his voice surprisingly gentle. "The number of trials you must stand in for are limited. When it is time for your own branding, I can make sure it isn't as bad as it could be."

He raised a hand, reaching under the sack over my head and smoothed his thumb over my cheek, his expression surprisingly gentle and he continued his intense gaze.

I was vaguely aware that another angel had landed next to us and that Cole had reached for the red-hot rod. He placed a hand on my shoulder and with next to no effort, made me bend and get on my hands and knees. My mind seemed to be on a standstill as the hair fell away from my neck.

The breath caught in my throat as the scream tried to escape when the iron was pressed into the back of my neck. My vision went black for several seconds and my head spun violently as the pain ripped through me. My arms and legs refused to work anymore and I collapsed onto the cold and bloodied stone. The only thought that processed was pain and that I wanted to die right then and there.

A pair of firm but gentle hands raised me to my feet and my vision slowly returned. It remained unfocused however, and my head lolled slightly from shoulder to shoulder.

"Judgment has been placed," I heard a beautiful voice say, though I could not make my eyes find the source of it.

My skin crawled for a moment before I could feel the flesh tearing in my back. The beautiful wings that I loathed erupted forth but this was nothing compared to the pain that was radiating from the back of my neck.

I did not even hear the laughter from the condemned ones, though I knew it was there, but I did see them spring from their seats and launch themselves toward us.

Before they were even halfway there, Cole wrapped his arms around me and tipped us over the side of the walkway.

CHAPTER TWENTY-NINE

When I woke it wasn't just my neck that hurt. My entire body felt as if it had been hit by a semi-truck, pulled through gravel mixed with shards of glass, and then dropped off a ten story building. My head throbbed so fiercely it felt as if a few of those shards of glass had to be protruding into my skull. As my brain sorted out all of the pain, my stomach heaved and I just managed to roll to my side, the contents of my stomach shooting into a bucket that was unexpectedly on the floor.

With a sharp intake of breath, I rolled back onto my back. Every movement sent new, raw shots of pain pulsing through my veins.

It took me a few moments before I realized I didn't know where I was and I felt sure I was not in the same place I had been when I'd fallen asleep last. Opening my eyes as little as possible, I looked at my surroundings.

There was very little light in the room. There did not appear to be any windows and the only light that did come into the room streamed in from a door that was open on the far wall. The room seemed to be bare of anything besides the bed I was lying on and a simple wooden kitchen chair. As far as I could tell the walls were plain white and I couldn't see the floor.

"The time I first saw you," I heard Cole's voice at the foot of the bed and watched as he stood, then took a seat on the chair. "I knew I had to have you. It was so strong, the drive, it nearly drove me mad."

I glared at Cole, sitting so relaxed with one ankle crossed over the other knee. I had never truly hated anyone in my life but hate could not even come close to being the right word for how I felt about Cole.

"It should have been easy to find you, for us to be together. Had you been the person who was on trial I should have simply had to go into the depths of hell and look for you. There wouldn't have been anywhere for you to hide. But when I saw you I knew there was something different. You were so frightened and yet you seemed to know exactly what to expect. None of the other council members seemed to notice you were not who you were supposed to be. But I knew something was wrong as soon as I looked into your beautiful face."

My body started shaking as hate and disgust flooded through me. I wanted to make him stop. I didn't want to hear what he was saying, to know the full truth of how he had come after me from a reality that should not have been real.

"It was then that I decided I had to have you for myself. It took me a little while but I figured out a way to follow you back into the world of the living. It was so strange, being back. The world has changed a lot since I last walked it. I suppose a lot should change in a few hundred years."

My mind was so twisted with fury I could not even make myself comprehend what his last few sentences meant.

Cole sat forward, resting his elbows on his knees. He stared into my face for what could have been a few intense seconds or several long minutes, I wasn't sure. His eyes were so severe, I could not look away. They drew me in, called to me like water would to a man who had been stranded in a desert for days without it.

I snapped my eyes closed and turned my head away. Something was wrong with those eyes. They did strange things to my thinking and I didn't like it. There was a power behind them that was all the more evidence he was not human anymore.

"You're dying, Jessica," Cole said, his voice hard and clear. When he didn't say anything else I looked back at him, trying to be careful to not lock eyes with him again. His eyes were hard, his jaw clenched, his fists knotted into balls that rested on his knees.

"I'm sick," I said with disgust in my voice as I struggled to sit up a bit. "That doesn't mean I'm dying."

"Actually it does," Cole said, his voice low. "You remember that lovely little conversation you had with your father yesterday? Everything he said was the truth. You were dying when you were a child. He made a plea to have more time with you and that plea was heard.

"You've been living on borrowed time for the last fifteen years but that time is quickly running out. Do you remember what your father said was wrong with you when you were a child?"

I didn't want to consider what Cole was saying but I couldn't help but recall the conversation. My father had said I'd had a horrible fever, chills, headaches, body aches, I couldn't eat anything without throwing up. Exactly like I was experiencing now.

"The same thing is happening again. Like I said, you've been living on borrowed time in exchange for standing trials. Time is up though. You don't have long left now. You're already becoming more like me with every passing day."

I didn't have to wonder for long what he had meant by that.

"You don't normally need to sleep for as long as people do. As an angel, I never sleep, nor do I eat. My needs are not the same. I know how everything looks so disorienting and clear to you now, it's the same with your hearing, but this is how it is for me always. You are making the gradual transformation into what you should have become fifteen years ago."

I closed my eyes as the room started tilting. I wanted to deny what he was saying, to tell him he was wrong. The most frightening thing was that everything he was saying made impossible sense. Things like this should never make sense.

"You will be standing your own trial in not too long. Do you know where you will be judged to go when that time arrives?" Excitement seemed to be rising in his voice as Cole continued.

"You should know as well as any council member that it takes a life of good living to be exalted. Are you sure you've done enough?"

He paused a moment as if to let me consider his question. I squeezed my eyes closed and shook my head, trying with everything I had to block out what he was saying.

I heard the chair squeak slightly and a moment later felt the bed shake as Cole sat on the edge of it.

"I can guarantee the after-life will not be as horrible as it could be if you agree to one simple thing. Stay with me. Give yourself to me as I wish to give myself to you. I can even get you into a position of power if that is what you want. A seat on the council is yours if you simply agree to be with me and me alone."

He picked up my hand that lay limply at my side. He brushed two fingers from my forearm down to my own fingers. A strange tingling sensation shot through my veins though it was not at all the repulsive recoiling sensation I was used to when Cole touched me. It was quite the opposite and before I even allowed myself to do so, I wished he would do it again.

"I can make you a *very* happy woman, Jessica," he whispered. I could feel his intense eyes burning into my face but I could not look away from the hand that held my own. He traced his fingers up and down again and I shuddered from the pleasant sensation.

"Hell's not that bad," I was startled by how close Cole's whisper was, his lips brushing against my ear.

His last words shook my head clear and I jerked my hand out of his. "I may believe you that I might be dying," I hissed as I finally met his eyes again, feeling the fire that burned behind them as the hatred poured out of me. "And if I am, so be it. But I will not be your queen of the condemned. I'd rather be a lowly, unimportant damned angel than your lover in hell."

Cole's expression was hard for a moment but quickly melted into a smug smile. "We shall see," he said before he rose and walked toward the door. "I would consider my offer very seriously, Jessica. I am not lying when I say you only have days left. Don't wait too long."

With that he left and I could hear him lock the door from the outside. I was plunged into darkness, locked in a prison with no windows and the leader of damned angels as my keeper.

X

There was no way to mark time as it passed other than a general guess from how often I was sleeping. This was happening frighteningly more and more often and I guessed that I was sleeping nearly once a day. The trials were happening all too frequently, though Cole did not return to them again.

Another form of altered consciousness was taking over me as my condition worsened progressively. I did not recognize what it was at first. It started only as a feeling of loss, of feeling like I had lost everything that mattered most in the world to me. It was difficult to tell that this strong, overwhelming feeling of despair was not completely coming from me. While I had no guarantee that those I loved the most were safe, I had given Cole no reason to hurt them. I had to believe that they were safe.

The hallucinatory visions soon followed. They were so strong and so vivid it was difficult to believe that they were not real. I wasn't entirely convinced that they weren't real in some way.

The first ones were of Alex. After searching for me for so long he had given up hope. His despair was heart wrenching as I watched him cry out my name, watched him sit awake in the dark at night. I wanted to call out to him, to assure him that everything would be alright.

His grief couldn't last forever though. The visions that came next were of Alex meeting another woman and quickly falling in love. He gave the ring he had bought for me to her.

I saw Sal, alone and scared in the mental institution. The staff was telling her that she had to leave and go home. They also told her that I had gone missing and that they presumed that I was dead. When Sal was alone in her room on what was to be the last night of her stay, she took her razor, ripped it apart till she could get the blades out, crawled into the tub, and slit her wrists. The staff found her the next morning.

The phone rang in my parent's familiar home and my mother answered it. They told her the same thing Sal had been told. My mother did not even look sad. No tears of grief spilled onto her face.

The most horrifying thing about these visions was the very real possibility of them having actually happened. Alex shouldn't have to grieve over me for forever, no matter how much it shattered my heart into a million pieces to imagine him being with someone else. What was to keep Sal from actually attempting suicide when she heard that her one true friend was gone forever? And as depressing as it sounded, it was not hard to believe that my mother wouldn't cry over the un-confirmable possibility of my death.

I tried to keep reality separated from what I hoped wasn't. What would Alex think happened to me? Would he have any reason to suspect kidnapping? It would have been difficult for someone to sneak onto the yacht and take me, without me making any kind of sound. Would Alex think I had left him in the middle of the night? I had no reason to think Cole didn't leave some sort of note for Alex, telling all kinds of horrific lies.

And Sal? I guessed she had about a week left in the institute before they would make her leave. What would happen to her after that? And when they couldn't get a hold of me? I could only hope that somehow Alex might be able to help her and possibly take over my role in her life. She seemed to like Alex enough.

Thinking of such devastating reality seemed to make my condition spiral downward all the faster. Pain was a constant companion; my skin burned fiercely with the fever while its polar opposite of chills shook my body uncontrollably. I had not eaten since I had last seen Alex, though I had no desire to do so.

I couldn't deny what Cole told me. I was dying and I knew it.

My thoughts wandered on their own accord, in an attempt to distract myself from the pain, to future possibilities. What life would become if I truly had lost and would lose everything and everyone important to me. I did not even have the strength of mind to block out the thoughts of Cole's offer.

Taking everything and everyone else out of the picture, would it really be so horrible to be with Cole? He could be charming and flattering and obviously he had feelings enough for me to go to so much trouble to come after me. Certainly an eternity of looking into the perfection of his face couldn't be so terrible.

I considered something else he had said as well. He was right; it took a lifetime of good living to be exalted. People in general were good but it was so easy to do something to condemn yourself. Had I done enough to gain blue eyes? What true good had I done with my life? I had abandoned my family years ago and lost most care for them. I had shut everyone out of my life. I had been selfish enough to drag Alex into this mess. I may not have been a criminal but what had I done with my life to better those around me? If I was to receive my own branding, certainly it would be better to be with Cole than to be one among the thousands, tens of thousands?

Cole *had* said that hell wasn't that bad.

Thoughts of Cole filled my head more and more frequently. I found myself pondering over his perfect features over and over. The strong set of his jaw, the straight line of his nose, those intense eyes. Any athlete would have traded his soul for Cole's body and build.

The memory of Cole's touch haunted me in a nearly painful way. I wanted him to touch me like that again. I wanted to feel his skin against mine again, just for the thrill it gave me.

Imaginings of what the possibilities could be with Cole consumed me. I thought of lying under a blanket of stars, wrapped in those impossibly strong arms and knowing they would never, ever have to let me go. I pictured how his hands would trace up and down my arms, wrap around my waist. How his lips would feel against my own.

The sound of his voice flooded my ears, telling me over and over how he loved me as no other man could love a woman. He told me of how he would do and had done everything he had to to be with me. He whispered how beautiful I was and that he never wanted to be with another woman in the rest of his existence.

As time continued to pass I did not know what was real anymore and what was not. My state of consciousness was so loose I could not tell if Cole was really there, beside me on the bed, whispering those words to me, touching me in the ways I longed for, or if it was only a figment of my imagination. It didn't seem to matter anymore. The feelings of unreality were better than the pain that ripped through me.

CHAPTER THIRTY

After what had to have been at least a week, pain sank into every corner of my body and it was all I could do to not scream out. No pleasant visions filled my head and all I could think of was the fact that I just wanted it to be over. I was tired of the slow descent toward death.

My brain did not even register the sound of the door being unlocked or the way light spilled into the room. I barely even noticed when the bed shook just slightly. An all too audible sigh slipped out of me though when the hands I had wished for softly traced down from my temple to my jaw.

"It will be over soon," the beautiful voice said. My eyes searched crazily for the face I longed to see. Everything around me seemed so blurry but when I finally found his face it cleared. I could see every devastatingly beautiful feature of him.

His face seemed sad, all too serious. A face like that should never look sad. I wanted to reach out and touch it, to tell him that everything was okay, but something inside of me knew it wasn't. I also couldn't muster the strength to lift even my fingers.

"The time is fast approaching. You must make the decision," he whispered. "Are you willing to risk that we might not be able to be together? That you might be taken away from me?"

My brow furrowed as he said this. I didn't like talk like that. Of course we should be together. I should listen to everything he said. He loved me. Everything he had done thus far was evidence of that. I gave a slight shake of the head, all I could manage through the pain.

With this Cole's eyes brightened a bit, his jaw unclenched just slightly. "There is something you must do before it happens, before you go. We must guarantee we will be able to be together. We must not take that risk, right?"

My head felt muddled and clouded as I shook my head again.

"You have to make sure where you will be placed," he said, his voice low and serious sounding. I felt something cold being placed in my hand, like metal of some kind. "The pain doesn't have to keep going on. You can make it stop and make certain that we will be together at the same time."

I lifted my head slightly to see the object that rested in my hand. It was small, hard, and a shiny silver color. The barrel curved beautifully and perfectly and the trigger begged for me to pull it. To end it all.

My eyes never left the gun, even as Cole rose again and left. Even when I was plunged back into darkness I continued to stare through the dark at where I knew it was in my hand.

He was right. I didn't have to keep suffering through the pain like this. I didn't have to deal with the sickness, the chills and the fever. And if I chose to end it all I could guarantee that Cole and I would be together. That was what I wanted, wasn't it?

I felt as if a heavy drug had been placed into my system and that drug was telling me that this was of course what I wanted. It weighed me down and made me feel sluggish. But it was so strong, I had a hard time fighting with it, telling it that I wasn't sure if that *was* what I wanted.

The gun sat in my hand, a comforting and yet terrifying weight. My head continued to spin and my body raged with aches but I couldn't bring myself to take that final step. I wanted for it to be over with but I did not feel ready to move on. There seemed to be something else I needed to do, something I needed to take care of.

As I struggled to clear my head, I thought of the reason I needed to wait, even for just another day or so. I needed to make sure those I loved would be safe when I left them behind. I had to get a reassurance from Cole.

I was anxious for Cole to come back into my room but thankfully I did not have to wait long.

"I've decided," I croaked, my voice sounding almost inhuman. "I'll do it. I'm ready for it to be over. But I need to know that they are safe. Is my family safe?"

Cole's look was triumphant as he took my hand in his. "Of course. They are safe at home; no harm has come to them."

"And Sal," I strained to keep my voice loud enough to be heard. "I need to see her before I go. I have to make sure she will be taken care of."

Cole's expression became serious as he considered this. He did not say anything for a good half a minute. "Alright," he nodded. "If you give me your promise, I will take you to see her in the morning. It's too late at night right now."

I felt that strange fog press more heavily on my mind but I only nodded, my lips unwilling to say the words I was still unsure about.

"Get some rest," he whispered as he stroked his hand along my cheek, sending the wonderful tingles shooting through my skin. "I will take you in the morning."

The next morning I woke feeling like a new woman despite the trial I had just experienced. While I still did not feel perfectly healthy, my body only slightly ached, the chills did not shake me and my skin felt almost normal temperature. The world did not tilt in sickening ways.

For the first time since I had come to be in my room, Cole let me out. I was not allowed to go far though. I walked out of my room and he helped me as I walked a few feet down the hall to a bathroom. The light was blinding and disorienting after sitting in the dark for days and days.

After Cole left me in the bathroom, I looked around to see he had set out soap and the necessities to wash my hair. There was also a stack of familiar looking clothes sitting on the counter. I began to wonder how he had gotten them but realized it would have been only all too easy for him to obtain them. No one would have seen him enter the house to retrieve them, even if they were looking straight at him.

The water felt like new life washing over me as I stood in the shower. My body suddenly felt disgusting and wasted. I had trouble even recalling when the last time I had showered was. At the same time, I realized I had not even needed the use of a bathroom since I had woken up here.

While I was reluctant to turn the water off, I was even more anxious to see Sal, as Cole had promised. I finished getting ready as quickly as possible.

When I emerged from the steamy bathroom, Cole was sitting at the bottom of a flight of steps that led to an unseen place. His expression was calm and I had no way to guess what thoughts were behind those captivating eyes.

"How do you feel?" he asked as he rose and stood before me. He placed his hands on the sides of my arms, rubbing up and down them slightly.

"Wonderful," I said.

"You should get some rest for a while," he said, his eyes suddenly burning into mine with intensity.

With those words the world went dark.

I woke from wonderful visions of Cole and I on a sandy beach to the pleasant softness of his voice in my ear, calling to me to wake. His eyes were intense as always yet soft in a way that threatened to melt me into butter at any moment.

"We are here," he said softly as he pushed a bit of hair out of my face.

I sat up straight, realizing we were in Cole's car, sitting in the parking lot of the institute.

"I will give you as much time as you need," he said, his voice low and intimate as he continued to look into my face. "Call me at this number when you are finished." He handed me a slip of paper. I didn't even look at it as I slipped it into my pocket.

Cole reached across me and pushed my door open. Without a second thought I stepped out into the grey, overcast day.

I was glad to see that the halls and front desk were deserted as I walked straight toward Sal's room. After giving three sharp taps on the door, I let myself in.

I did not see Sal right away when I entered the room and was almost panicked that she might not even be in here when I remembered Sal's old tendencies. After a moments search I found her curled into a ball with a blanket pulled over her head at the foot of the bed on the floor. She startled awake as I uncovered her.

"Jessica?" she whispered sleepily.

"Yeah, it's me," I whispered as I sat on the floor next to her, leaning my tender frame against the wall.

Sal struggled to disentangle herself from the blanket as she sat up. She rested her back against the bed, staring at me long and hard.

"You look terrible," she said quite clearly after a moment. "Like my cousin who used to do drugs, kind of," she sounded like her normal self an instant later.

I couldn't help but chuckle a little. Inside, my thoughts tried to clear and a faint voice tried to tell me how I *felt* a bit like I was on drugs.

"Is everything okay, Jessica?" Sal asked, her expression full of concern.

I didn't answer her immediately as that small voice in the back of my head tried to tell me something else. It was too faint to hear it. "It will be soon," I replied.

She seemed confused at my reply but I continued before she could ask any questions.

"I need you to request that your caretaker be switched to Alex," I said suddenly, unsure of the best way to word everything I needed to say. "He can help you with everything you need like I have."

"Why?" Sal asked, her voice sounding slightly hurt.

"Because," I said with a sigh. "I have to go away. I have to leave." This seemed the easiest way to put things. "Besides, you will be going home soon."

"No!" Sal said too loudly as she shook her head violently. "I can't! He's there; he knows where to find me!"

"Cole is leaving too," I said softly, not quite meeting Sal's eyes. "He will be gone soon so you can go home."

I could feel her eyes boring into my face but I could not bring myself to look at her.

"He's a bad man, Jessica. You can't go with him. You can't trust him."

I still couldn't look at her. "We have to leave. We can't stay."

She looked at me for a long time without saying anything. She was abnormally still as she considered what I had said. "I don't understand."

I didn't say anything for a while. Feeling stiff and sore, I slid across the floor to sit beside her. I put one arm around her shoulders and gave her a squeeze. "I am so happy to have met you Sal," I said, my voice low as I tried to keep tears out of it. "You've been one of the best friends I've ever had. I am going to miss you so much but I know Alex will take good care of you."

Sal continued her quizzical stare. "I don't understand," she repeated. "Don't leave. I don't want you to go."

A tear spilled down my cheek as I squeezed my eyes closed. "I have to. I don't have any choice. My time here is up."

"I don't understand," Sal whispered again, her bottom lip trembled slightly as tears of her own spilled onto her cheeks.

I met Sal's eyes and the tears poured down my face freely. "I have to go now," I whispered. "You know I love you, Sal."

She shook her head but with a tearful voice said "And I love you too."

Knowing that if I were to stay any longer I would be in danger of having a total meltdown, I placed a kiss on Sal's forehead and climbed numbly to my feet. I hesitated in the doorway. Sal's expression was so confused; seeing the tears running down her face sent a fresh wave of my own down my cheeks. "Good-bye," I said quietly.

I closed the door behind me and again glad there was no one around, I tried to wipe the moisture from my face. Without even looking in a mirror I knew I wasn't a pretty sight. Crying did horrible things to my face, combined with what being sick had done to my body, I was terrifying. I did not even know the person who had looked back at me in the mirror this morning. She was a skeleton, a ghost of the happy woman I had been just a few short weeks before.

It only took a few minutes for Cole to reach the institute after I called him. I didn't look into his face as I climbed into the passenger seat. My eyes didn't focus on much of anything and my mind couldn't seem to either.

"Can we just drive for a while?" I heard myself ask. "Just for a while?"

I didn't see Cole nod nor did he say anything but the car rolled forward and pulled onto the street.

The passing of the buildings behind us was numbing in a comforting way for some reason. I didn't know why I had made my request. Bellingham had been a refuge I had fled to I supposed but I felt no burning need to say goodbye to the city.

Eventually civilization fell behind us and Cole turned down a road that did not look well-traveled. The evergreens towered above us, growing thicker and thicker the farther we drove. Springy ferns started growing closer and closer to the road. A heavy mist descended from the sky, thick enough that Cole had to turn the windshield wipers on low.

The pavement fell away to gravel after a while, forcing Cole to drive slower as the road curved around. Eventually it ended with a parking lot that consisted only of two logs to indicate where to park. There was a short grassy stretch of a few feet before it gave way to small rocks that faded into the water.

My mind was blank as I opened the door and let myself out of the car. Cole remained perfectly still as he watched me walk out toward the ocean.

I didn't bother looking around for a large rock or a log to sit on. The gravel seemed dry enough, though I didn't particularly care, so I sat right down, the ocean lapping just a few inches from my toes. I stared out over the misty water to the green forms that loomed barely above it. I didn't come to the ocean often but from looking at a map once I knew the closest island I could see was Lummi, owned by a tribe of Indians, behind that was Orcas Island, and somewhere beyond that was Vancouver Island. I had been so close to them for nearly two years and had still never taken the trip out to visit any of the San Juan Islands that littered the space between the mainland and the huge Canadian island.

I closed my eyes and inhaled deeply, relishing in the strong sent of ocean life. I faintly heard the horn of a ferry sound off in the distance, trying to give warning to any smaller boats that might be hidden in the mist. I dug my hands into the stones and sand beneath me, enjoying the feeling of Mother Nature.

A small sense of closure had settled on me since I left the institute. I knew Sal would be alright. She would be confused and hurt but she would be fine. Cole had assured me that my family was safe. I had no reason to think that Emily might be in any immediate trouble. But there was still one very important person I had no guarantee about.

I had been very careful in not saying anything about Alex to Cole. A part of me knew that this was best, to keep my mouth shut. I had to think that Alex would be safer if he was left out of everything. I could never go completely satisfied, not knowing that he would be alright, but I had to believe he would be. Alex could take care of himself.

CHAPTER THIRTY-ONE

Eventually the mist turned into a light rain and it did not take long to soak me through. I wasn't sure if it was because of getting wet or if it was just the afterlife calling to me again, but my body started to tremble with chills, the aches slowly crept back into my limbs and my head started to throb.

I couldn't fight this any longer. It had to end.

The rain was suddenly blocked from my skin as something warm was wrapped around my shoulders.

"It's time," a beautiful voice said softly.

I could only nod.

Strong hands helped me to my feet but I didn't look Cole in the face as he helped lead me back to the car. The heat that blasted out of the vents couldn't do anything to calm the chills that shook me with incredible force now.

The tires found their way back to the pavement and the city came back into view then fell away again as we traveled south. It took a while before I registered we were going back to the lake. My suspicions were confirmed as we pulled into Cole's driveway. He had been holding me in his own home, just two doors down from my own. I couldn't bring myself to feel any emotion about it though. That was just the way it was; it didn't matter now.

With his hand on the back of my shoulder, Cole quickly led me out of the rain and into the house. The house seemed unnaturally dark for being early afternoon, all the lights were off and most of the drapes had been pulled shut.

As we started our descent down the stairs, I barely even noticed the few shards of broken glass that lay strewn on the floor before the back door.

We both froze at the bottom of the stairs, looking at the doorway of my room. Light was streaming through the door into the hall. Even though I had slipped out of consciousness before we had left earlier, I knew Cole would not have left the light on in there. He had never turned it on.

Cole's grip tightened at the back of my neck and I heard his teeth grind together as we stepped into the doorway.

My knees wobbled, threatening to collapse as I took in Alex standing in the room. In one hand was clutched the dirty clothes I had been wearing when I disappeared from the yacht, in the other hand was the shiny silver gun.

There was a long moment where everyone seemed to be frozen, each unsure of what exactly to do. It was Alex who broke the silence.

"It wasn't hard to figure out what had happened after I finally reached Jessica's father and talked to Sal this morning," his intensely blue eyes stared into my own as he spoke. I saw the emotions play across his face, terror, relief, horror.

Alex's words seemed to have shaken Cole from his stupor. With a hiss, he shoved me aside, knocking me to my hands and knees. His body seemed to shake for a moment before his shirt suddenly ripped into shreds. A pair of beautifully dangerous wings burst from his skin.

Seeing Cole standing there, in the real world, in his true form, was the most terrifying experience of my life. The thousands of times he had grinned in glee as he pressed the brand into my skin flashed through my head. The sound of the demented laughter that I had heard from him and those who were in his charge filled my thoughts. And Alex was in the same room with him, standing directly in his path.

These thoughts all passed through my head in only a moment. That was all it took for the wings to coil and launch Cole at Alex.

I didn't even hear my own scream as Alex and Cole collided into the far wall, just to the side of the bed. The sheetrock buckled beneath the force, dust exploding from the wall as they slid to the floor. Cole was on his feet again in a movement that was too fast to see. He grabbed the front of Alex's shirt and launched him across the room. Alex's body hit the space where the ceiling and wall met, the wall again crumpling, before he dropped to the floor.

Sobs and screams erupted from my chest as I tried to crawl over to Alex. He was struggling to sit upright, shaking his head as he briefly met my eyes, trying desperately to warn me to stay away.

As Cole slowly made his way across the room, I realized with horror there was a spot in Alex's left arm that was bulging in the wrong direction. Blood covered his face as it poured from his nose.

341

"You couldn't just leave her alone, could you?" Cole hissed as he reached for Alex again. He picked Alex up like a rag doll and slammed his body into the wall twice before he threw him across the room again.

Alex didn't move for a second that felt like a century. Then he rolled onto his side and he struggled to prop himself up on his good arm. He winced at the motion and even though he said nothing, I could see the pain that was in his eyes. I realized with horror one of his legs was resting at an angle that was just slightly off from what should have been possible.

"I will never give up on her," Alex said with clenched teeth as he glared at Cole. "You have no idea what real love is."

Cole crossed the room in three steps, this time grabbing Alex by the throat, pinning him against the wall.

"It's too late for her," Cole whispered, his nose only inches from Alex's. "You can't save her. I can give her something you never could."

Alex's hands, which had been clawing uselessly at Cole's, stilled for a moment. "That's where you're wrong," he choked, his eyes burning with intensity as he met Cole's livid stare. "I made a deal," I barely heard the words as Alex hissed them.

Cole's expression suddenly went blank. Slowly a look of realization, anger, fear, and defeat all mixed on his face.

"No," he quietly hissed.

"It's true," Alex whispered. "And you know there is nothing you can do about it."

Cole's face distorted with an emotion beyond anger. "No!" he screamed into Alex's face. He slammed Alex's head against the wall, leaving a dent behind it. I could see Cole's knuckles turn white and my screams poured out of me as I crawled across the floor.

With a sickening snap that filled the room, Alex's struggling form suddenly went limp.

With one final heave, Cole threw Alex's still body across the room, where it crumpled into a heap just behind the door.

I sat frozen on the floor as the world fell silent and seemed to stand still. I held my breath as I waited for Alex's chest to rise and fall, for him to stir in anyway. He didn't.

Cole looked from Alex's body to my face. As I looked back at him I didn't feel fear, I didn't feel anger. I couldn't feel anything. The perfect features now only seemed to emphasize the truth of what he was. His face twisted in anger that reflected the monster within.

Without saying a word, he turned to the door and walked out, his wings trailing behind him.

X

I held Alex's limp, cooling body in my arms for hours. The full truth of what had happened had still not hit. My body felt numb, I stayed detached from it; no emotions filled me. In truth I was probably in shock.

I didn't realize at first how the chills had disappeared, my body relaxed, my head had stopped pounding completely. My strangely enhanced vision and hearing seemed to still be intact and with how my head had stopped spinning the effect was amazing. It was hours before I realized that I felt perfectly normal again. Better than normal. At least that was how my body felt. Inside, I was beyond broken.

Eventually as I caressed Alex's cheeks, felt how they were no longer warm, felt the heat of his strong hands disappear, cold, cruel reality started to sink in.

Alex was dead. Cole had killed him.

The tears began first, building in intensity as they rolled down my face and spilled onto the top of Alex's head as I cradled it against my chest. Small sobs bubbled from my lips and grew into cries of agony and torment.

Through my grief I couldn't understand what had just happened. What had Alex's final few words meant? He had made a deal? There was nothing Cole could do about what? And why had Cole suddenly left after? Why didn't he just finish me off?

As no answers came, I realized something else. I had felt as if I had been under the influence of some kind of drug the last week or so. In a way I had. The feelings I thought I was having toward Cole, my strange, resigned behavior, it had all come from Cole. He had planted those feelings in me, made me see those awful visions of Alex and Sal. Planted things that weren't real about Cole and I into my head.

One thing I knew he had been telling the truth about though. I had indeed been dying. Now I wasn't.

The last traces of even room-temperature warmth faded from Alex's skin and it started to turn cold. The reality that Alex would never hold me in his arms again, never make another light hearted joke, never flash me his brilliant smile again was too much.

I was hysterical as I mourned over the loss of the man I loved more than I would have ever thought it was possible to love someone. Screams and wails poured from me and my crying did not stop when the tears ran out. Anger, frustration, sorrow, and pain ran though me, pounding me like a train wreck.

When I finally quieted on the outside, there were a few thoughts that kept running through my head, over and over. I couldn't go on without him. What was the point of living if the person I loved the most was gone?

As if in answer to my question, something shiny from across the room caught my attention. I crawled across the blood streaked floor toward it, sitting in front of it as I gently picked it up.

The gun had seemed so inviting before when Cole had given it to me. It had promised to end all the pain. While it was a different kind of pain now, it seemed to promise the same thing.

I sat with shaking hands holding the gun. Even though they shook, I felt suddenly very calm inside. I knew there was no way I could continue on now. There was no *point* in going on. The decision was so simple to make.

Without breathing, I raised the gun. The cool feeling of the barrel against my temple was calming and comforting. It would all be over soon. I wouldn't have to think about anything but my own branding in just a moment. I had endured plenty of those, this would be easy.

Taking a deep breath, I squeezed the trigger.
Click.

It took me a moment to realize what happened as the sound died. I drew the gun away and opened the chamber. It was empty. I then realized it felt lighter then when Cole had first given it to me. It was as if someone was trying to play a cruel, sick joke on me by emptying the gun that had held my only escape.

The gun dropped to the floor with a thud and a fresh wave of tears consumed me. The reality of what I had almost done and what I now couldn't do hit me like a ton of bricks. My head dropped to my knees as I pulled them into my chest, my shoulders shaking as I let the tears have me.

CHAPTER THIRTY-TWO

I was acutely aware of the sound of rustling wings as it disrupted the silence. I nearly sighed in relief. Cole had come back to finish me off.

I didn't turn around to see him come. I didn't want to look into those eyes again, to run the risk that he might make me feel things again that weren't real. I kept my back to him, wishing he would simply get it over with as quickly as possible.

The approach of the sound of rustling wings was hesitant, almost unsure as I heard it come across the room. This seemed strange; Cole was never hesitant about anything.

I felt the brush of feathers on one of my arms and I tried not to shudder. There were more rustling sounds, as if he was crouching behind me. I felt a warm hand touch my shoulder and a tear rolled down my cheek again as familiar sensations flooded through me. The touch was so warm, too familiar on a soulful level and yet I knew that touch would never be warm again. Cole was going to be cruel by trying to make me feel for him what I felt for Alex, even with his dead body still in the room.

"Please," I started to beg. I wanted to tell him to just get it over with but my vocal chords didn't seem to want to work.

The strong hand on my shoulder started to turn me toward him and I couldn't find the strength to fight it. I turned to face what I hoped was the final end to my pain.

A pair of steel grey eyes stared into mine, locking my gaze in a way that made it impossible for me to breathe. They were so familiar yet so foreign. The face that held them didn't belong. It was the wrong eyes with the wrong face.

Alex stared intently into my face with those foreign grey eyes. Yet he was so different. His handsome face seemed enhanced, his skin flawless and fluid. He was so radiating and beautiful it was almost painful to look at him. All evidence of the blood that had covered him was now gone, replaced by only impossible perfection. That perfection carried down into his body, whole and complete. His chest was bare, evidence of his shredded shirt strewn across the room.

I realized that the brush of wings I had felt earlier had not come from Cole. It had come from Alex.

Alex's own pair of massive wings sprouted from his bare back. Every feather was perfectly formed and in its place. Each one was the purest white imaginable but I knew how they would look in the sun, how the light would reflect back the impossible metallic color.

A horrifying realization hit me as I felt myself leaning towards him. This most likely wasn't real. I had seen Cole kill Alex and then leave. Cole was still around somewhere and he had made me see things that weren't real before. This glorious man before me could in fact be Cole himself.

I was on my feet and sprinting out the door before I even bothered to see how this man who looked like Alex would react. My step didn't slow as I took the stairs two at a time and bounded across Cole's living room to the front door. The rain that had poured earlier had subsided into mist and it clung to my skin and clothes as I bounded across the street and continued up the hillside.

Reason and thought held no place in my mind as I barreled through the woods. I tripped and stumbled through the tangled ferns, tree roots erupted from the ground and they seemed to try and hinder my path to nowhere. I didn't know where I was going or why exactly I was running. Had I not just been wishing for Cole to finish me off? Perhaps that was what he was going to do when I had fled.

With this thought I came to a standstill. There was no sight of any of the houses that surrounded the lake, nor could I even see the lake itself anymore. There were only towering trees that surrounded me on the hillside, thick and dense enough to absorb almost all sound. Had I been thinking straight I might have wondered how I had gotten this far up the mountain so fast.

If my sense of hearing had not still been so enhanced I would not have heard the almost undetectable footsteps that approached from behind.

He didn't say anything at first and I only faintly heard the sound of air as it flowed in and out of his nose. My body remained stiff and rigid as I waited for some kind of crushing blow I knew an angel could deliver. I had only slightly felt the evidence of Cole's inhuman strength; I had seen it first hand as he had thrown Alex's body around. But it never came and the man behind me kept his distance.

"I went to check on you that night on the yacht and saw that you were sleeping." It was unmistakably Alex's voice but it was so beautiful, I would have marveled at just the sound of it had I not been so doubtful and wary. "I wanted to stay with you but you were so adamant that you wanted to be alone. You had been acting so strange all night, I wasn't sure what to do or think."

"Cole was there," I whispered, still not turning to face him. I could see no harm in telling this. If this man who looked like my Alex really was Cole, he would know this anyway. He had been there. "You couldn't see him, I couldn't see him. He made himself invisible somehow. He threatened to kill the both of us if I didn't do as he said."

"That explains a few things I suppose," he said after a moment's hesitation. "I went to check on you again in the morning and you were gone. My first instinct was panic but I tried to reason with myself, that there was a chance you may have just gone for a walk or something so I waited anxiously. When you didn't return I started looking for you. I must have searched the whole city for you. Seattle's a big city.

"I called back to the house but you didn't answer. I didn't know where else to look. I didn't know what to think.

"I hadn't heard anything in the night, but I thought maybe you had been kidnapped. Perhaps I had done something to upset you and you decided to leave. There were all these possibilities but I didn't know what to think or do. And then I thought maybe your dad would know something, since you had talked to him that day.

"It wasn't too hard to track him down. Ucon, Idaho isn't a very big town and he was the only Bailey listed. I called him and explained that you were missing. I asked him if he knew anything, if something had maybe happened while you two were talking."

As the sun disappeared through the trees a strange grey hue settled itself into the mist, giving everything an unearthly like glow. It only enhanced the bizarreness of everything that happened in the last twenty-four hours.

"He told me everything about the conversation the two of you had," he continued. "He told me about why you started having the nightmares, how you had been so sick. I put the two together pretty quickly, that you were experiencing the same things now. He then told me that he had promised you he would return home, because you were afraid of a dangerous angel from your nightmares. That this angel lived just two doors down from you."

As Alex continued to reveal what seemed to be the truth, I started to realize that if this really were Cole in disguise this explanation would not be going the same.

"It wasn't hard to guess who that meant," the hatred in Alex's voice surprised me. I had never heard him sound hateful in any way.

"Your dad flew back to Seattle that night and I picked him up from the airport. The first place we checked out was of course Cole's but he never would answer the door. Most of the drapes had been pulled, all the lights were out and we couldn't see anything. All the doors had been locked. It looked as if he had abandoned the place.

"We went to the police and filed a missing person's report but they weren't exactly helpful. Your dad wanted to try and get a warrant to go into Cole's house but what evidence did we have? And even if there was any, why would they believe us?"

I agreed internally. I was glad they hadn't gotten too far with the police. It would have sounded crazy. With this thought, I admitted to myself that I was determining that the man behind me was not in fact Cole. My pulse quickened and I felt the spark of life ignite within me slightly again.

"We tried to think of everywhere you might have gone to hide. Perhaps you had just gotten scared and ran, to escape Cole. We didn't come up with much though; we didn't even know where to start."

I heard Alex take a step closer and my heart gave a strange flutter. I didn't retreat, didn't try to keep that gap between us.

"And then I had the idea to go visit Sal. I didn't know if I expected to turn anything up from it but it had been a long time since I had seen her. I figured it couldn't hurt to talk to her.

"Imagine my surprise when Sal told me you had just been in to see her not an hour before," Alex continued, his voice stiff. "She told me how terrible you looked. She kept telling me you had turned into a skeleton but that you said everything was going to be fine soon. She said you told her that you and Cole had to leave. That you couldn't stay. She said that you told her goodbye and Sal said she was afraid she wouldn't ever see you again."

I could hear Alex's frame stiffen and his voice sounded strained when he spoke. "I knew three things then. You were dying. Somehow you *knew* it was going to end soon. And Cole was involved with how it would end."

Alex grew quiet and I somehow sensed he didn't want to tell me the next part.

"What happened, Alex?" I whispered. As the words slipped out of my mouth I turned around to face him. He stood twenty feet away, his chest still bare but the glorious wings now gone. His steel grey eyes seemed to nearly glow as he gazed through the thick mist at me. I couldn't deny it anymore, couldn't fight it. This wasn't Cole playing a cruel joke on me. This was my Alex and he had done something in exchange for my life to become this way.

"I...I..." he hesitated and I could tell he wanted to come closer. "I made a deal," he whispered, his eyes never wavering from mine. "I could only hope someone was listening but I said that if you could lead a normal life, normal as in full and healthy and free of the trials, I would offer myself in your stead."

Before I could voice the protests of horror that filled my head Alex rushed on. "I went to Cole's and when no one answered, I broke in through the back door. I couldn't wait any longer, I had to find you. I found that awful room you had been in. I found your clothes and I knew that you had been kept there. I also found that gun and I was terrified of what might have already happened. I checked it and was slightly relieved to see that it was still full. Good thing I took the bullets out." Hints at that smile that I loved so much played at the corner of his lips.

It took me a moment to realize what he meant. He was referring to my little meltdown when I had tried to turn the gun on myself. I had been right when I thought it had felt heavier when Cole had given it to me.

"And then amazingly you walked through the door, alive, but looking only seconds from death. I nearly didn't recognize you.

"You know the next part but basically Cole sealed the deal when he, well, killed me."

I cringed as he said the word. It confirmed all the more the horrific truth. Alex was indeed dead; this wasn't a human anymore that stood before me.

Alex took one hesitant step forward, followed by another. His eyes held mine intensely as he did so, seeming to give me permission to tell him to stop at any moment. I didn't.

"I knew the trials terrified you and I believed you had good reason for being so afraid. I never imagined it was as bad as the truth. As I stood before the council members there was quite a stir among everyone as they debated my fate."

A light clicked in my head. "You haven't been judged yet," I blurted out, awe filling my voice.

"How did you know?" he questioned, his brow furrowed.

"Your eyes, they're grey now. When you are judged, you either receive blue eyes or black. Only those who aren't judged yet have grey."

Alex's expression seemed genuinely surprised. Cole would have known this without a doubt. I couldn't deny it anymore and an extreme sense of calm and gratitude filled me as I extended my hands toward him.

"Show me," I said quietly, my voice barely audible.

Alex looked uncertain as he slowly closed the gap between us. He stopped just a foot in front of me, not yet taking my hands.

"I don't know how," he said as he looked down at my hands.

"Cole could make me see things. I know most of them weren't real but I'm afraid some of them might have one day become real," I said as I swallowed hard. "Just try and think about it. I want to see what happened."

This was only partially true. While I trusted Alex with more than just my life, I didn't want to go back to seeing things that weren't real, to have my head feel like it was in a fog again. But I wanted to know the truth, to understand what exactly it was Alex had done.

His eyes were hesitant as they met mine but he took both of my hands in his. As he did so, a sense of rightness and calm flooded through my system and at the same time it felt as if a fire had been let loose in my veins. There was no doubting it, this was my Alex. This was the man I loved more than I thought anyone in the world could love someone.

Alex's eyes burned intensely into mine and as he did so the trees that surrounded us melted away and the mist seemed to form into solid stone walls. The cylinder that I knew all too well encircled us, the demented voices of the condemned and the singing of the exalted mixing into a chaotic chorus.

I was standing at the mouth of the tunnel that led back to the prison cell I knew so well, watching as Alex stood with his hands bound in the golden cord before the council. Seeing him there sent waves of terror through my system. He didn't belong there, he shouldn't have had to stand there for many, many years to come.

"What this boy has done is against nature," one of the condemned council members cried out. In all the trials I had stood I had never heard them deviate from their normal jargon of the trials. I stood frozen in my place, intrigued as much as I was horrified. "Who is he to make a plea like this?"

"Have you ever seen an act so selfless though?" an exalted woman asked as she leaned forward in her seat, looking into the faces of all the council members. This seemed to quiet the condemned members protests.

"Please," Alex said, and despite his claim of being terrified, his voice sounded confident. "I only want for her to have a normal life. She doesn't deserve to stand trial for things she didn't do. She's..." his voice filled with emotion and he glanced down at the floor. "She's one of the most amazing people I've ever met. I will do anything."

The council members were silent for a moment but those seated on the stairwell that wound around the cylinder erupted with more noise. The exalted made aweing sounds, their faces serene and caring looking. Those with the black eyes hissed and protested with words unknown to human ears.

It was the leader of those with blue eyes who spoke first. "We shall put it to a vote," he said as he stared intently at Alex. "I vote to grant your request. I also vote to allow you to return to the human world and give you more time with this woman you are willing to trade so much for."

With these words all hell broke loose. Wings bat anxiously and furiously from all around, the hissing grew to shouting and gasps escaped the mouths of most all.

Each of the condemned council members gave their vote, all but the leader of the condemned denying that Alex should be allowed to return and denying Alex's request for my life to return to normal. The new leader simply did not cast a vote on either matter.

The votes of the remaining four exalted council members took much longer to be heard. They each debated internally as to what both of our fates would be but in the end both counts were voted to be granted.

Shouts of joy and excitement came from one crowd while the other seemed to have had enough. They coiled their powerful wings and plunged into the fiery depths below.

"I would like to make one more request," Alex suddenly spoke as the sounds of chaos died down. Each of the council members froze as their eyes bored into Alex. "One of your own is still in her world. With his task failed I fear for what he might do in order to exact revenge. I ask that her family and dearest friend be protected from him somehow."

Alex's bold request more than shocked both the council members and me. Had he not already asked something huge and impossible? Now he wanted something more?

While the black eyed council members simply raged in protest, the others debated for several minutes. It was the female council member who spoke this time.

"Young man, what you have already asked is more than should be given. But, we have never seen such a display of selflessness and for that we commend you. You have our guarantee that this woman's family and friend will not be harmed by the angel who has wrongfully escaped."

"Thank you," Alex breathed as his signature smile nearly burst forth on his face. "Thank you."

As soon as he said this, the smile on his face faded and twisted into a look of at first confusion and then into agony. I could see the skin on his back ripple and shiver and after just a moment a beautiful, massive pair of wings burst from his skin. When he looked back up at the council the blue in his eyes was washed out into grey.

At this the lines that defined everything around me started to fade and blur and the scene seemed to shake.

"You must know you will not be returning as a human. Your human form has died, things are not going to be…" the voice was fading away as everything turned to a smoky grey and we were suddenly standing back in the forest.

I couldn't say anything for a very long time as I simply looked into Alex's face as he still held my hands tightly in his. I didn't notice nor did I care that tears were slowly rolling down my cheeks. There seemed to be no words grand or sincere enough to express the feelings that were surging inside of me. Knowing I was never going to be able to express in words what I was feeling, I closed that small gap between us, pressing my lips to Alex's and wrapping my arms around his waist. As my hands drifted over his back, I felt two thick raised scars on the insides of his shoulder blades, evidence of the wings that could appear there.

I felt in no hurry as my lips moved greedily with his and I breathed in the familiar scent that was Alex. It was impossible to comprehend the love that I felt in that moment, the love that I knew would last me through the rest of my days. Alex had sacrificed the greatest thing he could for me and I knew I would have done the same thing in a heartbeat if there had been a chance.

When I did finally pull away, my face was still streaked with tears. I looked intently into Alex's eyes, my forehead resting against his.

"I don't deserve you," I breathed. Before he could protest I continued. "I don't deserve you but I am going to try and be worthy of you. It's going to take a lot of work but I am going to do everything I have to do to be worthy of you."

That half smile cracked on Alex's lips before he pressed a short kiss to my lips. "Just be you," he whispered as he looked back into my eyes. "That's all it takes. I am yours for forever and even longer."

"I love you, Alex," I said as I tightened my arms around him. It should have been impossible, literally holding an angel in my arms. Even more impossible knowing this angel loved me enough to become one in exchange for my survival and freedom.

"And I love you, Jessica," he breathed. He pressed his lips very gently to mine before he stepped away. Keeping one of my hands in his, he led the way back down the hill to our house.

I knew things weren't perfect. Cole was still out there somewhere and even though I knew he couldn't touch those I loved, I still knew what he was capable of doing. And even though I had Alex back, he wasn't human any more. There would be complications and challenges. But despite everything that wasn't right in my world, for the first time, I slept without enduring a trial and branding for things I did not do, in the arms of an angel.

ACKNOWLEDGEMENTS

There are a lot of people I need to thank for supporting me and for telling me to never quit writing. First thank you to my husband for his unexpected, enthusiastic support. And to my kids for taking naps long enough that I could write Branded. Thank you to Halley, for loving my story enough while I was writing it to keep me going. Thank you to my mom and my sister Ashley for reading this in the beginning and pointing out its flaws. Thank you Jenni for taking time away from your own writing to create this amazing cover image for me. And thank you to the rest of my family and friends for your support and wonderful influence.

KEARY TAYLOR is the independent author of Branded, Forsaken, Vindicated (*Fall of Angels* series), and Eden. She lives on Orcas Island in Washington State with her husband and their two children. To find out more about Keary and her writing process visit her at

www.KearyTaylor.com
or
http://kearytaylor.blogspot.com

DON'T MISS THE NEXT INSTALLMENT OF THE

FALL OF ANGELS

SERIES,

AVAILABLE NOW!

AND THE THIRD AND FINAL VOLUME

COMING 2012

Made in the USA
Charleston, SC
15 April 2014